# Framed For Murder

by

## Marla A. White

*A Pine Cove Mystery*

**Framed For Murder**

Cover Art by *Diana Carlile*

The Wild Rose Press, Inc.
PO Box 708
Adams Basin, NY 14410-0708
Visit us at www.thewildrosepress.com

Publishing History
First Edition, 2024
Trade Paperback ISBN 978-1-5092-5429-3
Digital ISBN 978-1-5092-5430-9

*A Pine Cove Mystery*
Published in the United States of America

## Dedication & Acknowledgements

A HUGE thank you to all my beta readers, particularly Carolyn and Jen. I couldn't have done this without you.

And a loving thank you to firefighters everywhere who keep the very real mountain top cities like my fictional Pine Cove safe from devastating wildfires at the risk of your own lives.

# Chapter One

## *Palm Springs*

Night had long since fallen on Palm Springs, though the city lights made it impossible to confirm the stars were still shining in the sky above, even from Poppy's viewpoint atop the positively Spartan glass and concrete office building. However, she considered herself to be an optimist and had no reason to fear the stars had winked out of existence. Besides, she had other issues to *consider*, not *worry about*, mind you. Poppy Phillips never worried despite her dangerous line of work, but she always thought a situation through before leaping. Well, most of the time.

This time of year, with the holidays over and the chill of January in the air, there was only a smattering of tourists about in the city enjoying the nightlife. If she listened closely, she could catch a whisper of music from the nightclub because while she'd climbed to the top of the tallest office building in town, this being Palm Springs, the edifice stood just seven stories tall. She struck a pose like a cocky highwayman on an old movie poster she saw as a kid, legs spread wide and hands on her hips. Although some might think because of her slender figure and diminutive size she more closely resembled a pixie, she believed what she lacked in size she made up for in confidence. She inhaled the crisp desert air deeply and smiled, her arrogant grin hidden behind her favorite black balaclava.

A cautious person, no matter what it might seem like, she checked her complicated climbing rig fixed to the roof one last time before looping her lean, toned arms through the straps of a sleek backpack. With a roll of her shoulders to ease the adrenaline-fueled tautness, she snapped the rope to her climbing harness and walked down the side of the building, facing the pavement a dizzying distance below. Seven floors is a far cry from her last job scaling the forty-one floors of the Eamon & Leet Plaza in downtown Los Angeles, but a fall from that height would still kill you.

The rope fed out at a steady pace, allowing her to make the vertical stroll between the rows of small, decorative balconies without a care in the world. After a descent of three floors, she nimbly stepped over the railing of one of them. A little bored at the ease of her task so far, she unhooked the rope, slipped off the backpack, thrust a gloved hand inside, and withdrew a slim blade. She slid the tool into the doorframe and, in seconds, unlocked the door.

She entered and took a moment to appreciate the well-appointed office. The thick, plush carpet made it easy to pad noiselessly through a deserted reception area. In truth, if the floor had been littered with broken glass her steps would still be silent; she appreciated the quality of the floor covering, all the same. She reached the destination specified in her instructions, the closed door off to the right. Curious about its mate to the left, she ignored the door for now to focus on the task at hand.

The door opened, without so much as a creak of a

hinge, at the slightest touch. She crept in and studied the wall behind the large, OCD neat desk where a bland landscape in oil hung. The so-called artwork displayed in an over embellished gold frame served as further proof money can buy you almost anything, including love, but not taste.

Not the time for pondering, however. She glided across the room, gripped the edge of the frame, and tugged. The gaudy wood swung open to reveal a wall safe. Poppy did the only inelegant thing she ever did and cracked her knuckles and neck before flicking on a tiny penlight. Holding it in her mouth, she dialed the combination she'd memorized from her contact's brief. The safe opened with a *snick* and, ignoring the stacks of cash and paperwork, she removed a rectangular box as directed. She cracked it open to peer at the necklace inside, shrugging at its unremarkable collection of common gemstones strung in a clunky arrangement by a copper-colored wire.

She pivoted to exit, paused, and returned to the safe. What the hell; they'd never miss one stack of cash. The money and the necklace secured in the backpack, she slid the satchel over her shoulders. Then she tiptoed back out the way she'd come in and stumbled over something large and soft. *I never stumble*, she thought with an irritated *harrumph*. Curious about what caused the anomaly, she retrieved her penlight and clicked it on. The tiny circle of illumination revealed a shocked expression on a dead man's face.

With a small gasp, she switched off the light and sprinted toward the balcony door until someone suddenly blinded her by flipping on the harsh overhead lights. She stopped in her tracks, blinking back her vision. A shot rang out from the office on the left, prompting her to fly out the balcony door. She glanced up and then down her climbing rope. Either direction would take too long and leave her exposed. Another shot encouraged her to run. Cool as if she were stepping onto an elevator, she opted to go sideways, parkouring to the next balcony and the next before dropping to the floor below, unbothered by the idea of plummeting to the pavement if she didn't stick the landing. Because she never doubted she would.

After a brief flight, she made a graceful superhero landing on the balcony below. She touched a gloved hand gingerly to her shoulder where a sliver of pale skin shown through the torn shirt. The glove came away slick with blood. A third gunshot rang out, but by then she'd disappeared into the night, leaving a smudge of blood on the balcony railing.

****

*Pine Cove*

A trickle of sweat rolled down Mel's spine as she searched the climbing wall for her next handhold. She'd made it half-way up the advanced climbers' wall in record time, for her anyway, but now was stuck trying to figure out where to go from there. The chalk marks on the well-used wall made for a pretty good guide, but at five foot four Mel was a little shorter than the average climber. She dipped her hand in the chalk bag attached to her harness, her hands clammy and slick.

"You all right, sweetheart?" asked Jackson Thibodeaux, his voice laced with a New Orleans drawl. The accent only appeared when it suited him, she noticed, including every time he called her sweetheart. The first time had been a couple of months ago when she moved to the tiny mountain resort of Pine Cove. The endearment annoyed her initially but, like Jackson, it had grown on her. However, she'd never admit it to him.

"I'm fine and I thought we agreed you wouldn't call me that?" She allowed a secret smile to dance at the corner of her mouth.

"Not even when we're out on this romantic date?" he said loud enough for everyone in the climbing gym to have heard. And at this time of night, during the gym's peak hours, the number was higher than she cared to think about.

"This is not a date. You offered to help," she retorted.

"You claim it's not a rendezvous, but you put on lip gloss. In fact, from this angle I'm getting a better view than most guys on actual dates."

She risked a downward peek. He smiled at her, his aquamarine eyes sparkling in amusement. Okay, she had taken an extra few minutes to get her girliness on, something she'd actively worked against back in her days as a patrol cop in Los Angeles. Mel had rationalized she needed to soften her image in her new home, but had she subconsciously primped for Jackson? Rather than debate it, she sprinkled some of the chalk down on his dark curly hair and returned her focus to the fake rock wall in front of her.

Encouraged by the reminder he was there to belay for her in case she fell, she lunged for her next handhold. She quelled her whoop of excitement. This wall barely scored a blip on the Yosemite Decimal System and would have gotten nothing but her scorn before. Back then, she scaled mountain peaks with her brother Liam. Now she scrambled to secure her toe-holds and plot her next move on this small fake mountain. She glanced down for a moment to find a steadier hold, but that was all it took. The debilitating acrophobia she thought she'd finally gotten control of held her in its icy grip.

Panic-stricken, Mel hugged the wall tight even though clinging to the side threw off her center of balance. Rigid with tension, the aptly named "Elvis leg" soon kicked in as her muscles jumped and vibrated. She tried to shift her position to change the pressure on her feet, but no matter how much she willed them to move, fear locked her legs in place. Instead, she made a wild grab at the next chalk mark. Her knees gave out and when her hand connected, her sweaty palm failed to get a grip. She expected to drop a few feet before the belay rope would halt her descent, but when she kept going she let out an involuntary yelp. Finally, four feet off the ground, her fall ended with a jolt.

Furious, she unclipped the rope and dropped to the floor. "Asshole," she hissed at Jackson as she sat on the gym's soft mats and yanked off the climbing harness. "You weren't even paying attention. You know what I'm dealing with, and you dropped me." Humiliated, tears stung her eyes. He was one of the few people outside of her family who she'd trusted to tell about her fear of heights ever since a rooftop chase ended in a crushed ankle and early retirement. The fall and the fear were the biggest failures of her life, a weakness she hated to reveal to anyone, and he'd thrown away her trust like it was nothing.

He sunk down next to her, but she ignored him, her head bowed in defeat until he hooked a finger under her chin and guided her to face him. His solemn gaze met hers. "Emmeline O'Rourke, I would never let you fall. But sometimes you have to slip a little to learn you're going to be okay."

Her cheeks flushed with anger. No matter how noble his intentions might be, how dare he decide how far it's okay for her to fall? "Thanks, Dr. Freud. Next time I'll get one of the other climbers to belay for me. Somebody who will take the job seriously." Jamming her gear in her duffle bag, she marched out the doors and never looked back.

Chapter Two

The next morning, Mel woke up cranky and unsettled, though whether she was still angry with Jackson or herself for lashing out at her friend who was trying to help, she wasn't sure. All she was certain about was she was in no mood for surprises when she walked through the door connecting her living quarters to the office of the Babbling Brook Bed and Breakfast. Her family had joined forces in order to help her buy the place after her fall. Unfortunately, it didn't matter if she was in the mood for a surprise or not, because one awaited her.

Through the window of the small lobby, she spotted a shiny red sports car that hadn't been there last night. It didn't belong to any of her guests because she always asked what kind of car they drove when they checked in. Which meant someone was abusing her woefully inadequate lot by parking where they didn't belong.

With a growl of irritation, she marched toward the kitchen to start the coffee going before her guests made their way to the cozy dining room occupying the back half of the Great Room. She'd call Deputy Sheriff Gregg Marks to see about getting the car towed but didn't expect the sheriff's department to jump into action. Heck, last month when she found a dead body in front of the fireplace of the Great Room, they hadn't been able to come for an entire day because of a record-breaking snowstorm and lack of manpower to deal with both situations at the same time.

Rounding the corner to the kitchen, Mel stopped short. Curled with her feet tucked daintily underneath her in one of the wing-backed chairs sat a petite brunette, head bowed, reading the paper and sipping a cup of tea. She'd checked in all their guests personally and didn't remember this woman. Still, she hadn't seen every member of one or two of the groups renting the larger cabins, so she held her temper.

"Excuse me, is that your car parked out front?" She struggled to maintain a polite tone.

The woman's head snapped toward her, her perfect lips making a surprised little 'o' before breaking out in a broad smile. She removed her wireless earbuds, blasting classical music across the room. A swipe to her phone silenced them, and she got to her feet in a fluid motion, stepping toward her with the grace of a ballet dancer. "Officer O'Rourke, how good to see you," the woman gushed in a lilting British accent. "Or should I just call you Mel?"

"Poppy?" She was too astonished to squeak out more.

"In the flesh." The lithe woman beamed but stopped short of wrapping her arms around Mel in an enthusiastic hug. So many questions rattled around in her pre-coffee sluggish brain, but she blurted out the most obvious one first.

"How did you get in here?" She'd locked the front door after the posted eight o'clock closing time last night. The guests all had keys to their own cabins or rooms and had instructions to call if they needed her after eight. The safety protocol was a habit she'd stuck to religiously after finding a murdered man sitting in a chair right across from the one vacated by her...nemesis? Acquaintance? She shook her head, unable to put a label to their relationship.

"Well," she purred, her brown eyes sparkling behind long fake lashes, "I drove up early this morning and it was too cold to sit in my car until your eight a.m. opening time." She gestured to the sign in the window stating lobby hours. "So I let myself in. I knew you wouldn't mind."

Poppy Phillips was a thief. A notorious cat burglar, sometimes called "The Ghost" by social media outlets and more whimsical members of the public. Many police forces had been chasing her for years, including the LAPD. They knew she'd committed a multitude of crimes, but never found the evidence to make the charges stick, until last year. Mel, hot on her heels in pursuit after a daring robbery, got within an arm's length from grabbing her with the stolen items on her person when the thief nimbly jumped from the roof of the building they were running across, over an alley, to land on the one next door.

Mel tried to follow, but slipped and slammed into the side of the building instead. With her partner too far away to help, she clung to the rooftop by her fingertips until they cramped from the strain. She started reciting the Hail Mary for what she thought would be the last time when two strong, slender arms pulled her to safety. It was Poppy. She could have kept going and escaped, but she came back to save Mel's life.

As they both collapsed to the roof, breathless and laughing at the absurdity of the situation, she cuffed herself to the thief and arrested her. Rather than lashing out and trying to escape, she just sat there and laughed some more. It was almost insulting how chill she was about the whole thing. But, since one rescue deserved another, she convinced the prosecutor, a member of her extended family, to drop the charges in light of services rendered. So what was she doing here?

Making a mental note to change the lock and check into a security system to prevent another surprise visit from potentially less amiable thieves, she persisted. "Yes, but what are you doing here? In Pine Cove?" She narrowed her eyes at the intruder. "Are you on the run?"

Poppy's eyes grew wide in a nearly convincing guise of innocence. "No," she huffed with the perfect blend of indignation and hurt feelings, "why would you say such a thing?"

"Experience?"

After mulling her statement over for a moment, the Brit gave her a crooked grin. "You got me there but seriously, after our run in on the rooftop and you managed to keep me out of the nick, I got to thinking, is this what I really want to do with my life? So, I decided to turn over a new leaf. When I heard about your lovely B&B, I says to meself, 'Poppy, that's the ticket. Go work for your old pal Mel.' And here I am." She spread her arms wide like a magician who had performed a trick and awaited her due applause.

Mel scrubbed her face with her hands. "This is too much conversation before coffee." She pivoted on her heel and headed down the hall into the kitchen, where she grabbed the carafe from the coffeemaker. Turning, she almost dropped the glass pot, shocked to find Poppy on her heels. The thief's quick hands snagged the container, saving it from shattering on the tile floor, and filled the carafe with water while humming a happy tune.

"What are you doing?" Mel grabbed the full carafe out of her hands and finished the coffee prep herself.

"I'm auditioning for the job, poppet."

She wasn't sure what a poppet was but from her teasing tone, she suspected the thief just called her an idiot. The other woman took advantage of her flustered state and rummaged through the fridge. Eggs, milk, and butter appeared on the counter, while Mel opened and closed her mouth with squeaks of protest. "While I waited for you to wake up, I noticed your sorry little breakfast menu and the idea struck me you could use my help."

Coffee brewed, Mel poured some into her cup, where milk and a pinch of sugar sat at the ready. She sipped, grimaced, and added more sugar. Sadly, Poppy had a point. Toast and rubbery scrambled eggs maxed out her breakfast making skills. When the family opted to buy the Babbling Brook, the idea had been for her older sister Vinnie to spend a week in Pine Cove helping her master some simple dishes. A week turned out to be not nearly enough time, however. After years of living alone and eating mostly takeout or frozen meals, she just never developed a knack for cooking and never cared until now. Even her coffee tasted terrible.

Satisfied with the ingredients she'd collected, Poppy took off her down coat to get to work. Caught up eyeing its cute fur-trimmed hood, something she could never pull off without looking like a cartoon version of an Eskimo, she almost missed the wince of pain skitter across the woman's porcelain pale face before vanishing.

"You okay?" She might be skeptical of her, but in a sort of Javert-versus-Jan Val Jean kind of way, they'd known each other for a long time, and she didn't want her to be in pain.

"No worries—" she shrugged off the question "—just pulled a muscle is all. Almost like a sign from the Almighty, I'm getting too old to run around scaling walls, eh?" Mel raised a dubious eyebrow as she tied on an apron before measuring some flour and folding the ingredients together.

A pulled muscle would explain why she was stirring with her left hand, but the ex-cop in her liked to think her bullshit detecting skills far outshone her coffee making skills. She wanted to press for more details, but the phone at the front desk rang.

"Don't take any of the silverware, I'll be right back," she called over her shoulder as she hurried through the door to the small lobby.

"Good morning, Blabbling Book Bread and Breakfast," she stumbled over the tongue twister of a greeting.

"Hey Mel, it's Liam." Oh great, she had to fumble the name when her brother called. She'd never hear the end of it. "I'm going to be a little late, but I should still be there sometime this morning." They'd agreed Liam, who ran his own contracting company, would come for a few days to do some maintenance around the place. She'd been expecting him any minute now since he preferred to drive up at the crack of dawn to beat the traffic out of L.A. Then a thought occurred to her, and she grinned.

"Had a late night, did you? What's her name?" she teased him.

"What? No, nothing like that, I—" and then some noise in the background interrupted him. Was someone shouting?

"Is everything okay?"

"Everything's fine, I'll see you later." She was so confused, a full second passed before she realized he didn't crack even one joke about her being so tongue-tied. No matter what he said, something was definitely going on, but she couldn't do anything about it until he made the two-hour and change trip to Pine Cove. In the meantime, through the window she noticed the family who checked in a couple of days ago leave their cabin and head toward the dining room. Shoot, breakfast service should have started ten minutes ago, and she hadn't even set the tables.

She popped her head into the kitchen and was met with an array of amazing smells. Bacon, new coffee, and...blueberry? Satisfied Poppy had breakfast under control, she hustled out to the dining room with napkins, silverware, and mugs for the family just before they sat down at a table big enough for the five of them. She whirled around to get them glasses of water and, for the second time that morning, found Poppy right behind her.

Cool as ever, the other woman didn't even so much as jostle the plates she delivered to the surprised family loaded with blueberry pancakes, bacon with a mouth-watering maple smell, and fresh melon cut into neat squares. That was weird. She didn't even know they had melon. In a final splashy twirl, her new cook pulled the syrup out of her apron pocket.

"Oh my gosh, this all smells so good," the father exclaimed. "And this bacon is delicious."

"It's crack bacon," Poppy beamed. "Got the recipe from a little hidden gem of a restaurant in Hollywood."

"This is so much better than yesterday's breakfast," the young son blurted out as he stuffed a piece in his mouth, his parents shooting Mel embarrassed apologetic glances. The Brit brazenly winked at her, but she had to admit the spread in front of them ranked ten times better than the sad burnt French toast she'd made yesterday. She busied herself filling their glasses with water while her new chef took their orders for how they wanted their eggs done.

"Show off," she muttered as Poppy passed her on the way back to the kitchen. She didn't even realize there was a difference between sunny side up and over easy, not to mention how to cook them.

The rest of the morning was a blur of activity and more heavenly smells. Word of mouth must have gotten around about the improved food because twice as many guests came for breakfast compared to yesterday. Mel scurried clearing tables and resetting them until the service ended, then helped Poppy clean up the kitchen. She tried not to worry about Liam, who still hadn't arrived by the time she'd put the last glass in the dishwasher and hit the start button. Traffic was always unpredictable, but there was something off about his voice.

"So boss, what do you think?" Poppy asked, bringing an involuntary shudder like someone walking over her grave. Her previous employee cheerfully addressed her as "boss" right up until she tried to kill her.

"All right, you're hired as long as you never call me 'boss' again. Let's just stick with Mel."

"Fantastic," she gushed, sounding way too relieved. "You won't regret this."

"My last employee killed one of the guests, so the bar is pretty low," she joked, gratified when her frenemy laughed. At least she got her dark sense of humor. Many of her new neighbors in Pine Cove did not. "If you hand me the broom, I'll go sweep the dining room floor and then set you up with a place to stay." As Poppy took hold of the worn wooden handle, she winced again. Pulled muscle my ass, she thought, but she only had the bandwidth for one mystery and right now it was Liam.

Chapter Three

After tidying the Great Room, Mel led Poppy up the narrow, wooden exterior stairs on the main building of the inn, to a small room on the second floor. Most of their guest accommodations were standalone cabins within easy walking distance to the Great Room where they served breakfast, but there were a few rooms in the lodge itself.

"You can take the room as part of your compensation or, if you find something else in town you'd rather stay in, I can bump up your wages within limits, so don't expect a lot." She glanced back over her shoulder and frowned at her new employee. "Assuming you stay that long."

Her suspicions rose when she offered to help Poppy move her things from the red sports car to her room and the woman hastily refused. "No worries, I've got it, mate," she responded with a broad smile and pulled a small duffle out of the trunk—using her left arm instead of the injured right.

"That's it? You decided to make a huge change and packed your whole life in one bag?"

"I figured if I'm going to start over, I might as well make a clean break with the past." She patted the duffle, adding, "Out with the old and all that."

Mel was no stranger to the concept of starting over, having just done the same thing herself, but she still required a rental truck to carry the things she needed to make the inn feel like her home. Possibly Poppy was better at not being too attached to possessions. Since she'd made a living stealing other people's property, maybe she'd seen the folly of loving things too much. Or she lied about starting over and was up to something. Only time would tell.

**\*\*\*\***

Once she showed Poppy to her room, she retreated to the office where she futzed around with some unimportant paperwork to avoid her real assignment. Scrutinizing the grocery bill for corners to cut was much more up her nuts-and-bolts alley than the homework her cousin Gemma, who ran the website for the inn, had given her—a worksheet to fill out on "branding" their business. A forty-three page worksheet, as if she wasn't spending every waking moment running the business.

Her cousin had been bugging her for weeks about this branding nonsense, explaining she needed to identify her values to get the Babbling Brook Inn noticed. She even wanted her to decide on her favorite colors for the marketing materials. And everything started with something called a mission statement, according to all the articles she'd been bombarding her with since the family invested in the rustic bed-and-breakfast.

"Easy for you to say," Mel grumbled and then realized talking to herself out loud was probably "on brand" with being a weirdo. With a sigh of resignation, she clicked open the document and started reading. The first question asked, "Are you ready?" What if her answer was no?

The growl of a big vehicle pulling into her gravel parking lot caught her attention. Way more curious about who arrived than about figuring out her personal strengths and weaknesses, she walked through the office into the lobby to peer out the window. A flood of relief washed over her. The sight of Liam's truck, safe and sound, took a huge weight off her shoulders. Relief turned to bewilderment when Liam helped Grandma O'Rourke out of the passenger side.

While Liam's oversized pickup fit his construction work, Grandma's diminutive build made an assist necessary. Her feet, clad in sensible orthopedic shoes, dangled eight inches off the ground. They must have used a step stool for her to get in, she thought, as she mentally rifled through the possibilities of why her grandmother chose now to visit.

Great, one more unexpected visitor. Maybe that was her brand, "Come to the Babbling Brook, where every day has a new bombshell to deal with". Probably not useful if they were trying to entice people to come and relax.

\*\*\*\*

"Grandma O, what a nice surprise!" Mel rushed outside to greet the matriarch of the O'Rourke family. Her once glorious head of red waves was still thick but snowy white, and her face showed the laugh and worry lines of a long and interesting life, but her hazel eyes crackled with intelligence. And just a touch of crazy.

"Wasn't my idea. This one," she snarled and jerked a bony thumb at Liam, "kidnapped me." She rubbed her arms vigorously despite the heavy down jacket she wore. "Christ on a cracker, it's cold here." She marched toward the front door, her step spry in spite of her age.

From the bottom of the stairs, she took in the Babbling Brook's main building. She'd been ill with a kidney stone when the family did the walk-through to buy the place and had never seen the inn before. "So, this is what your father bought," she harrumphed before turning back to Mel with a pleasant smile. "Lovely to see you, my dear." And with that effusive greeting, she disappeared into the lobby.

Mel gaped slack-jawed at her brother, whose palm covered his face. "Why did you kidnap Grandma?"

"I did not—ugh!" He answered from behind his hand before shaking off his frustration and moving to the back seat of the truck to grab their bags. "Mom forced me to bring her. That's what the delay was all about. She's been driving her crazy, and then this morning she lit the kitchen on fire."

"She what?!"

"I wasn't there, so I don't know exactly, something about the toaster and a curtain. Anyway, Mom convinced her she should come help you out and halfway up the mountain she wove this kidnapping story."

"Help me? How, by greeting guests with her charming personality?" She loved her grandmother, but her salutation and scathing condemnation of the inn with just one glance were pretty mild for the old woman. When she really got on a tear, the best thing was to go to a movie until she wore herself out.

"Beats me but pro tip, do not let her in the kitchen." Balancing the bags in one hand, Liam enveloped her with his free arm. "At least, not until we make sure the insurance covers curtain fires."

"No need to worry, I just hired someone today who

is great in the kitchen."

He looked at her askance. "Great as in better than you or someone who is actually a good cook?"

"Shut up." She laughed in response to the insult. "The guests this morning raved about the food. For however long she stays, I think she'll be a plus in the breakfast department, anyway."

"Where did you find this culinary genius? Did you put out an ad already?" He held the door open for Mel and they entered the lobby.

"We didn't, she found me." She looked around. "Where's Grandma?"

The echoes of laughter led the siblings into the Great Room where their grandmother sat in front of the fireplace chatting away with Poppy. They turned toward Mel and Liam as they entered.

"Mel, your mother is a hoot," she gushed.

She narrowed her eyes at the alleged ex-thief, who had to know perfectly well the woman in front of her was too old to be her mother. Grandma O, however, took the compliment to heart and patted Poppy's hand, gracing her with one of her rare beaming smiles.

To Mel's surprise, Liam skidded to a dead halt. She turned back to see why and received the icy blast of the unmistakable storm in his eyes. She'd seen the same dark expression in the mirror when she was furious. What did he have to be so angry about? Before she could ask, he dropped their bags and launched into full hissy fit mode.

"You!" he bellowed at Poppy.

The brunette seemed sincerely surprised at his response. Swiveling her head to see who else was in the room and finding no one, she met his gaze and pointed to herself with an exaggerated, "Who, me?" expression.

Her brother spun, targeting his rage at her. "Don't tell me this is who you hired?"

"You're only being a grump because you haven't tried her bacon," she joked, hoping to deflate the situation. Years of trying to nail her for any number of jobs she'd pulled off had frustrated Mel, but she had to admit she always liked her style. Despite her suspicions when she found Poppy in the lobby this morning, so far she'd been nothing but charming and kind of fun, so what had she done to piss off easy-going Liam in the two minutes since they met?

Her brother crossed his arms, stubbornly jutting out his square jaw. "There's no way that woman is working here. She nearly killed you once, I'm not giving her a second chance."

"You two have met?" The information surprised her, so she let the macho b.s. slide for now. She didn't need anyone to protect her, but his anger rolled off him so calling him on his chauvinism skittered close to throwing gasoline on a fire.

"We had to watch her on the news sound bites, taking her bows for saving your life, while you lay in that hospital bed, broken and in agony." Mel had never seen his eyes blaze with such fury before. She'd been so focused on her own suffering she'd never thought about what her family had gone through. Liam clearly had been carrying steamer-trunk sized baggage. "Nobody bothered to mention she's the one who put you in danger in the first place. Or that you're crippled for life, thanks to her."

"Crippled?" Poppy's brows furrowed, her eyes darkening.

"Easy, drama queen," Mel snarled, "nobody's crippled."

"We used to go rock climbing and now you can't even mount a set of stairs without getting dizzy." His exasperation exploded as he paced to the far end of the Great Room to stare out the floor-to-ceiling glass door at the patio and brook beyond. What really hurt was he sounded more bummed out for himself losing a climbing partner than concerned about her.

"Is that true?" Poppy sprang up.

"I'm working on it." Embarrassed by the whole conversation, she busied herself with tidying the morning newspapers the guests had left strewn around the sitting area.

"She nearly killed you, she's not working here," Liam repeated without turning away from the view outside.

Grandma O'Rourke rose to her feet with more nobility than agility, stood between her two grandchildren, and pronounced, "I like her, and I say she stays," before tottering off to the kitchen in a self-professed search for the infamous bacon.

Of course, she liked Poppy, she just paid her a huge compliment. Never mind if she was guilty of what Liam accused her of doing or not. After putting the last section of the newspaper back in place, Mel noticed the below the fold story on the front page and tightened her fist until she almost tore the paper in two.

*Scientist Killed in Daring Heist*

Skimming the article, she found out the victim, an engineer for a large oil company named Kyle Lange, surprised a burglar robbing the safe in his office in a downtown Palm Springs high-rise. There were reports of multiple shots, so the intruder must have been a lousy aim but finally hit his target. They left their fancy rigging on the roof in their rush to escape, but no gun was found at the scene. The Palm Springs Police Department asked anyone with further information to come forward.

Mel glanced over to make sure her brother continued to brood by the back door before stalking to Poppy and grabbing her by her right elbow, the arm she'd been favoring all morning. Her thoughtful frown shifted to a full-on grimace of pain.

"Oh, did that hurt?" she murmured without a shred of sympathy. "We need to talk."

Chapter Four

Mel propelled a complaining Poppy into her office and shut the door. Hopefully, if the phone rang, or a guest needed to check in, Liam could handle it.

"Oy, yes that bloody hurts. What's wrong with you, mate?" she carped.

"You want to tell me about this, *mate*?" She shoved the paper at her. "And don't even try to claim you don't know anything about the robbery. Is that how you 'pulled a muscle'? Murdering a man? Sit." She pointed to the chair on the opposite side of the desk and picked up the phone. "Don't bother running, because I'm pretty sure Deputy Sheriff Marks would love nothing more than chasing you down."

"Wait," the thief exclaimed as she lurched forward. Mel's murderous intent must have shown on her face because the other woman eased back into the chair, holding her hands out in surrender. "Look, I'm truly sorry if you're suffering ill effects from our frolic across the rooftops, but you have to admit, I did save your life. You owe me at least the courtesy of hearing my side of the story.

"Yes, I wasn't completely forthright with you, but I need your help. Every cop between here and Las Vegas would love to pin something on me and here's their big chance, all wrapped in a bow, but I didn't do it. Simple case of wrong place at the wrong time, mate, I swear.

Hear me out, and if you want to ring the coppers after, then I'll go quiet as a lamb."

She was so tempted to call Deputy Marks and be done with it. This woman had been at the inn for roughly two hours and had already lied to her. Mel didn't need any more confusion and uncertainty in her life right now. She was in way over her head running a bed-and-breakfast as it was. Being a cop had been so much easier—all she had to do was chase bad guys, not worry about details like fresh flowers in the rooms. But she trusted her instincts and inexplicably, every one of them screamed the thief was telling the truth. She laid the phone back in its cradle.

"All right, I'm listening."

Poppy's shoulders sagged in relief, which surprised her. She'd always imagined the thief to be unflappable. She certainly styled herself after all those elegant, daring characters found in British spy thrillers. She heaved a sigh and launched into her story.

"An anonymous person contacted me out of the blue via Salutations, offering to hire me for a simple safe job."

"Salutations?" she interrupted, "What's that?"

For the first time since Liam blew up at her, Poppy's lips curled in her signature smirk. "A bit in the dark ages, aren't we love? 'Salutations' is a texting platform where the message disappears thirty seconds after being read. It's all very cloak and dagger if you ask me, but clients seem to like it."

"Clients?"

"I'm not denying I'm a thief, a girl's got to make a living after all. But in all the years you've been chasing me, have I ever used a gun? A weapon of any kind?"

She didn't have to consider the question before answering. Never. Besides her parkour style of dramatic entrances and exits, refusing to carry a weapon was part of "The Ghost's" distinct persona. She had no delusions it was because the Brit took an anti-violence stance. Every smart criminal knew if they ever got caught, any evidence of deadly force, even if by accident, meant a much stiffer prison sentence.

"Point taken. Go on."

"The message was anonymous, but that's not unusual." Poppy leaned forward, telling her tale with enthusiasm since the threat of the sheriff being called had passed. "The weird part was they described in great detail the only item I was to nick out of the safe."

"You mean you didn't take everything?" She frowned. The paper made it sound as if the thief had emptied the safe of all its contents.

"No, I swear, I only took a necklace, as instructed. Although I can't imagine why. The thing is hideous looking," she said with an exaggerated shudder, "and as far as I can tell can't be worth spit."

She was the expert jewel thief, so Mel took her word for it. Then a horrible suspicion bloomed in the pit of her stomach as she put together the pieces of the thief's story. "And where is this necklace now?"

Poppy broke eye contact, suddenly fascinated by the toe of her own shoe. "That's the thing. Ani," she swept her gaze to meet Mel's with a small smile, "that's what I've been calling the anonymous client. Anyway, Ani had given very specific instructions as to the day and time to pinch the necklace and directions to meet at the big hotel and casino at the bottom of your mountain afterwards to exchange the goods for the money, but no one showed."

She crossed her arms and narrowed her eyes, her suspicions growing. "Stop avoiding the question. Where's the necklace?" Possession of stolen property, even if she didn't steal it, could land Mel and possibly her family in jail. Bad enough the cops could accuse her of being an accessory after the fact for not turning in a wanted criminal. She wouldn't let the whole O'Rourke clan suffer because she owed this woman something for saving her life.

"I'm getting there, 'ang on." The woman's accent got heavier as her frustration rose. She tried to mimic Mel's crossed arms but hissed in pain. "The thing is, everything was going tickety-boo when out of nowhere some bloke flips on the lights and starts shooting at me."

The location of the necklace took a backseat for the moment. She got to her feet and stood over Poppy, the torn muscle story suddenly making a lot more sense. "How bad are you hurt?"

"It's a scratch," she waved her concern off, but used her left hand to make the gesture. An obvious clue that the wound wasn't nothing. And the black turtleneck she wore did a pretty good job of hiding blood.

"I'll be the judge of that."

"What, here? Now? It's on my shoulder, I'd," she dropped her eyes and voice demurely, "I'd have to take my shirt off."

Mel's palm met her face. "For the love of…it's just us girls here. You don't have anything I haven't seen before."

Reluctantly, she pulled her wounded arm out of the

sleeve of her sweater and shoved the material aside, allowing Mel to see her bicep. She scoffed. "Who knew you Brits were such prudes? Like you've never taken your shirt off in public before."

Poppy's chuckle morphed into a moan as soon as she touched her arm. "There was one time at Mardi Gras...so many beads." The last word was cut off with a hiss of pain as Mel inspected the tidy DIY bandage wrapped around her upper arm. The wound might be minor, but bright red stains were already seeping through the strip of white cotton.

"Come on," she insisted, grabbing her jacket, "let's get your boo boo looked at. You can tell me the rest of the story on the way." *Like where you've stashed stolen goods and please tell me not in my hotel.*

"This isn't the first wound I've had to dress," the woman remained in the chair, carefully threading her arm back through her sleeve. "I did a fair job if I do say so myself. No need for a doctor bill, I'm well aware of how you Yanks and your medical system like to price gouge."

Exasperated, Mel stood with her hands on her hips. "I'm not kidding. It might seem like nothing, but if bits of cloth from your shirt are still in the wound, it could get infected. Or it might require stitches and without proper treatment you'll have a scar."

The thief turned in her chair and batted her lashes at her. "Aw, Officer O'Rourke, you really do care about me."

"Me? No way, heart of stone, ask anyone. I just don't want to cook tomorrow because your arm got gangrene."

All humor faded from Poppy's face and her gaze

grew intense, the pain more visible now she knew to look. "It's a gunshot wound. Even in a quaint little town like yours, the doctor will have to file a report with the police. I don't think I left any blood on the scene, so the coppers aren't necessarily keeping an eye out for bullet wounds being treated, but I can't be sure."

Dammit, she had a point. When had she gone so soft? She'd forgotten about that. Still, the growing bloodstain concerned her. The thief wasn't a friend, but she enjoyed having someone around from her old world. And if she truly was innocent, she shouldn't have to hide. In fact, she couldn't hide forever, not even here in Pine Cove, so they might as well deal with the situation.

"Don't worry about the Doc, I'll handle her." She met Poppy's gaze full on and hoped her sincerity was clear. "It'll be all right, I promise. Now stop bleeding all over my hotel, and let's get you patched up."

She prayed the promise was one she could keep as the other woman trudged to her feet and followed her out of the office. She meant to try, but what's the saying about the road to hell being paved with good intentions? Somewhere out there roamed the person who killed Kyle Lange, and they either did a solid job of framing Poppy or got a lucky break and were going to make the most of it.

Worst-case scenario, if they think she can identify them, they'll be searching for her to finish what they started.

****

"This is a nice change of pace, dark gloomy cloud cover instead of all that sunshine," Poppy commented as they crunched through the light snow covering the ground down to the other end of town and Dr. Linda Hart's office.

"Are you kidding? This *is* a sunny day in Pine Cove." Mel had only lived here full-time for a few months and still struggled to adjust to the weather. Having grown up in Los Angeles where the sun shone ninety-five percent of the time, she had no idea how different the climate just three hours away could be, but to paraphrase an old movie, it wasn't the miles but the altitude. The cold temperatures she'd expected, but the almost constant cloud cover had been a surprise. Doc assured her the sun did shine here, but she had very little experiential evidence to support the claim.

"Ooh, what a grumpy Gus you are today," Poppy said teasing. "Look at this lovely small town! There's an adorable candy store, a florist, an artist studio—everything a girl could want! And painted in such bright, pretty colors."

"Yeah, yeah. I live here, remember?" She actually hadn't noticed most of the places the Brit pointed out. She'd been too busy learning how to run a bed-and-breakfast to get out much.

Inhaling deeply, she ignored her defensive statement and chattered on. "Mmm, and the fresh scent of pine. No matter how hard they try, you can't bottle a smell like that." This bubbly young woman defied the expectations she had of the master criminal she'd chased most of her career. Jaunty, cocky, arrogant—those were the adjectives she'd always applied to her. "Nice" had never been in the mix. She scowled as the thief smiled and waved at strangers, throwing out a, "Hullo!" as they passed by.

"Okay, enough of the Mr. Rogers act, let's get back

to this crime spree of yours. You broke into this guy's office, stole the necklace, and someone started shooting at you. What happened next?"

"Did I mention the part where I tripped over the dead body?"

Mel tried to tamp down her frustration, but it's not like the woman was a civilian. She was a thief who specialized in leaving not a shred of traceable evidence, for Pete's sake. She knows what details are important and a dead body is a pretty big detail. "No, you left out that part. Where does this trip fit into your timeline?"

"I, um, well, had just closed the safe and switched off my torch, so the office was dark. I headed toward the door when my foot caught on something. There he was, sprawled out on his back. I mean, he must have been there the whole time, but I'd gone round the other side of the desk going in and didn't see him."

The hesitation in her story caused a blip on Mel's bullshit radar, but she'd get back to that. Right now, she needed to hear the whole story to get the full picture of how much trouble Poppy was in.

"Did you get a look at the dead guy? Did you recognize him?"

When she didn't answer right away, Mel stopped her habitual scanning of the street, looking for trouble and studied her companion's face. Her eyes looked haunted, and she wore a horrified expression she'd never seen on her before, not even when she was in cuffs. She shook her head in answer to the question, and there was an authentic catch to her voice when she finally spoke. Or the woman was a damn good actress.

"At first, I didn't know what I stumbled on, but when I caught myself by putting out my hand and met something soft, I got curious. I switched on my penlight and thought someone had fainted or fallen asleep. Then my torch lit his face, and I saw his mouth hanging open and his eyes, unblinking, staring at the ceiling." The jerky shudder of her shoulders wasn't a staged act. "I was legging it out of there when the lights flipped on, and somebody started shooting at me."

"How did you get away? Did you go out the office door? Could any cameras in the halls or stairwells have caught you?"

She shook her head once in a vigorous motion, as if dispelling the vision of the dead man from her brain and then her standard light-hearted expression fell back in place. "Nah, the bugger stood between me and the door, so I left the way I came in, dashed across a few balconies, but he kept shooting at me so I dropped a floor and capered on."

Mel stopped, getting queasy as she visualized the scene. "What does 'capered on' mean? Did you climb down the outside of the building without a rope?" The nonchalant lift of a shoulder she got in response made her throw up a little bit in the back of her throat, her own vertigo returning by proxy. "Were there any cameras? Did anyone see you?"

The woman huffed; her face puckered in disapproval. "What do you take me for, some kind of amateur? I cased the building three nights running. There were no cameras on that side, very little foot traffic after ten and fortuitously, the nearest streetlamp was out."

"Oh, the light just happened to be out, did it?" Poppy's smirk answered her question. She wasn't surprised. Her careful planning was what made her so hard to catch. They turned the corner and reached Doc Hart's place.

The doctor's home and practice were located off the main circle drive of Pine Cove in a white clapboard, one-story building accented with gleaming black shutters and door. The doctor had done away with the holiday display of red and gold foil covered pots of poinsettias lining her small porch the day after Christmas. Presumably for Linda Hart, December twenty-sixth marked the end of the holiday, time to move on. Personally, she'd still have the Christmas tree in the Great Room if the dried-out Douglas fir hadn't become a fire hazard. She put a pin in the idea of using a fake one next year to keep the decorations around longer.

She noticed a truck parked in the Doc's tiny gravel parking lot to the left of the building. Her brows crinkled, and she hesitated. If the Doc was seeing a patient, perhaps they should wait until they were gone to be on the safe side. Unfortunately, either Poppy didn't see the truck, or the safe side was a place she never visited. Before Mel could stop her, she raised the shiny brass knocker on the door and rapped a few times. A few moments later, a gruff, "I'm coming, hold your horses," sounded from the other side.

The door swung open and there stood Dr. Linda Hart, her kind round face and full head of gray hair contrasting with yet another one of her many T-shirts advertising a rock band. "Mel, good to see you," she greeted her with a warm smile but no outstretched hand. The Doc had long been a believer that shaking hands was an exchange of germs, not sentiment. "How's your ankle? Irene tells me you haven't come down to see her for physical therapy. Those wounds won't heal themselves."

The doctor glared at her over the top of her spectacles, her double meaning crystal clear. She was one of the few people in town who understood how much her fear of heights interfered with Mel's life and had been encouraging her to see a professional to deal with her phobia.

"Sorry, business has been picking up, and I haven't had the time," she mumbled, ignoring Poppy's questioning glance. "Can we come in?"

With a sweeping gesture of her arm, Doc Hart welcomed them both inside. "Business or pleasure?" she asked. The answer determined whether they turned to the left or the right in her small foyer, the separation between her home and her medical practice.

"Business, but nothing urgent if you're already seeing a patient," she explained.

The older woman gave a dismissive wave of her hand. "Just finished an annual physical for someone who is annoyingly healthy. He's in the other room putting his clothes back on, so come on in." She opened the door to her small clinic and ushered them in. "What seems to be the problem?"

The two women exchanged sheepish looks—who should do the talking? While Mel struggled to formulate an answer factual enough to get by, Poppy dove in.

"Cheers for taking the time to see me, Doctor Hart. Mel's told me so many wonderful things about you."

"Oh? Are you a friend of her's from Los Angeles?" Doc Hart was pretty sharp, and Mel suspected something about her story already sounded wrong from the way her brow puckered.

"We've known each other for ages," she babbled, and it was mostly true. They had known each other, but to say they were friends was pushing the truth.

"What part of England are you from?"

Doc's question surprised Mel. Did it matter? She never could tell a Liverpoolian, if that was a word, from a Londoner.

"Oh, a small town you've never heard of, Herefordshire."

The older woman looked unconvinced but switched focus to the matter at hand. "So, what can I do for you?"

"Ran into a spot of trouble and my friend here insisted I have you take a look at my arm," Poppy replied cheerfully.

Her vagueness earned them both the stink-eye from the doctor. "Go on then behind the partition," she waved toward the standing privacy curtain, "take off your shirt so I can examine it. I'm good, but I don't have x-ray vision."

She'd just disappeared behind the divider when a deep voice from the other side of the room rumbled, "Emmeline O'Rourke, fancy meeting you here."

*Oh shit.* Gregg Marks, clad in jeans and a plaid shirt he hadn't buttoned, walked into the room. The man's impressive six-pack wasn't why the sight of him sent flutters through her stomach, though it didn't help. They'd had their disagreements, but he wasn't an idiot. If he saw Poppy, eventually he'd make the connection between the robbery with "The Ghost's" MO written all over it and figure out who she was.

"Deputy Marks," she greeted him in a raised voice,

stressing the deputy part for Poppy's sake. *Please take the hint and stay out of sight.* "I didn't know you were here."

He gave her a cocky grin, equal parts charming and irritating. "What, you mean the doc didn't sell tickets to my annual physical?" he teased as he buttoned his shirt.

"Oh brother," the doctor muttered as she put a firm hand to his back and pushed the man out of the exam room. "You're almost as perfect as you think you are. Now scoot so I can get back to work. I'll send the paperwork to the department later today."

As soon as the door closed, Poppy stepped out from behind the partition wearing a paper gown in place of her sweater. "Yum," she whispered with a wink as she took her place on the exam bed.

"What have we here?" Doc cut the bloodied bandage off her arm and frowned. "I'm no expert, but that looks like a gunshot wound."

Poppy and Mel exchanged loaded looks, and both started talking at once, tripping over their own fairy tales about how the injury happened. She put a hand on Poppy to silence her, exhaled sharply, and confessed.

"You're right Doc, it was my fault. I accidentally shot her this morning when I was showing her how to load a gun. I'm kind of hoping we can keep this between us?"

"Yeah, so not what happened, at least not this morning. Try again." She pursed her lips and gave them both a harsh glare, silently demanding an explanation.

Mel's cheeks grew hot, like they always did when she got caught in a lie. That's why she rarely did it, not out of any moral code, but because she was a terrible liar. Her mind churned at what to say when Poppy gave a little sob. Surprised, she glanced over to see the thief blink rapidly a few times, a feat she had to admire considering the long, thick false eyelashes she had on. On the fourth blink, a tear rolled down her cheek, and she gave the doc a brave smile.

"Don't blame Mel, she's covering for me. The truth is," she looked at the floor, then raised her luminous gaze to the doctor and amplified her emotions to a whole new level. "She's helping me run away from my abusive arse of a boyfriend. We had a fight last night, and he took out his gun. Luckily, I'm pretty quick on my feet but not quite quick enough." She raised her arm like a chicken wing to emphasize where this fictitious boyfriend shot her. "Mel told me to file a complaint once she realized what had happened, but he's friends with cops back in LA. If this gets on an official report, he'll hear about it and find me."

On the $f$ of find, she put a tremble in her lip so it came out as "f-f-f-ind" and barely squeaked out the "me". Hell, Mel believed the story, and she'd watched her spin the fable on the spot. The doctor put a sympathetic hand on her shoulder, her narrowed gaze shifting back and forth between the two women.

"You're sure that's a good enough reason not to report this?" Her voice was kind, but there was a shadow of doubt and suspicion in her eyes.

"Doc, Poppy and I go way back, and she really does need my help to figure a way out of this situation." This time the lie was close enough to the truth that her cheeks didn't turn bright red.

The doctor heaved a big sigh and shook her head. "Do not make me regret doing you this favor." She waggled her finger at them both, scolding, "And if this boyfriend shows his face in Pine Cove, you're calling Gregg Marks immediately. Do not take any chances and confront him yourself."

Mel didn't let herself heave a sigh of relief until after the doc bandaged the bullet wound and they were heading back to the B&B. Had they gotten away with it, or was Doc Hart on to them?

****

"Your doc was rather reasonably priced, not at all what I expected from you Yanks and your infamous healthcare." Poppy commented in a chipper tone, possibly because of the topical numbing agent the Doc had put on the wound. It had required several stitches and a prescription for an antibiotic, so at least the trip and exposure of the bullet wound had been worth the risk. She flexed her arm, but Mel would bet she'd be sore tomorrow.

"The Doc gave you a big discount because of your tale of woe, and don't worry, you'll be working off what you owe me for paying your bill."

"Of course, love. You have my word. Besides, your copper, he's quite bev," the Brit cooed, "well worth sticking around for."

She stopped cold. Her companion gave her a shrug. "What?" Misunderstanding the continuing silence, she explained, "Means he's handsome."

"Yeah, I get what the expression means. You need to take this more seriously. If he sees you and recognizes you, there's nothing I can do to help."

The career criminal waved off her concern. "Please, not the first time I've avoided the cops. Besides, I don't stand a chance with him."

"What? He's a man, one bat of those eyelashes and

he'll be following you around like a puppy, which would not be a smart move, so stay away."

"No love, I meant because he's sweet on you."

"Shut up." She couldn't deny there'd been something between them, but whether the spark was attraction, the bond between cops, or friendship, she didn't know and definitely didn't want to talk about it.

"Come on, he obviously—"

But she was no longer paying attention, her eyes focused on the furry, red beast gamboling through the trees dotting the neighborhood to her right.

"Chewie," she called, but the dog ignored her. "Chewbarka, come here, boy. Come on." The big dog's head swiveled until he found who was calling his name. When his gaze locked on Mel, his floppy ears perked up and he galloped toward her. She braced herself for the blow when forty pounds of Labradoodle put his front paws on her chest. "Chewbarka, did you escape again?" The right color and same expressive eyes, the dog resembled the heroic sidekick. His response to her question was to lick her face.

Jackson's puppy—and despite his size, the dog was still a youngster—had developed a knack for getting out of his yard at home where he hung out with Hugo Thibodeaux, Jackson's dad, whenever he wasn't with Jackson at his café. More than once she'd seen the big goof making an adorable nuisance of himself greeting people enjoying a cup of coffee or a meal at one of the outdoor dining areas dotting the town square with a slobbery kiss. She'd gotten in the habit of carrying a few treats in her pocket to make catching him easier. She wondered if he escaped just to get a treat. Even though she suspected she was teaching him a bad habit, she couldn't say no to those brown eyes and gave him a cookie.

"Who's your furry friend?" asked Poppy.

"This is Chewbarka, he belongs to a friend of mine who owns that café." Mel nodded her head down the street.

"The Hungry Puppy, eh? Aptly named."

"Jackson has an unusual business model. He creates food for people and their pets."

"Seems to be doing well," Poppy observed. Even the tables outside under the portable heaters had a wait list. Mel imagined the inside dining room must be packed.

"Come on, we better take this goofball back home before he gets into any trouble. Last week when he got out, he went to town digging a bunch of holes in the small local garden store." Not hearing a snarky response, she glanced at Poppy who smiled at her. "What?"

"Nothing, I just never pictured the Officer O'Rourke I knew so…happy. Which makes me think either you really like this dog or its owner," she said with a self-satisfied smirk.

"Shut up," she countered again, cringing at her own weak comeback, especially when it prompted Poppy to hum an obscenely cheerful tune.

\*\*\*\*

The firm hold Mel kept on Chewie's collar proved unnecessary. As long as she had treats in her pocket, the dog stuck to her side. Thank goodness it was a short walk to the Thibodeaux home, or she might have run out.

When they arrived at the sleekly modern two-story

house Jackson shared with his father, Hugo, the gate to the four-foot-tall horizontal wooden picket fence around their yard swung open. She ushered the dog and Poppy inside before securing the latch. The simple metal clasp snapped in place when she closed the gate, so either someone hadn't shut it properly or...

"Chewbarka, have you figured out how to open this gate?" It seemed unlikely the rambunctious puppy could operate the latch himself, but it wasn't like Jackson or Hugo to be so careless. If the dog had mastered the latch, he wasn't fessing up. The front door of the house opened and a fit man in his fifties stepped onto the porch. His mop of brown curls matched his son's except for the streaks of gray weaving through them.

"Mel, how are you doing? Jackson's at work, was he expecting you?" Even after a decade of living in Pine Cove, his faint Cajun accent still tinted his words.

Scratching Chewie behind the ears, she explained, "No sir, I'm just returning your escapee."

"Chewbarka, where did you get off to this time?" He admonished the puppy with a grin. Father and son shared the same deep dimples, which made it obvious when his smile faded away much too quickly. She'd only met Hugo a few months ago, but couldn't remember seeing him without a happy expression on his face.

"Mr. Thibodeaux, is everything okay?"

"Hm?" he asked as if he hadn't heard her. "Oh, yes, yes darlin', everything's fine. And I told you before, please call me Hugo." He seemed to shake off whatever was distracting him as he walked down the steps and the dog left her side to ram his big head into the man's thigh. Clearly Jackson got his Cajun charm from his father, as Hugo enveloped her in a warm hug. After he released her, he appraised Poppy with a smile. "And who is this enchanting vision with you?"

"This is my...er," she hesitated. How did she define Poppy? She hadn't considered her a friend before. Did her coming to Mel for help make them friends now? The thief studied her with a crooked grin, as curious as Hugo to hear what came next. "My new assistant at the B&B, Poppy Phillips." The woman cast her eyes downward, but did Mel glimpse dejection?

"Poppy, what a lovely name." He opened his arms in an invitation.

"Can't take credit for it, have to thank my mum for that," she said, accepting the offer and stepping into his embrace.

"Very nice to meet you." After a brief hug, he turned back to Mel. "Thanks for bringing him back home. Guess I'm going to have to look at fixing the gate."

"The latch locked when I closed it," she nodded toward the now secured entry. "But it was open when I got here, so either Chewie has figured out how to work the latch or your son left the gate open."

"Oh, I must have done it when I got the mail," he admitted with a frown. "Danged if I can remember leaving it unlatched though. I'll be more careful from now on. Can I offer you some pie to make up for your troubles? Don't worry, Jax made it, not me," he added with a chuckle.

Poppy skipped toward the door with a smile when Mel stopped her. "We'd love to, sir, but I left my brother in charge of the Babbling Brook and, well, he's better with tools than with people. I should get back before he causes a minor catastrophe."

She gave him a small wave and started toward the gate when he asked her, "Have you talked to Jackson today? It surprised me when he came home so early last night and was in such a bad mood. I know it's none of my business, but I can tell you from experience if you two had words, the best thing is to talk about whatever is bothering you and clear the air."

Suddenly the distance to the gate and her escape from both his fatherly concern and Poppy's peaked interest seemed like a mile away. "No sir, I haven't seen him, but I'm sure everything's fine. We're good." With her hand on her new assistant's back, she propelled her out onto the sidewalk, waited until the latch *snicked* into place and then hustled toward the inn. She ground her teeth while Poppy chanted, "Jackson and Mel sitting in a tree, k-i-s-s-i-n-g," as well as another verse featuring Deputy Marks, under her breath the entire way there.

Chapter Five

"You swear to me you didn't stash that stolen necklace in my hotel?"

In order to get Poppy to stop singing her annoying song, Mel questioned her all over again about the necklace and if she'd taken anything else. She needed to protect her family and their liability at all costs.

"For the hundredth time, he hired me to take the necklace, so that's all I stole, and it isn't in your bloody inn. The hideous thing is in the boot of my car." They'd reached the inn, and Poppy stopped, putting a hand on the rail of the stairs leading to her room. "Do you mind if I take a quick kip? Even by my standards, the last twenty-four hours have been buggered."

Mel nodded, well aware of how much her arm had to be hurting. She studied the woman as she escaped to her room and her tail did indeed seem to be dragging, as Grandma O might say. But she'd also seen her put on an Academy Award worthy performance at the Doc's place, convincing the doctor she was escaping an abusive boyfriend. How much could she trust of what the Brit ever said?

****

Guests were out and about, leaving her little to do at the front desk, so Mel left her grandmother in charge while she sat at her computer to dig into the murdered man. According to her story, and her gut said Poppy stuck mostly to the truth, the Palm Springs PD had more than likely found her climbing equipment, which put her name on a very short list of suspects. The elegant cat burglar schtick was her signature, so it wouldn't be long before they started looking for "The Ghost" if they weren't already. If she was going to help her, she needed to come up with a list of plausible suspects, and fast.

A computer search for Kyle Lange scored dozens of hits. He and his partner, a woman named Leigh Pemberton, owned Badger Corp, a subsidiary of a Nichols Oil, a much larger oil drilling company. The science was above her pay grade, but according to their newsletter, Badger Corp made ceramic pellets that made oil extraction easier, as well as products to eliminate spills.

Looking beyond his company website, she found numerous articles praising his inventions mainly from news sources by and about the petroleum industry. Eco activist bloggers and environmental sites damned those same formulas for ruining the planet. No big surprise there. There were also several links connecting him, or at least his money, to charity, but that didn't make him a saint. When you're wealthy, donating a few thousand dollars to feed puppies is a good way to soothe a guilty conscience without a lot of suffering.

"Christ on a cracker, there's no need to get your knickers in a knot, lady," a voice at the front desk bellowed. Mel put her hand to her face, understanding now why her mom sent cranky Grandma O to chill out in Pine Cove for a while. But they couldn't afford to offend guests or get bad reviews when they'd just re-opened, so she hustled out to the front desk to soothe whatever feathers the cantankerous old woman had ruffled.

When she left the office and saw who her grandmother was talking to, a wave of dread washed over her. Mrs. Oberdingle, the mayor's wife, stood primly at the front desk with her little long-haired black and white dog in an oversized purse, its eyes bugging out more than usual. Forced to buy her clothes in the teen section of the store because of her peewee height, today her bright yellow flared pants and cheerful sweater jacket clashed with the death stare she was giving Grandma O. A nosy busybody with a great deal of influence over the Chamber of Commerce, she was the last person Mel wanted her grandmother to get into a tussle with. A bad review on a trip site they could weather. A vengeful Mrs. Oberdingle wouldn't be so easy.

"How dare you suggest Cio-Cio has to stay outside? She is my service animal, and legally, I have every right to take her with me wherever I please."

Technically, that wasn't true, but then again, the dog also wasn't an emotional support animal in the first place. The mayor's wife didn't need any emotional support. She had quite a healthy ego and if she got into a situation when she needed backup, Mel was sure she kept the mayor's balls in her purse right beside the mopsy dog.

"Well then, I guess you'll have to stay outside too because that walking flea circus isn't going one paw further into this hotel." The older woman leaned over the desk, towering over Mrs. Oberdingle. Mel hid a smile behind her hand. The O'Rourkes were not tall people, so this was probably the first time since her grandkids hit puberty that Grandma O held the higher ground over anyone.

Under different circumstances, it would have been funny to let the two harridans duke it out, but she couldn't see a good outcome no matter who won, so she jumped in between them.

"Thanks for keeping an eye on the front desk for me, Grandma, but I've got it from here. Why don't you go take a break?" She beamed sweetness and light when she faced Mrs. Oberdingle, but when she turned toward her grandmother, she shot the older woman a glare to prove she wasn't kidding. The old woman harrumphed and left, but not before clandestinely flipping the mayor's wife the bird. Mel, aware of her grandmother's crude gesture, ignored it and focused on her guest, smile plastered back in place.

"Mrs. Oberdingle, how lovely to see you again. What brings you to our inn?"

Her grandmother muttered, "Kiss ass," but Mel ignored her.

"I see you've got some scruffy young man hammering away at the rickety cabin in the middle of your *compound.*" She sneered as she sputtered the last word.

For reasons she couldn't fathom, Mrs. Oberdingle blamed her for losing the town's annual Christmas charity bake-off. Her ire made no sense. All of them, even Jackson, were beaten by the local grade school kids whose parents were strong-armed by the principal into bidding so much money for their tasteless lumps of unidentifiable sweets that they won hands down. Still, the woman seemed to hold her personally responsible, sniping at her every chance she got.

The old saying about catching more flies with honey never made sense to a very literal-minded Mel. Who wants to catch flies, anyway? But the first week out on patrol, her training officer showed how to throw cranky, aggressive people off balance with a polite smile. The tactic kept her from punching many an obnoxious person in the face, but Mrs. Oberdingle put the theory to the test. "That's my brother, Liam," she ground out through gritted teeth. Scruffy? Luckily, her grandmother hadn't heard the bothersome woman call her favorite grandchild scruffy. "He's going to be here for the week to do some repairs."

"Well, he'll have to hammer more quietly or do it another day. The Ladies Auxiliary is having a luncheon next door, and we can't hear each other through that unbearable racket."

Ever since her historic cookie loss, the mayor's wife found reasons on a weekly basis to complain about something Mel or the Babbling Brook had done wrong. Carping about Liam's *unbearable racket* was another exaggerated protest, but asking him to hold off until this afternoon would be easier than reasoning with her.

"I'm so sorry, I had no idea the repairs were bothering anyone." She pulled her phone out of her pocket. "I'll text him right now and tell him to stop."

Without another word, the tiny woman stomped away, grumping under her breath as if she'd told her to suck it instead of getting her way.

Text sent and acknowledged with a reply of *WTF,* a shrug emoji, face palm emoji, and a smiling poo emoji. She laughed. He was doing her a favor by spending the week here fixing things, and now Mrs. Oberdingle and her cronies were harassing the poor guy. What does a ladies' auxiliary do, anyway?

She realized with a jolt of alarm she hadn't heard anything from the back room since Grandma O's retreat from the Oberdingle fracas. Mel had already moved into her own place by the time her grandmother came to live at her parents' house, so she wasn't sure what to expect from the septuagenarian. Did she normally nap during the day? Her father had insisted his mother live with them to make it easier to keep an eye on her, but tales of her constant antics sounded like his strategy had backfired. She'd assumed the old woman had withdrawn from the field of battle to the inn's living quarters to turn the TV on at its highest volume and watch her "stories" like her maternal grandmother used to do before she passed away, so the silence worried her.

Since new arrivals shouldn't be arriving until later, she thought it was safe enough to leave the desk unmanned for a moment to go check on her. Slowly opening the creaking office door in case the older woman was asleep, to her shock, she found her grandmother clacking away on the computer keyboard.

"Grandma?" She hurried around the desk to read the screen, praying she hadn't gotten hooked on some on-line gambling site. What she saw surprised her even more. Her grandmother had created files about Kyle Lange. Among them was one marked *articles*, another *social media*. The one labeled *legal issues* caught her eye.

"Oh, hello dear," her grandmother greeted her. "I noticed you were looking into this Lange fella, so I thought I'd lend a hand."

No one could blame Mel for being stunned at her

grandmother's computer skills. The last she heard, Grandma had a hard time opening e-mails. "What...how?" she mumbled, flabbergasted.

Instead of being insulted, her wrinkled face broke into a sly smile. "Not so crazy after all, am I? I'm assuming you're reading up on the poor man because he was murdered? I would have thought you'd abandoned all that police work nonsense once you moved here and focused on finding a nice young man to settle down with, but if you want my opinion, one of those tree huggers did him in."

She opted to ignore the "nice young man remark" and shifted a chair around to sit next to her grandmother and share her view of the computer screen. "What makes you say that?"

With a few strokes of the keys, the older woman called up Lange's Tweedle account. "His feed is full of posts about the great work Badger Corp was doing for their parent company, Nichols Oil."

She'd deduced as much from the articles she'd found about him. Several eco-friendly groups blamed him for damaging the environment. "Okay, but Tweedle battles happen all the time. All sound and fury—"

"Signifying nothing, yes I know the quote, dear. But this one," she clicked a few times on the screen to highlight a particular account, "This EcoWarrior69 fellow looks suspicious. I mean, obviously that's not his real name, so something's hinky. Hopefully, there were sixty-eight other EcoWarriors before him, or he loves the planet way too much."

"Grandma!" Mel felt her skin grow red-hot with embarrassment all the way to her hairline.

"What? Grow up, Emmeline. Anyway, his profile pic is one of those cartoon thingys of the planet in a cape armed with some sort of laser beam. If that doesn't say guilty, I don't know what does."

She read through the brief profile under @EcoWarrior69, less concerned about his "cartoon thingy" than his many long, rambling posts baiting Lange. He taunted the scientist, taking credit for actions he'd taken to stop oil drilling by the parent company. Some legal, others not so much. A few of the posts must have crossed Tweedle's fluid lines because they'd been taken down for content, but the remaining ones blamed Lange for an oil leak from one of Nichols' wells that devastated a coastal marshland last year. The scientist didn't respond.

"Now, on the other hand," Grandma highlighted various social media accounts for Lange's younger wife, Heather, "the second Mrs. Lange hasn't met a muffin she isn't compelled to post all over everywhere, including SpinChat."

With the stroke of a key, the white-haired woman showed a post Heather had put on the social media platform Mel had always associated with kids twerking. She displayed a cupcake from her favorite bakery in Palm Springs, with video hastily cut together showing the stages from batter to decorated cupcake set to a pop tune. The boring snippet had gotten a few thousand hits, so someone must have cared. Still, it was weird hearing the words "SpinChat" coming out of her grandmother's mouth. "How on Earth do you know about SpinChat?"

"Fiona told me about it and showed me how to post."

"You have a SpinChat account?" She squawked,

certain if she found out one more incredible thing about her grandmother, her mind would be thoroughly blown. And why did her sister Vinnie let her precocious nine-year-old daughter Fiona anywhere near SpinChat? A dull headache began knocking behind her eyes as Grandma O pulled up her account and played one of her videos. Oddly enough, the clip of the sunrise was pretty good. Much better than Heather Lange's cupcake.

"That's what happens when you have nothing but time on your hands, dear. I can make you one if you want?" What the heck would she even post to SpinChat and why? Then she realized the motive behind her grandmother's ploy.

"Is this more of your love connection efforts? Believe me, the last thing that would attract a man to my door is seeing me doing something stupid on a social media platform with kids doing the floss dance."

"Don't be silly," her grandmother said as she patted her knee. "I meant for this...inn." She didn't even try to keep the disdain out of her voice.

"No, thanks," she assured her. "But I appreciate all of this research, you saved me a lot of time."

"Good, then you can pay me for my hard work by buying me lunch." She rose to her feet more easily than Mel did, her damaged ankle having stiffened while they were sitting. "Why were you looking into the murder, anyway? Are you thinking of writing a book or something?"

"Yeah, why are you investigating some rando guy you never met," asked Liam from the door, "who was killed during a robbery the night before a thief comes to our inn asking for a job?"

Dammit, she knew he was quick but hadn't

counted on him staying on top of the local news. "I was curious what leads they had, that's all. Once a cop, always a cop. Where do you guys want to go to lunch?"

The hard, thin line of his pursed lips and the spark in his hazel eyes, so like her own except for the gold flecks that right now took on more of a steely shade, said he was far from dropping the discussion about Poppy. But instead of hashing it out, he switched gears as he held out his arm for their grandmother, who took it despite her spryness. "At the hardware store, one of the guys raved about this place, something about a puppy? Let's try there."

She cringed, which of course stoked her grandmother and brother's curiosity. "Meh, it's more of a place to go to eat with your dog, you guys wouldn't like it."

Grandma's eyebrows shot skyward, and her brother coughed "bullshit" in his hand. The matriarch poked him, letting him know she'd heard that, before bestowing an angelic smile on Mel. "Nonsense, dear, it sounds lovely."

The last place she wanted to go was The Hungry Puppy, where she almost certainly would run into Jackson, the owner and the culinary genius behind the food. She owed him an apology for being such a jerk last night and had no problem giving him a sincere *mea culpa*. Saying it in front of her nosey family, however, was another matter.

"Hey, did someone mention lunch?" Poppy asked from the doorway.

"No way," her brother squawked, planting himself to prevent anyone from exiting or the intruder from entering.

"Liam," Mel growled, in no mood for his over-protective b.s.

"If you're okay with her working here, that's your business, but I'm drawing the line at sharing a meal with her." The anger in his voice surprised her. All this time, she'd blamed herself for being unable to deal with her fears. She had no idea her brother held such a grudge against the thief. Whether the rest of the family shared his opinion, she learned in the next breath.

"Liam Gerard O'Rourke, get over yourself," Grandma O demanded as she shoved past his wide shoulders to put her hand on Poppy's arm.

Kill me now, Mel thought, as she grabbed her jacket and led the way to her doom.

## Chapter Six

As they walked down the street, looping through town to get to The Hungry Puppy, a light dusting of snow reminded the little group that January in Pine Cove meant any weather was possible. They could have made the trip in half the time if they'd taken the bridge over the brook the B&B got its name from. The ancient, narrow structure connected the back of the inn to the café, but Mel blanched when her grandmother headed toward the shortcut.

The one time she'd successfully crossed the span with a fifteen-foot drop to the churning, frigid waters below was to save Jackson from her murderous employee. It was humiliating when her seventy-something grandmother blithely put her rubber booted foot on the wooden bridge and Mel sucked back a gasp of air so loud all three turned to stare at her.

Poppy's brows furrowed in concern, which drove Liam to scowl at the thief, but even her grandmother avoided citing the reason for her sudden fear of heights. Ignoring the elephant on the bridge, so to speak, the foursome strolled down the sidewalk instead, taking in the unique shops along the way.

It almost seemed like Pine Cove had passed a statute banning big name chain stores, preferring mom-and-pop ice cream stands, coffee houses, and clothing boutiques. Even the sole movie theatre was locally owned. Grandma O reclaimed Poppy's arm and the two of them prattled on about each shop, bakery, and art gallery along the way.

When the older woman slipped on a tiny patch of ice, Liam rushed to support her left side. His glare at Poppy over their grandmother's head went unseen by his adversary, but Mel noticed and sighed. As kids, sibling rivalry between actual siblings in their family often raged to epic levels, and she didn't relish the idea of reliving the havoc now between her brother and whatever Poppy was becoming to her. But her bigger problem lay a mere hundred feet ahead of them, when the threesome would meet Jackson and the speculating about their relationship would run amuck.

He was a great guy—smart, successful, and funny, all topped with his southern charm, not to mention his gorgeous mocha skin and startling aquamarine eyes. But she'd had enough upheaval in her life over the past year. Her accident had forced her to retire from being a cop, the only job she'd ever wanted. Living in Los Angeles with the ghost of the life she could no longer have broke her heart, so she'd come to Pine Cove to clear her head. The family used to visit the small town when she was a kid and those memories were always happy ones.

Walking around town lost in a funk, she'd noticed the empty inn and took the "for sale" plastered on the window as a literal and metaphysical sign. After talking the move over with her family, she uprooted her life to start over again in this small mountain community. She didn't need to add any romantic entanglements to complicate things.

Her grandmother and brother, however, loved to

meddle. From the time she started dating, Grandma O perceived every male acquaintance of hers as a possible love match. A few years ago, Mel took her to a doctor's appointment and by the time they left, she was picking out names for great-grandchildren. The pushy old woman had gone so far as to get the single doctor's phone number, but she'd been too mortified to give the poor man a call.

Liam was just as bad, but in the opposite direction. All through high school, any boy he didn't deem suitable, which included the majority of males except for a few of his rugby buddies, got the stink eye. Even though he was two years younger than her, a glare from her brawny brother deterred most prospective dates from coming near her or her sister. The pit in her stomach grew wider as she thought about what would happen when these two intrusive forces united against a common target.

She didn't have to wait long. As they approached the sunny yellow building with its white trimmed wrap-around porch that comfortably fit a dozen tables and the necessary heaters to keep diners and their dogs warm, a familiar head of dark, curly hair turned their way. Jackson saw the group and a warm, inviting grin lit his face. Bidding *au revoir* to the customer he was chatting with, he bounded down the porch steps to greet them.

"Mel, I was afraid I wouldn't see you again after last night." Three sets of eyes snapped toward her and she read the very mixed thoughts going on behind them. Her cheeks flushed at Poppy's very obvious smirk of pleasure. She definitely thought they had sex. Noting the heat of Liam's glower and the mischievous delight in her grandmother's eyes, Mel realized they were all thinking the same thing but reacting to the mental image of them getting naked together differently.

"Jackson has been helping with my height phobia by taking me to the climbing gym," she explained in a tone she hoped clarified they should all be ashamed of themselves. It pissed her off when none of them looked like they believed her, but she ignored their childish behavior and turned her attention to the man in front of her.

Jackson was as different from Gregg Marks as red wine was from white. While Gregg was broad and muscular like Liam, Jackson had a deceptively slender build, possessing the lithe strength of a dancer or figure skater. His features made him more welcoming than Gregg's, and he always smelled of brown sugar and caramel from the time he spent in the kitchen concocting his next culinary creation. A genius level chemical engineer, he'd left his career to devote his talents to creating tasty food as opposed to synthetic additives capable of mimicking the real thing.

"It was my fault, I'm sorry I was such a jerk," she apologized in a rush. "You were just trying to help and you're right. I have to get comfortable with the idea that stumbles are going to happen, and I need to recover from them, not quit."

Jackson shook his head, dropping his gaze. "No ma'am, I shouldn't have let you fall so far. Next time I'll be more careful, providing you're willing to try again?"

A whole flock of butterflies exploded in her chest at the thought, but she nodded and did her best to smile. "Of course. How about later this week? My more immediate problem is I've got some hungry employees.

Do you have a table open?"

"For my neighbors?" His lazy grin curled one corner of his mouth and lit his dazzling eyes. "Always. Unless your new crew plans on murdering me like your old one tried to do."

Apologizing for the hundredth time and getting a laugh in return, she made the introductions. "This is my Grandma O'Rourke, my brother Liam, whose pictures you've seen, and—"

Before she could finish, Poppy did a weird thing, gliding forward in a burst of energy like a speed skater to close the gap between them. In the blink of an eye, she stood within inches of Jackson. "I am your biggest fan," she declared in a breathy voice, adding more strokes of her luxurious eyelashes. "I read the article about you in *Tasty Cuisine* and even though I don't have a dog, I admire your work. Offering your canine menu in to-go 'doggy' bags? Genius. And donating the leftovers to the local shelter? So inspiring."

Mel's jaw dropped. She lived a stone's throw from the man, saw him every day and didn't know about all of his activities. When did Poppy become so knowledgeable? More to the point, what was she up to? Jackson clearly didn't share her suspicion of the woman's motive, flushing with delight at her praise.

"Why thank you ma'am, I figured my dad and fifteen other people were the only ones who read that article." Then he directed all of his charm and dazzling gaze at Grandma O, taking the arm Poppy had abandoned. "Here, young lady, let me show you to a nice warm table inside."

\*\*\*\*

As he guided them to their seats, Mel got her first

good look at his newly expanded operation and was impressed. He'd made room for more tables while losing none of the café's original charm. But something was missing. She didn't see Hugo helping with table service or chatting with customers on the porch with Chewbarka, a first since she'd known them.

"Where is your dad?" she asked as Jackson pulled out her chair after seating Grandma, leaving Liam to either pull out Poppy's for her or come across as a jerk. With all the enthusiasm of a patient getting a root canal, her brother did the polite thing before flopping down in his own chair in disgust.

"He, uh, stayed home today," he mumbled, tipping her off something was wrong.

"Is he okay? Poppy and I ran into him this morning after catching your furry escapee, and he seemed out of sorts."

His eyes darted furtively around the room before admitting, "We got an email the other day from my mom, alerting us to the fact she's flying in from New Orleans for a visit." His grim expression told her this impromptu reunion wasn't a joyful one. "She should be here tomorrow morning, so he's busy fussing over the house for her majesty's arrival."

When Mel first met Jackson and Deputy Marks as they stood over her murdered guest, their ugly history kept the two men from being civil to each other. The cop acted like there was nothing to tell and she hadn't been able to pry much out of Jackson beyond he and his dad had moved to Pine Cove from Louisiana when he was a high school freshman. Starting over as a teenager had been tough, but he'd understood why his father, heartbroken after his wife asked for a divorce, had to leave his home state.

"I don't think my dad ever got over Mom in all these years, and the idea of seeing her again is hitting him hard," he confided.

It explained why Hugo was so distracted this morning, but her gut told her there was more to the story. "How are *you* doing?"

He tried for a casual shrug, but the stiffness to his body spoke volumes. "We've been in touch since Dad and I moved away. I visit her a few times a year, but I can't imagine why she's coming here out of the blue." With a family as big as hers, she understood how sudden calls for no apparent reason were cause for suspicions. Most of the time, like Grandma O's unexpected appearance this morning, some sort of disaster followed. "It's been nice meeting you all, but those burgers aren't going to make themselves. Enjoy your lunch, it's on the house as my welcome to Pine Cove gift." This time, his bright smile didn't light up his face like before. His mother's surprising visit was visibly bothering him.

Returning her attention to her own familial mess, she noticed perusing the short but mouth-watering menu choices gave Liam something else to do other than glower at Poppy. His efforts to intimidate her had done him no good. The effervescent woman kept chatting on anyway, somehow managing not to turn to stone despite his death stare.

While Mel oscillated between a salad to be healthy or a burger and fries to be happy, she wondered how she could help the Thibodeaux men. She hated seeing the nicest, most laid back people she knew so tense.

When the server arrived to take their orders, she

decided on happy. Life was too complicated some days to take the high road. After he took their menus and left, Poppy's hand brushed her arm.

"I did a little research on ways to get over phobias and, according to one article, the best way is to take up a hobby that's more Zen than what you're afraid of, like knitting, or scrapbooking. Something to get you to focus on details you can control."

Mel rolled her eyes as her grandmother ridiculed the idea. "Pfft, knitting sucks."

"You've tried it?" She couldn't picture her eccentric grandmother doing anything so domestic. She was an extraordinary baker, but that was the extent of her grandmotherly instincts. When she was a little girl, Grandma O was supposed to take her and Vinnie to see an animated kid's movie, but took them to a gangster flick instead, swearing them both to secrecy since their parents would lose their minds if they found out.

"That senior center your mother took me to for a while insisted we old broads spend an hour a day doing some stupid craft. It was supposed to keep our minds sharp and hands moving or some such twaddle."

"You mean the place you got thrown out of?" Liam snickered. "Gee, I wonder why."

Poppy shared a laugh with him and Mel noticed he thawed a few degrees as she pressed on. "I think if you start small and do something you have complete control over, where you can fix any mistake, it'll build your confidence. Eventually you'll realize you have domain over bigger things as well. The climbing gym is a great idea, but maybe attacking your fear from the side instead of head on will work better?"

"Or knitting might bore you so much that rock

climbing looks a lot more appealing," her brother offered. "I hate to say it, but that's a good idea."

Their food arrived and smelled so divine she had no regrets about skipping the salad. Between fries, she argued she was way too young to take to a rocking chair and knitting needles. Liam reminded her their thirteen-year-old cousin Aislin knitted her a sweater last year for Christmas.

"All right, we can go check out the yarn store after lunch. They probably have classes or a book or something."

The Brit bounced in her chair in excitement. Liam begrudgingly agreed to take Grandma back to the B&B and keep an eye on her in case she got into any more confrontations with the locals or guests.

"But hurry back, I want to pick up where I left off fixing the porch railing on cabin six now that the meeting of the noise police has wrapped up."

She assured him she wouldn't be more than fifteen minutes behind him. How long can a visit to a yarn store take?

****

The Yarn Barn was small but brightly lit, with floor to ceiling windows on the front and side. Even with the sun scarcely peeking out from behind the grey clouds, the place had a cheerful ambience. The rainbow of skeins displayed on open wire shelves allowed the light to bounce around in a welcoming way.

The assorted textures of the yarns drew her attention as much as the colors, from curly ones that reminded her of Chewie to silky soft mohair. Half of the back wall was crammed with books on how to knit with patterns for everything from blankets to baby clothes. The other half held dozens of different sized and shaped needles and a wide variety of crochet hooks. Mel, who had faced down hardened criminals without flinching, found this strange new world intimidating.

"Welcome to the Yarn Barn," a sturdy woman with thick waves of honey-blonde hair and an infectious smile greeted them.

"Thank you, love. My friend 'ere is looking for a new hobby and I thought knitting would be just the ticket." Surprise trumped her irritation at someone doing the talking for her. And there was that friend label again. Truth be told, she didn't have many women friends and none in Pine Cove other than Doc Hart.

"Then you've come to the right place. I'm Dortha Jo, by the way."

Again, Poppy jumped in and made the introductions before Mel even opened her mouth. The woman, who turned out to own the shop, peppered her with questions about what kind of project she wanted to start with.

"Something super easy," she asserted before her self-declared new bestie got her in too deep. "I'm not much of a crafty person."

"Then I've got just the thing for you." The shop owner seemed undeterred by her lack of enthusiasm and led them over to a rack of patterns for scarves. They all looked daunting to master, and if she couldn't be perfect at something, what was the point, so Mel's attention wandered while the other two women blathered on. She meandered around another display and was surprised to see a familiar face.

"Melanie, how nice to see you," exclaimed Kendall Bard, the realtor who sold the Babbling Brook to the

O'Rourke clan. She bit back her inclination to correct her. Again. No matter how many times she told the woman her name was Mel, she insisted on getting it wrong. There was no point in correcting her, other than to quell Poppy's snorted laughter. Great, perfect timing for her to come join her.

As a former cop who prided herself on her powers of observation, she was embarrassed to admit she almost didn't recognize the realtor. In her defense, she looked so much more casual, with her ample figure clad in jeans and a sweater instead of her usual power suit. Especially since the jeans fit her, which made her think the woman would be better off owning her plump self rather than wearing suits one size too small.

"I was beginning to think you'd become a recluse and never left your hotel. How's your family doing? Are they happy with their investment?"

"Aw, I didn't realize your whole fam got together and bought the inn. How sweet." Poppy's eyes grew wide and—was that a tear? It touched her for a moment until she remembered the woman's proven talent at faking emotions.

"Things are going well, Mrs. Bard. A little tough at first," *what with the dead guy found in the lobby and all,* "but business is picking up." Mel bit her tongue, worried her neighbor would pry for juicy details about the murder she'd solved, but the woman had fresher dirt to dish.

"Did you hear about the killing last night in Palm Springs? What a tragedy, the Langes are such nice people." She *tsked* and shook her head, setting her ponytail of processed blonde hair swinging wildly, but Mel didn't buy her sincerity for a minute. The gleam in the woman's eyes indicated she had more dirt she was dying to tell. She normally didn't listen to gossip, but considering Poppy's involvement in the crime, it seemed prudent to gather all the information she could.

"Did you know the victim?" From the way Kendall's lip curled in disgust, she realized her official cop-speak must have been off-putting. "I mean, was Kyle Lange a friend? I'm so sorry for your loss."

Her ruffled feathers smoothed, the realtor nodded. "I sold him and Heather, his wife, their charming little A-frame cabin down on Beaver Way a few years ago. Quite a find, too. Those are hard to come by, as they rarely go up for sale."

Mel's frown had almost nothing to do with her new bff's muffled titter at the street name. *Real mature for someone named Poppy*. Because the bigger question was what were the odds of the dead man owning a cabin in their tiny town AND the person who hired Poppy arranging to meet her just down the road to make the exchange? "Is that normal? Palm Springs is only an hour away. Why would the Langes own two homes so close together?"

"Oh, a number of people from Palm Springs prefer to spend the summer in the cool mountain air rather than in the searing triple digit heat down below. In fact," the realtor's face lit up like she'd just thought of a brilliant idea, "I wonder if Heather plans to sell?" Kendall put her yarn down and pulled her over-sized cell phone out of her equally over-sized purse. As if no one else could see or hear her, she swiped at an app and said into the phone, "Ask Heather Lange when she's in town about the cabin." She turned her attention back to the people staring at her, stunned. "Like I said, the market for A-frames is very hot right now."

"She's coming here now? So soon after her husband's murder?" Why would a grieving widow leave town, no matter how short the drive? There'd be funeral arrangements to make at the very least, not to mention questions from the police.

"Oh yes," she bobbed her head, pleased to have information they didn't. "Caitlin at the nail spa said her assistant made an appointment for tomorrow afternoon. I suppose she wants to get her nails done for the service."

"And they say *criminals* are heartless." Poppy mumbled under her breath.

All out of hot news to share, Kendall purchased her yarn, said her goodbyes and hustled out the door, recording more memos to herself in her outside voice. In her wake, Dortha Jo's mellow timbre as she walked Mel through some options for her first knitting project was a soothing balm. Eventually the crafter talked her into making a beanie out of soft, eucalyptus green wool.

"The color goes so well with your red hair and sets off those eyes of yours. I promise, I've had a sixth grader make this in under three hours," the maternal shop owner assured her. Mel retained a healthy dose of skepticism, but bought the supplies and agreed to give it a try by attending her upcoming knitting class.

****

The sun had broken through the morning cloud cover and shone as the two women made their way back to the B&B, each carrying their bag of knitting supplies. Mel hadn't seen what Poppy purchased, but assumed the yarn was wild and bright to match her personality.

"So, is Mel short for Melanie?"

She narrowed her eyes at Poppy's mischievous grin. "No, and don't ask."

"Oh, I already know," she said with a carefree wave of her hand. "I heard your deputy call you Emmeline earlier. Your grandmother is quite chuffed with her choice. What she can't fathom is why you shortened your beautiful name to 'Mel' and not something more feminine, like Emma."

Her jaw clenched so hard she might have cracked a molar. Hopefully not. "I didn't choose the name, my oldest brother couldn't say Emmeline, so he called me 'Mel' and it stuck. If she wanted me to use the name Emma, why didn't she tell my parents to name me that?"

Feeling guilty after not consulting the matriarchs before baptizing their first born, her parents had allowed her grandmothers to have a hand in naming her and her older sister, Vinnie. Since their oldest brother Sean had shortened Lavinia down to Vinnie, she'd have thought they'd have learned their lesson and chosen a name a toddler could pronounce, but no, they had not. In truth, neither she nor Vinnie cared, or they would have demanded the family address them differently long ago. O'Rourkes might have a warped sense of humor, but they weren't cruel.

Poppy nattered on about how therapeutic the knitting project would be while Mel remained silent, percolating on an idea she kept to herself. As they climbed the front stairs of the inn, she stopped, frowning. Realizing she hadn't moved, her companion rushed back to her side.

"Are you having a panic attack? I thought you'd be

more," Poppy made a face imitating the famous painting *The Scream*. "But you do you, I guess."

"What?" At first she was confused, but then she figured out what the Brit meant. "No, I'm not...ugh," she grunted in frustration. "And for the record I never looked all," and she did her own version of *The Scream*. "I was thinking if the Lange's have a house here standing empty until at least tomorrow, we should go check it out. See what we can learn about this guy the police suspect you killed."

"Ooh, I like the way you think." She vibrated with excitement. "Let's take my car."

She crossed her arms and refused to budge, even after Poppy unlocked the doors with her key fob.

"Now what? Afraid of red cars or something?" she asked with a crooked grin. "Or of my driving?"

"More like afraid of going to jail if you get pulled over, and they find stolen goods in your car," she countered, ignoring the roll of Poppy's eyes. "We'll take my nice, normal, inconspicuous car. If we're going to do a little B&E, standing out like a sore thumb in your sports car is a bad idea."

****

Fifteen minutes and a few wrong turns later on the twisty, narrow, poorly marked private roads, Mel parked her blue compact and let out a low whistle. Some distant relative in Michigan once took the O'Rourke family on a vacation in their woodsy cabin. The lakeside getaway consisted of one room with intermittent electricity, no TV, uncomfortable mismatched furniture, and bare wood floors. This so-called cabin was a work of art.

The neighborhood was a collection of uniquely

designed homes meant to blend in with the forest. There were no lawns, with the landscaping contrived to appear natural. None of them were huge, and the Lange's fell in about the middle of the pack, but they all glittered in perfect proportions. Some were built around the trees, like tree houses for adults. The Lange's was as Kendall described; a perfect two-story A-frame made of cedar. The front and back walls were solid glass that sparkled even in the shaded light of the heavily wooded area. Small balconies cut into the side of the A shape had sliding glass doors to let nature in on all four sides. She could understand why the realtor was drooling over the potential of selling the place for Mrs. Lange. The property had to be worth a fortune.

She was so awestruck by the place she didn't keep track of Poppy until the woman waved to her through the front window. From inside, grinning like an idiot. Mel swiveled her head, nonchalantly checking to see if anyone noticed them. The homes looked empty, as if they were used for weekend getaways, not as permanent residences. Satisfied no prying eyes spotted them, she hustled to the door Poppy opened, way too pleased with herself for Mel's comfort.

"You broke in?" She hated the high pitch incredulity gave her voice.

"Hardly," the expert cat burglar scoffed, examining her perfect nails in feigned boredom. "I mean, the lock was child's play and the alarm system is rubbish. The place was begging to be broken into."

"Fine." She had to admit walking through the front door was easier, but she didn't have to like it. "No more rash moves. Let's split up and 'cautiously'," she emphasized the word, hoping the warning would take the bounce out of the thief's step, "look around. We're searching for any correspondence—"

"You mean like letters?" Poppy asked. "What, do they not have computers and email? Did I go through a time warp or something on my way here?"

Lips thinned in irritation, she ground out, "Yes, smarty pants, some people do send letters. Bills, birthday cards, the post office is still a thing. But yes, we're also looking for a computer. It's probably locked with a passcode, but we might get lucky. You check the bedroom and bathroom upstairs. If you find any prescriptions, take a picture. Don't steal the bottles or they'll notice."

With a snappy mock salute, she climbed the wrought iron spiral staircase to the second floor while Mel headed into the spacious and spotless kitchen. The cupboards were stocked with non-perishables by height with boxes on one side and cans on the other, but the fridge was empty save for a bottle of wine. Evidently, the couple hadn't been here for a while.

The kitchen equipment was of professional quality. The appliances were two notches above the ones they'd chosen when they refurbished the inn and looked new. The inside of the oven was pristine. Either they had the kitchen redone recently, their cleaning crew was amazing, or the setup was all for show. She ventured into the hall and descended three steps into the sunken living room.

A baby grand piano sat in the corner, and a large sofa faced the fireplace with coordinating chairs on either side. A quick poke proved this furniture, unlike her Michigan relatives' decor, was supremely comfortable and no doubt had a hefty price tag to match. A modern original oil painting hung above a mantle laden with photos in bright silver frames of a smiling woman with a variety of dogs. Mel assumed that was Heather, who Grandma told her was the second Mrs. Lange.

*What happened to the first Mrs. Lange?* The current wife appeared pretty but not stunning, and had an intelligence behind her eyes that made her seem like more than just some piece of arm candy. However, there were no pictures of the Langes together, not even a wedding photo. How much in love can you be if you don't even have a picture taken with your significant other?

A flash of movement out of the corner of her eye caught her attention. She ducked behind one of the many huge houseplants and shifted the curtain to peek outside. A Sheriff's department SUV parked in the driveway, lights flashing. *Shit.*

Chapter Seven

"Please don't be Marks," Mel prayed over and over until a knock sounded at the door and...of course, it was Marks. Was he the only deputy the department had? Did the man never take a day off? She might have stood a chance of talking her way out of the awkward situation, reasoning with any other cop, but he had a knack for seeing right through her.

"The alarm system was 'rubbish'," she grumbled in a terrible imitation of Poppy's accent. There was no point in trying to hide behind the fiddle leaf fig and hope he'd go away, so she swung the front door open. She graciously waved the cop inside as if she was the rightful hostess welcoming him in for tea. "Good afternoon deputy, what a pleasant surprise to see you twice in one day." Fortunately, Poppy chose this moment to embrace her moniker and disappear. The last thing she needed was the cop coming face to face with the thief.

His gaze bore into her. "Imagine my disbelief when the alarm company reported a break in and I drive up to find your car outside the house of last night's murder victim. Didn't we go through this before, when I told you to leave the investigating to the authorities?"

*You mean when I had to bend a few rules to convince you the man's death wasn't from natural causes and Jackson was almost killed before you got involved?* But even Mel had enough of a filter to recognize reminding him of the incident wouldn't be a smart thing to do while standing inside the house she'd broken into.

"Give me one good reason not to haul you in right now?"

"Oh, for Pete's sake," she shot back, hands on her hips in defiance, "the vic was killed in Palm Springs, so this isn't the crime scene. I ran into Kendall at the Yarn Barn and she said the place might be on the market soon, so I wanted to take a sneak peek."

"What were *you* doing at the Yarn Barn?" Incredulity laced through his words.

"Why are you saying it like that?" Even though she would have asked herself the same question, his judgy tone irked her. "I can do all kinds of crafty things. Point is, Kendall thought I might be interested in the cabin, so I dropped by to take a look."

"She gave you the keys, did she?"

"Not exactly. I was looking in through the patio door, gave the handle a try, and it slid right open. Someone must have forgotten to lock it," she shrugged. "Needless to say, I didn't know about the alarm system or I never would have stepped inside."

"Stay right there," he commanded before checking and relocking the back door. Then he rejoined her, consulted his phone, and entered a code on the keypad.

"What are you doing?" Her throat closed in panic. Poppy couldn't escape now without setting off the alarm, and even the Brit wouldn't be able to talk her way out of a second call about a possible burglary.

"Re-setting the alarm. Why, are you planning on breaking in again?" The deputy put a hand on the small of her back and, considering the situation, gently ushered her outside. Then he locked up and showed her to her car. "Let's make sure this is the last time I see you today, at least on official business," he said as he opened the door for her.

She futzed around, torn between stalling to give Poppy a chance to escape or fleeing, and letting her take her chances. Unfortunately, he took the choice out of her hands. He stood there, ostensibly intent on staying put until she drove away. Backing out of the driveway and heading home, she heaved a sigh of relief.

"Someone has the good deputy wrapped around their pinky," snickered a voice from the back seat.

"Jesus H!" She yelped, jumping out of her skin as Poppy beamed at her over the back of the seat. "You scared the—what are you talking about? I'm lucky he didn't arrest me."

"Mel O'Rourke, you're an excellent cop, but an idiot when it comes to men. Anyway, at least our little adventure wasn't for naught," Poppy said as she took something out of her inside coat pocket. "I found this taped to the bathroom mirror." She held a plain eggshell-colored business-sized envelope.

"You stole a piece of evidence?"

For the first time all day, possibly for the first time since she'd met her, Poppy grew serious. "You and I are the only ones who are going to look anywhere else but in my direction. I couldn't leave the first clue that might point to the real killer in the hands of cops who aren't even considering other potential suspects. This is my life, I'll do whatever it takes to clear my name." Then her mood brightened as fast as if she flipped a switch. "So let's go back to the privacy of your inn and see what the note says, shall we?"

"Why wait? Open it now," Mel insisted, curiosity getting the better of her.

"What, and miss out on the chance for a little suspense? Where's the fun in that, poppet? I bet you were the kind of cheeky little nipper who snuck around trying to spy your Christmas gifts before they were wrapped."

"No," she grumped because of course she had been. "But for all we know, the envelope contains the bill from the cleaner."

The amused grin on Poppy's face grew broader as she shook her head. "No, I'm sure this is from the killer."

Right, she thought, cat burglar and soothsayer. "You already looked inside, didn't you?"

"Just a quick peek," the other woman admitted unabashedly. "We follow the clues, figure out who really killed that bloke, and Bob's your uncle, I can go back to my life in L.A."

She felt a sharp, unfamiliar sensation. Loneliness? Was she hurt Poppy wanted to leave so soon? She shook off the idea as being ridiculous as she drove back to the Babbling Brook.

\*\*\*\*

They entered the B&B to death stares from Liam, who manned the front desk.

"What took you so long at the yarn store?"

"Why?" Mel scoped out the lobby and entrance to the Great Room. "Where's Grandma O?"

"I'm coming, I'm coming," grumbled the old woman as she shuffled out of the public restroom

Marla A. White

behind the Great Room. "Sheesh, a lady my age can't hold it forever, kid."

"You've been in there for twenty minutes." Liam divided his heated glower between Mel, Poppy, and his grandmother. "I'm here to do repairs, not sit on my a–" shifting his eyes to his grandmother, he changed his word choice, "keister answering the phone."

"Are you implying running the front desk is women's work?" Poppy arched an elegant brow at him.

Mel struggled not to laugh at her brother's flustered expression. She'd never seen him so off-balance before.

"No, I-I…"

"Whatever. Grandma, are you okay manning the desk by yourself for a little while longer?" She ignored her brother. A lifetime of experience taught her that was the best way to deal with him when he got bratty.

"I fended off Angela Kemp when she tried to grab the last package of toilet paper in the Covid panic and she works out at a cross fit gym. I think I can handle a tourist or two dragging their sorry butts across the threshold."

In no way did her grandmother's response comfort her, but she was dying to see the stolen note. Damn Poppy and her insistence on keeping her on pins and needles. The cop in her, however, reasoned they should put on gloves and at least try to reduce the number of fingerprints in case they ended up turning in the evidence to the police.

She waited until Liam stomped out the back door before dashing into the kitchen to grab a couple of pairs of nitrile gloves. The last thing she needed was him making fun of her for playing detective. She got enough of that from Deputy Marks.

Mission accomplished, the two conspirators slipped into the office and closed the door. She sat behind her desk while Poppy perched on the corner. Pulling on the gloves to prevent any more fingerprints than were already on the envelope, she tugged the piece of evidence out of her purse and laid it on the desk.

First, she studied the envelope, searching for any clue of where it came from and who left it. A bland ecru color, the stationery was thick, much better quality than a standard envelope. There were no markings, not even a name of who the note was meant for written on the front. The flap had been left unsealed.

After going over the envelope one more time and still coming up empty, she slid the note out and examined it. Like the envelope, the paper was of good quality, something you'd buy at a stationery or office supply store. She judiciously unfolded the note to read what it said. It didn't take long. Printed out by a computer, the message read, "If you go through with your plan I will destroy you."

"Huh," Poppy grunted. "Not much to go on there."

She shot her an icy glare. "*That's* the tantalizing clue you couldn't just tell me in the car?"

"The threat didn't mean anything to me, but I was hoping you could crack the code." She shrugged.

*Ugh.* Shifting into cop mode, she studied the note more closely. She hated when the bad guys went all Mr. Mysterioso. Or Mrs. Mysterioso. No need to continue sexist stereotypes. "Well, it's a start, at least. Someone has a grudge against one of the Langes and since he's the one who's dead, the sensible thing is to focus on Mr. Lange. We should investigate his business contacts, see if there was some deal he was about to close or call off."

"Or," Poppy got to her feet, tapping her finger on her chin in thought, "could the note be from the missus? Maybe he planned on leaving her? What if Mrs. Lange is the one who hired me to steal the necklace before he hid the bloody thing from the divorce courts or gave it to his new chippy?"

"Then why shoot him on the very night she instructed you to steal it?"

"Maybe she was trying to frame me. Who would they believe, her or me?" She crossed her arms, looking very insulted at the idea of her spotless record of being a non-violent thief was now in tatters.

"If someone wanted to frame you, why hire you to steal a necklace, kill Lange, and then never show to collect jewels?" Mel frowned at all the variables that didn't make any sense. A necklace the expert claims is worthless, an anonymous contact hiring Poppy to steal it, and a Tweedle battle with an environmentalist. A tenuous thread connected all the clues, but she was no closer to unraveling it when raised voices erupted from the lobby. Again.

"What do you mean you need to see another form of ID?" A man's voice warbled in rage even through the closed door. "That's my picture on my driver's license."

Her grandmother's muffled response was, "Oh yeah? How did you suddenly grow all that hair? Hold on, are you're wearing a rug?"

She shook her head and muttered an impolite word as she got to her feet, but Poppy put her hand on her shoulder. "Don't worry, I got this. It's the British accent," she said with a wink. "I'll have him eating out of the palm of my hand in no time,"

Moments after she entered the lobby and closed the office door behind her, the Brit's voice cooed something, and the man laughed. Damned if she wasn't right. One problem solved, Mel returned to the file her cyber ninja grandmother had pulled together for Kyle Lange. The best place to start poking around seemed to be his office at Badger Corp.

****

"I'm sorry, what paper did you say you were from again?" After three phone transfers, Mel was eventually connected to Peter Mullins, Kyle Lange's assistant. His guarded tone made her suspect this wasn't the first time a member of the fourth estate had come calling. Considering Badger Corp's main function was helping its parent company extract more oil from their wells, environmental consequences be damned, multiple reporters hounding them was a distinct possibility.

"Yes, of course sir, I'm from the *PalmSpringmoutainviewtimes*," she slurred together for the third time, hoping he'd feel too dumb to demand she repeat it again. The last thing she needed was Mullins calling a real paper and finding out she was a fake. Impersonating a reporter wasn't a crime, but it wouldn't look good if he caught her. "We want to do something a little more than the standard obituary for a person who contributed as much to the world as Mr. Lange."

After a lot of wet sniffling on the other end of the phone, the man spoke again. She was getting a sinus infection just listening to him. "As I told the police," he said when he pulled himself together, "everyone loved

Kyle."

"So, he was a good boss?"

Mullins produced an ugly sound, a combination of a hiccup and a snort in response. "He was more than a boss, at least to me. He was a mentor and a friend. But his death is a tragic loss for more than personal reasons. He was on the verge of a new discovery that was going to change the world."

*Wow, over the top dramatic much?* "Oh? What was this discovery, sir?"

"I'm sorry, I'm not at liberty to say," he replied tersely.

"I understand you can't make an official statement, sir, but what about, you know," she tried to put a *wink wink, nudge nudge* purr in her voice, "off the record? To give me an idea of the kind of man Mr. Lange was beyond the company bio."

From the long hesitation on the other end of the phone, her cop instincts told her there was something else going on. Why wouldn't he want to at least hint at what this life-changing thing was? Most people, no matter how ironclad the NDA they signed, would crow just a little if they were on to something as big as he claimed.

"I...I'm not sure what he was working on," he admitted sheepishly. "Usually he would have included me on any new formula from the ground floor, but this time his partner insisted Kyle keep what they were developing a secret, even from me."

You didn't need to be Freud to catch how the resentment in Mullins' voice doubled down with jealousy when he said the word "partner". Could the note Poppy found have been from Mullins? Was he threatening to destroy Lange if he went forward without him on this new discovery? Mel grabbed a little spiral notebook out of her desk drawer and jotted down his name and motive to come back to later.

"Oh? Perhaps I can speak to his partner then?"

If she hadn't caught the gist before, Mullins' bitter laugh would have told her the degree of animosity he felt for this partner. "Good luck. I'm...er, was, his assistant for almost ten years and that bitch never gave me the time of day unless Kyle forced her to."

Wow. So if this partner ever turned up dead, she was pretty sure who the prime suspect would be. Unless everyone had the same reaction, including Lange? "We here at the obit desk can be very persuasive, if need be," she assured him. "If you gave me their contact information, I can get in touch for the sake of writing a more fitting tribute to Mr. Lange."

"If Leigh Pemberton had a nice thing to say about anybody, it would be a first," he huffed, before surrendering her phone number there at Badger Corp.

"Thank you, Mr. Mullins, you've been a great help. You have a good day," Mel said, about to end the call until another thought occurred to her. "Oh, one last question, sir, if I may?"

"Listen, I want to be helpful, but if this is about Pemberton you need to talk with her."

"Oh, no, sir, I was wondering about the break in. I understand Mr. Lange was killed when he interrupted a burglary." He swallowed down a hiccup, no doubt fighting off his veneration of Lange. The thought occurred to her that he might know the significance of the necklace, so she worded her question carefully to avoid giving too much away. "I was wondering if you could tell me what the killer stole?"

"That's the real tragedy," Mullins snuffled. "They killed the poor man over ten thousand dollars."

"There's cash missing?" she said with a start. "Nothing else?"

"What were you expecting, the plans to his formula?" Her sympathy for the man dropped at his snide tone. "If someone was after corporate espionage, they're morons to think it would be in the safe. Cash, his passport, and deeds to his properties are the only things Mr. Lange kept there."

"Oh? What about his wife's jewelry?" she pressed. "I understand she has quite a collection." Honestly, she didn't have a clue, but figured it was a reasonable guess.

"Anything of hers would be in their safe at home or the safe deposit box at the bank. Now, if you don't mind, I have a splitting headache."

Mel thanked him again for his time. A headache was a convenient excuse to get off the phone, but a quick check of his social media showed he'd been out last night partying hard with the Sonoran Desert Gay Men's choir. That could explain the headache and give him an alibi, at least for now. She'd dig deeper into this bar crawl he'd been on later if need be.

Leaning back in the worn leather office chair, she let what Mullins told her tumble around in her head. Poppy swore all she took was the necklace, but the assistant claimed there's cash missing and nothing else. So either he's lying, or Poppy is. Or both.

The cops called him after they found Lange's body in response to a report of shots fired and if they were decent at their job, they would have asked if there was anything missing from the safe. He could have taken the money himself, realizing this was his only shot at a severance package, and blamed the thief. Or, and before hanging out with her today this would have seemed the most logical choice, Poppy lied to her about not taking any money.

She absently twirled one of her auburn curls, deliberating why the thought of the thief lying to her bothered her so much. They weren't friends. Most of the time they'd spent together over the years involved her chasing the thief. But now she'd spent a little time with her and gotten to know her beyond her rap sheet, she saw a different side to her. *Or,* the part of her that missed her family and felt isolated in Pine Cove suggested, *are you so desperate for a friend you latched on to the worst possible option to fill the role?* One thing was for sure, she needed to be a lot more guarded around the charismatic cat burglar until she sorted out the truth.

Despite her doubts about Poppy, she decided to call Leigh Pemberton and find out what she knew about Lange. Whether or not she lied about taking the money, she'd given the woman her word she'd look into the crime, and she intended to keep her part of the bargain.

Two digits in, a knock sounded at her office door. Positive her grandmother would never bother to knock, and the office was the last place Liam would be caught, that only left Poppy.

"Come in," Mel called out, curious as to what she wanted.

The tiny Brit bounced in the room, a big shit-eating grin on her face. She braced herself. In her experience, no person wearing that expression was the bearer of good news for anyone but themselves.

"I just had the most marvelous conversation with your cousin Gemma about your marketing and branding campaign."

"You what?"

Poppy sauntered to her desk and took a seat on the edge, oblivious to the unspoken accusation she was interfering in her family business.

"You did ask me to mind the phones, so when she called, I answered."

"You should have taken a message. I would have called her back," she growled through gritted teeth.

"It was my pleasure," the Brit gushed, sounding one hundred percent sincere. "Besides, she says you're ditching her calls. Anyway, we got to talking about your marketing plan and the thought occurred to me since Valentine's Day is around the corner, you should have some sort of special or event."

"What? No," she asserted. "That's just too, I don't know, ew."

The tiny brunette smirked. "You own a hotel, you do realize people have sex in your rooms, don't you? Why not cash in on romance and lure them here for a romantic getaway? In fact," she leaned closer to Mel and dropped her voice, "seems to me you've got a couple of hot prospects in town yourself. C'mon, it's time to let your hair down and have a little fun." She leaned back to make a quick inspection of Mel's jaw-length bob cut. "Figuratively, anyway."

Heat rose to her face, although whether from picturing all their guests humping like bunnies at this very moment or the insinuation she was somehow the object of either Gregg or Jackson's lust, she couldn't say.

"I appreciate the suggestion," she stammered, "but please don't help me beyond cooking breakfast and housekeeping stuff." Figuring out her involvement with Lange's murder complicated her life enough. She didn't want to think about how her last housekeeper turned out to be a crazy killer.

"Say no more," Poppy responded without a hint of annoyance or wounded feelings in her voice, her hands held up in surrender. "Shall I call Gemma back and tell her the promo package is a no go then? I think she's putting the word out on your social media pages."

How did things spin out of control so fast? She wanted to blame the Brit, but that wasn't fair. Truth was, she *had* been avoiding Gemma. "I'll take care of it. I just need to step out and grab a bite to eat first."

"Ooh, Amy at Pastry Village has a fresh batch of mulled apple cider chai crullers that are absolutely mental. You should stop by and get one while they last."

She stopped dead in her tracks and slowly pivoted back toward Poppy. Just how last minute had her decision to come here been, anyway? "I've been here three months and I've never even heard of Pastry Village. You've been in town less than six hours. How do you know about it? Have you been researching Pine Cove?"

She tilted her head and made a show of putting on a pouty frown. "I do this crazy thing called talking to people. While you were on the phone, Tom dropped by and we chatted."

"Who?"

The other woman huffed at her. "Tom Horton.

He's staying in cabin three with his wife? Retired couple?" She shook her head with a sad smile, eyes full of compassion. "I appreciate Officer O'Rourke kept a keen eye out, but civilian Mel needs to quit seeing suspects and start finding neighbors and friends." Adding quickly, "After you suss out the real killer, of course."

She harrumphed past her annoying employee, grabbed her coat, and walked out the door. She had a business to run. Who had time to stop and talk about donuts?

"Shall I keep answering the phones, then?" Poppy called after her. "I think your grandma went to go take a nap." The question was legitimate, but the tone in her voice betrayed her absolute pleasure in tweaking Mel. This time, she didn't even try to resist the urge to give a particular gesture with her hand and got a loud laugh in response.

**** 

The only one place Mel wanted to go for a snack and a sweet distraction was The Hungry Puppy. Jackson somehow always knew what to say to shake her out of a dark mood, whether that meant making her smile or pissing her off.

To her dismay, an impromptu sign hung on the door saying they were closed for the afternoon, no explanation or reason given. Then she remembered his mother was coming to town. He'd probably had to drive to the Palm Springs airport to pick her up. You can't exactly get a ride service to drive all the way to Pine Cove, after all. The guilt over giving his competition a try lessened as she trudged down the block to Pastry Village.

The coffee shop was tiny compared to Jackson's place, but then it didn't have to be big. Their focus was strictly drinks and pastries for to-go clientele. There were a few tables inside and a limited number of chairs outside, where a smattering of people drank their lattes or smoothies. She blinked several times as her eyes adjusted from the bright sunshine to the dark wood interior before taking a seat.

After one bite, she begrudgingly had to admit Tom Horton was right—the apple crullers were mouth wateringly delicious. But then she guessed a guy named Tom Horton would know his breakfast pastry.

She slumped at a table by the window, a mug of coffee warming her hands, while she regarded the cruller crumbs and wondered how her life had gotten so out of control. A Valentine's Day special? How did that fit in with this search for her so-called brand? Because Mel couldn't think of anything less on target with her "authentic self" than pink hearts and flowers.

She was so absorbed in all of her deep thinking she didn't see Marks until he pulled out the chair opposite her. The scrape of wood against wood made her jump and slosh her coffee onto the table. "Jesus, why do you keep sneaking up on me?"

"Jumpy much?" He narrowed his gaze. "Did I catch you committing another crime? Was that an apple cider chai cruller you just murdered?" A crooked grin slid across his face, causing little crinkles at the corner of his cornflower blue eyes.

"If you had my grandmother and brother badgering you all day, you'd be jumpy too." She tempered her grumpy words with a gentle upturn of her mouth.

His good mood didn't last long though, as the

deputy got down to business. "This isn't entirely a social call. I was looking for you, and your new assistant told me I might find you here. Let's hope she's less murder-y than your previous one, by the way. Anyway, I need whatever information you can give me about the cat burglar you were chasing when you..." He glanced down at her ankle. It was the wrong ankle, but she knew what he meant and barely avoided a spit take. If he had any idea how close he'd been to the suspect, he'd kick himself. And her as well, Mel suspected.

"Why?" she asked, stalling for time. "The charges against the suspect were dropped a long time ago."

"You remember the dead guy's house you broke into?"

"Technically speaking, I didn't break, just entered. I told you, the door wasn't locked."

The deputy gave her a dismissive wave of his hand. "Whatever. Anyway, the Palm Springs PD found some fancy climbing gear that matches your burglar's typical MO, but they've hit a dead end on tracking it back to her. If you can give me any information to help me find 'The Ghost', I'd be in your debt. I'm up for a promotion and catching her would be a boon."

Even though Poppy had admitted to breaking into Lange's office, lazy police work bugged her. "If they can't trace the equipment to a specific burglar, how did they make the leap to bringing "The Ghost" in for questioning? Especially since she never used a weapon in any of her heists. It sounds like they're trying to pin the crime on her rather than doing good, solid police work."

All traces of his earlier playfulness fled the

deputy's face. "And here we are again, with you telling me how to do my job. I did you a favor by not reporting your unauthorized visit to Lange's house. Is it so much to ask that you do this one thing for me? Help me catch a killer and boost my career as a bonus?"

Well aware she had the single piece of evidence that might solve the crime hidden in her desk, a stab of remorse ate at her. She promised herself she'd make it up to him somehow and put her hand on his arm to stop him as he rose to leave. "Gregg, you're right, I'm sorry. I have no place telling you how to investigate this man's death. And I want to help you get your promotion, I really do. But honestly, I don't know anything more about the burglar than what's in the files.

"She goes by dozens of aliases and after that debacle on the rooftop with me where she managed to get off by the skin of her teeth, if she's half as smart as everyone gives her credit for, she's in another continent by now." Mel forced herself to make her eyes meet his and put that extra flutter to her eyelashes the way Poppy did. Not having the fake extensions, she wasn't sure how much good the flirty move would do until the deputy broke the gaze first.

"Whether it's me, the PSPD, or Interpol, someone is going to bring her in. My career aspirations aside, considering how ticked off the cop I talked to is, it would be better for everyone if it was me."

She considered his words after the deputy left. He was right. It was a matter of time before somebody figured out who and what Poppy was. If she kept hiding her, she might get the whole family involved in charges of aiding and abetting a fugitive. But if she turned her in, she'd be breaking her word and condemning her for

91

a crime she was more certain than ever she didn't commit. Her entire case came down to the threatening note. What was the plan Lange was about to put in motion that was worth killing him over?

The bigger question was, how could she keep her word to Poppy without putting her family in danger?

\*\*\*\*

Mel searched for twenty minutes before she found Poppy sitting alone on the stone patio outside the Great Room. Despite the chill in the late afternoon air, she'd left the gas fire pit unlit as she huddled in her puffy down coat, elbows on knees and chin in her hands, to stare at the brook.

The rushing water crashed along the rocky creek bed thanks to the recent rain and snowmelt, but it was hardly worth gawping at for so long. Huh. Swearing softly, she opened the door to join her. Might as well get this over with now, like ripping off a bandage in one quick pull to minimize the pain. The problem was, it still hurt.

She'd decided on the walk home she had no choice but to tell Poppy to leave. To run as far and as fast as she could, before Marks or the Palm Springs PD caught her. She didn't have enough to go on to unmask the killer before someone put the cat burglar in jail.

Sinking down on the bench next to her, however, Mel felt like crap having to break the news to her. A tiny wave of relief lapped at her feet when the other woman spoke first.

"Listen, I appreciate what you've done for me, but I've been thinking it's best if I leg it now before your copper friend gets too curious. I kept my face hidden behind the computer screen when he came looking for you earlier, but running in to him three times in one day? Mate, it's like fate is sending me a signal."

Mel let out the huff of air she'd been holding, almost giddy to hear she'd come to the same conclusion but stopped. The flatness of her voice, the sag of her shoulders, tripped an alarm. She wasn't wrong. She'd gone days without seeing Deputy Marks, so three times in one day was unusual. But of all the places she could have run to, she'd come to Pine Cove for Mel's help. What if she didn't have any other options?

"Where will you go?"

"Oh, it's a big ol' world out there. I'll think of something." The normally vibrant brunette plastered a grin on her face, but it had none of the mirth of her usual smiles.

"And yet here you are. What other trick do you have up your sleeve?" She shouldn't ask. Plausible deniability in case Marks questioned her was the smart way to go, but she had a bad feeling the Brit was out of options. Especially since she hadn't been able to look her in the eye.

"Honestly? Not a clue. Can't go back to L.A., that's for sure."

Knowing she was going to regret doing something hardly ever prevented Mel from taking action. This time was no exception. "Stay the night. We'll figure out a new game plan in the morning."

Poppy's gaze left the brook to meet hers. She was stunned to see tears in her eyes. "I swear to you, I didn't know until we met your estate agent in the yarn shop that your family bought this place. I'd heard you'd come here to run an inn and you've always been one of the good ones. I figured if anyone could help, it would be you. It might have put you in a spot, but you'd weather it okay.

"Then I got to know your grandma, Gemma, and even crabby Liam, and I'll be damned if I let my problems spill over onto them." She jumped to her feet and moved to the door, swiping her eyes with her sleeve. Mel caught her by the arm, realizing too late it was the injured one.

"Sorry, sorry," she apologized, dropping the contact. "Just wait, give me a second to think." Poppy paused before surrendering and plopping back down on the bench. Confident the woman would stay put, she paced the length of the patio. She did her best thinking on her feet, and she needed to consider all of her options.

"Sure, my life would be easier if you turned yourself in, *but,*" she talked over the other woman's objection, "you're right. Once they arrest you, they'll stop looking. God knows you've committed numerous crimes you never got busted for, so you doing some time won't weigh on my conscience. However, I'm positive you didn't kill anyone, so if you take the fall, the guilty person gets away with murder and *that* irks me. I didn't become a cop to let killers go free."

"But your family, all the work you've put in this place. I don't want anyone to suffer because of me."

"We've got a couple of good lawyers in the family tree, we'll be okay." *I hope.* "But you need to lie low and stay away from Gregg Marks."

Poppy jumped to her feet and hugged Mel before she could stop her. "I'll do anything you say. We'll catch this bugger, I'm sure of it."

## Chapter Eight

The next morning meant another one of Poppy's amazing gourmet breakfasts. Today it was perfectly cooked eggs benedict with a side of fresh berries. Or cinnamon rolls for the non-egg eaters. Liam had both, grumbling the entire time he stuffed his face. While Mel did the dishes and swept the Great Room, Grandma O worked her computer wizardry and dug up some interesting tidbits about Leigh Pemberton.

"So kiddo, the first thing I found was her page on the company website, come see." Grandma patted the chair someone had put next to her at the desk. She took a seat while Poppy left her customary perch on the corner to hover behind them.

"Christ on a cracker, her puss looks like she's sucking on a lemon. And her ring of...what would you call that color? Plum? Those permed curls look like a magenta helmet." She studied the picture and had to admit her grandmother was right. The color wasn't a cool, hip, *I'm a free spirit who uses a crazy color*. It looked like she was trying to achieve some sort of natural looking tint but failed. Thank God some ancestor from long ago gave all the O'Rourke's a distinct shade of red in their DNA.

The older woman sighed. "The Good Lord didn't give everyone bonuses in the looks department, but doesn't this Pemberton broad know Photoshop is a thing?"

Mel tried to stifle her laugh and asked Poppy, "Do you recognize her? Was she the shooter?"

She leaned in to peer more closely, but shook her head. "It all happened so fast I didn't get a good look."

Frustrated at the dead end, she asked, "What else have you got, Grandma Snowden?"

Her grandmother chuckled at the computer hacker reference. "Not a lot more, sorry to say." She clicked through a variety of social media platforms. "She and Lange founded Badger Corp back in 2009, then sold the company to Nichols Oil and remained a subsidiary. A lot like her partner, she kept a low profile on social media. No funny cat video shares, not even so much as a like on Graffer for the otter picture on her feed. I say she's your killer. Only a monster wouldn't have liked that."

While Mel wasn't prepared to declare her guilty based on that scant amount of evidence, she had to admit the snarl of a smile in her portrait was chilling. "Yikes. Let's see if she's any friendlier to chat with," she said as she dialed the phone.

When Grandma O settled in to make herself cozy, she gave her a pointed look. "No wonder Mom sent you off into exile, you nosy old thing. Both of you, go find a job to do or a guest to annoy," she instructed as she shooed her grandmother and helper out of the office.

The same bored receptionist who forwarded her to Peter Mullins yesterday droned, "Badger Corp, making tomorrow brighter today, how can I direct your call?"

From the lack of enthusiasm, she doubted the woman had the ability or desire to brighten anyone's day. "May I speak to Leigh Pemberton, please?"

"One moment," she muttered before putting Mel on hold. No surprise there, but why would a corporation bragging about being an award-winning green, sustainable company use a cheesy elevator version of an '80s punk hit for their hold music?

Five minutes later, she understood why.

Driving a pencil through her eye would have been preferable to standing one more minute of torture. The only reasons she hadn't thrown in the towel were because she was curious about Pemberton and more stubborn than their receptionist. Fortunately, the woman came back on the line before Mel did something rash.

"I'm sorry, Ms. Pemberton is taking a week of bereavement leave." She waited for them to offer to take her information down, but after a few moments of dead air it became clear that was never going to happen.

"Okay then," she muttered, "thank you so much, you've been incredibly helpful."

Sarcasm must have been out of the phone robot's repertoire because she grunted a surprised, "You're welcome," before Mel hung up.

All of which left her investigation, if you could call it that, at a dead end. She was no closer to finding who had a motive to kill Lange and worried Poppy's stretch of luck was about to run out. Deputy Marks, and whenever she thought about the case, she thought of him as Deputy Marks rather than Gregg, was bound to put two and two together and figure out "The Ghost" had been hiding under his nose. But she'd pursued all of her leads, short of driving to Palm Springs to talk to Pemberton in person.

Thinking about the drive conjured the memory of the zigzagging mountain road with steep drop offs she would have to travel to get there. Suddenly, going back to the branding workbook seemed to be a much better alternative. Until she opened the pages and re-read, "What are your core beliefs?" How was she supposed to answer such an overwhelming question? The page continued to ask what was her mission statement? Her message? "It's a hotel, not a higher calling. My mission statement is 'sleep here and you won't get bed bugs'," she groused, throwing down her pen. She put her head in both hands and rubbed her temples.

A jolt of inspiration hit her out of the blue. Kendall said Mrs. Lange had made an appointment to get her nails done this afternoon. She forgot which nail spa she'd mentioned, but in a town the size of Pine Cove, how many could there be? A quick Internet search, however, proved there were a surprising number. Who knew? Certainly not Mel. She got mani-pedis sporadically for special occasions like the Dodger's winning the World Series or the Kings taking the Stanley Cup. So almost never. She set off in search of Poppy to see if she remembered or God help her, she'd have to go to all fifteen salons in search of Mrs. Lange.

\*\*\*\*

"Were you singing just now?" Mel sputtered, stunned to have heard a pretty fair rendition of an old Broadway musical coming through the open cabin door.

Instead of being embarrassed at being caught like most people would be, she launched into her impression of the main character to boast, "Why yes, Guv, it were me." Her singing was even better than her acting. She shook off the realization to refocus on her bigger fish to fry.

"Do you remember the name of the nail salon Mrs.

Lange made an appointment with?"

Poppy continued dusting, amping up her swagger with a knowing grin. "In fact, she didn't say, but I asked the girl who delivered the flowers for the rooms and she said Nailed It is the best place in town. My money is on Mrs. Lange going with nothing but the best."

"You wouldn't want to come with me, would you? It would be the perfect cover, two old friends taking a girl's day out."

Was she imagining things or had the other woman gone pale? "Me? What do you need me for? You used to shoot bad guys. Surely you're not afraid of one person with a file and cuticle buffer."

Her gaze dropped to her chipped, ragged nails. "Yeah, but I've been here for over three months and have never gone for a manicure. Won't it seem weird to suddenly show up just when Mrs. Lange is there?"

The other woman hesitated, then shook her head. "These rooms aren't going to clean themselves. I better stay here and get everything done. You go enjoy yourself, propose a little cross-business dealing. You let them put their cards in every room in exchange for placing your hotel brochures near the door. No one will think twice about your sudden interest in your cuticles."

A pang of disappointment zipped across Mel's heart and she had to remind herself again she and Poppy were not and never had been friends. As soon as they identify the killer, the Brit would go back to L.A. so fast it'd make your head spin.

****

Nailed It was a short walk from the Babbling Brook. The small salon was located in a neon green, squat building next to the gift shop with the giant snow globe over the doorway. Yep, Pine Cove was a strange little town. As she hurried along, worried she might be late for the last minute appointment she'd grabbed, Mel thought about what Poppy said yesterday and inhaled deeply, catching the pine scent the thief was so enamored by. She had to admit she'd gotten so used to the fresh, clean aroma she'd pushed it to the background instead of enjoying the mountain air.

Unfortunately, she had no time to stop and smell the pine needles today. In moments she found herself at Nailed It, swung the door open and a nauseating wave of a completely different bouquet hit her in the face— one of acrylics, varnish, and heavy perfume.

There were several reasons she rarely got her nails done besides the expense, and the stench numbered among them. The pungent chemical odor tickled her nasal passages deep inside her head and drove her to sneeze several times before she got it under control.

"God bless you," exclaimed the middle-aged woman at the reception desk as she handed her a tissue, eyes wide in alarm.

"Thanks, allergies, nothing contagious," she assured her. "I'm looking for Caitlin?"

"Over here, doll," waved a grinning woman who couldn't have been much older than Mel. It seemed odd for a person in her thirties to address someone as "doll" but then again, giant snow globe over the shop next door, so...*Pine Cove is weird.*

Caitlin wore a bright orange tie-dyed Henley that reached the top of the her knees, cinched around the middle with a wide, tan, hand-tooled leather belt. Coal colored leggings and cowboy boots that matched the belt completed the ensemble. It was a strange combination, but somehow she wore it like a ray of sunshine.

She shook off the odd thought when she arrived at Caitlin's station and realized it butted against the one where a matron with perfectly coiffed salt and pepper hair sat, soaking her hands in a small sudsy bowl. Although her tanned skin glowed with the youth of someone in their thirties, the information her grandmother dug up about Heather Lange listed her as being in her late forties. Mel wondered what she did to stay so youthful looking. Whatever it was, she was certain she couldn't afford it, not with the close to non-existent profit the B&B brought in at the moment.

"Go on and pick a color," Caitlin instructed her, gesturing to the row upon row of nail polishes. They ranged from clear to a garish lime green and all the colors of the rainbow in between. Ten out of ten times she picked a muted light pink, but almost of its own accord her hand drifted to a dark violet hue and lingered there. As she pondered her choice, a familiar face popped in the door.

"Doc Hart?" She was the last person Mel would have expected to see there. The older woman who played guitar and had a penchant for heavy metal didn't seem the type to fuss with her nails.

"Oh, stop with the gawking. So sue me, I treat myself to a mani-pedi every week." The doctor flashed her fingertips, each nail featuring a different colored, meticulously painted daisy. After all the time they'd spent together, how had she not noticed? "I am surprised to see *you* here, however."

And this was why she'd wanted to use Poppy as

her excuse for a girl's day out. She fumbled for a good reason until she latched onto the other problem plaguing her brain. "Me too, but my cousin has been on my case about figuring out our 'brand' for the B&B. Nothing has popped, so I thought going outside my comfort zone might shake something loose."

"Then you definitely want to go with purple," Doc Hart teased. "I would have bet my last dollar you'd be more of a wimpy pink kind of person."

She bit back *what's wrong with pink* and defiantly snatched the purple off the rack before retreating to Caitlin's station. The Doc snorted a laugh as she followed her manicurist to the last empty station in the small salon. It happened to be on the other side of Mel, causing her to scowl. She considered the doctor to be one of her first friends in Pine Cove, but having her so close was going to make questioning Mrs. Lange on the down low ten degrees trickier.

"Purple will look so cool with your hair," Caitlin praised, pointing to her auburn waves. She hadn't thought about that. Maybe the color was too bright? But before she could go back to the rack to reconsider, the manicurist shoved her hands into shallow bowls to soak. She obeyed with a dollop of suspicion while, next to her, Heather Lange sighed in contentment as her manicurist took her hands out of a matching set of bowls and dried them.

"As always, your touch is magical, Miguel."

"You sure you don't want to do the whole mani-pedi, Mrs. Lange? You know how much you love soaking your feet even more your hands." The bespectacled man with his dark, slicked back hair gave the older woman a concerned frown. She must be a regular for him to remember her preferences. How often does she come all the way up here to get her nails done and why?

"Would that I could, darling, but I don't have the time today," she lamented. Mel saw her opportunity and jumped in.

"Oh my goodness, are you the Mrs. Lange in the news? I'm so sorry about your husband. You have my deepest condolences." Next to her, Doc frowned. Okay, she might have been a little over the top; she wasn't as accomplished an actress as Poppy.

"Thank you, that's very sweet. I miss him already." The words were sort of the right ones, but the new widow sounded sadder at the idea of having to skip a foot soak than she did over her husband's death. As Caitlin patted her hands dry, she pushed on.

"If it's of any comfort, he did so much good for the world." The only thing she knew for a fact he did was help oil companies pump money out of the ground, environment be damned, but she banked on rich people believing helping giant corporations turn bigger profits as a good deed.

Mrs. Lange's non-committal shrug made her rethink painting rich people with too broad of a brush. "That might be what his employees believed, but then they saw more of him than I did."

"So he put in a lot of overtime? Is that why you weren't worried about him working so late?"

"What do you mean?" the other woman shot her a venomous glare.

"Sorry, the papers said the, uh, incident happened very late or in the early hours of the morning. I just thought if you were home and he wasn't, you might have been concerned."

"I was at a charity function for my dog rescue the night he was killed. I'd invited Kyle, of course, but he claimed he was too busy."

"Married to his work, was he?" The only marriage she had to measure theirs against was her parents' and the Lange's fell short in the love department. Why wouldn't he have gone to support his wife?

"One good thing about Kyle's passing is I won't have to sit through anymore dinners with his sycophants gushing over him or that dreadful business partner of his."

She must have been talking about Leigh Pemberton. Mel pondered which thread to pull first— her dislike of Pemberton or the lack of grief over her husband's death? The woman had said "one good thing," as if it were one of many benefits to his murder. She continued, careful to avoid rousing the widow's suspicion.

"Ouch, must be tough, kind of like being married to two men instead of just the one."

Mrs. Lange's lips slid into a languid smile. "If only. Now *that* might have been interesting. No, his partner is a horrible, ferret-faced c-word who, after the funeral, I hope to never see again."

The manicurist put the last coat of a very classy peach color on the woman's fingers and then placed her hands under a fan with a UV light to dry. Her time was running out, she had to take her swing now.

"You don't think they were having an affair, do you?" Her question made both the Doc and Mrs. Lange's heads snap toward her. Apparently, her approach lacked the subtlety she was going for. She might as well have asked if she had a motive to kill the man. *Tell me, Mrs. Lange, did you leave a threatening note in your cabin for your husband?*

After a pause large enough to drive a truck through, Mrs. Lange let out a long, loud guffaw that brought tears to her eyes she dare not wipe away without risking smudging her newly painted nails. "If you ever saw Leigh Pemberton and my husband, you'd understand how funny the idea they were having an affair is," she wheezed between laughs.

"Kyle was good-looking and charming, I'll give him that." Her voice grew wistful and a little sad. "I don't doubt he slept with other women. He slept with me while still married to his first wife, so I entered this with eyes wide open." Wistful morphed into venomous as she snarled, "But sleep with Pemberton? He'd sooner cut off his own cock. Not just because she's unattractive, although that's reason enough, but anyone would realize before they got through the first course of a meal with her that her heart is as black as they come. Besides, he didn't trust her as far as he could throw her."

"Oh?" Mel asked and didn't have to work hard to sound confused. "I heard they were working on some big project together?"

Heather Lange snorted. "Some new micro-organism, blah blah blah. I didn't pay attention to what the thing did, but I know it was worth big money and, unlike all their other patents, this time my husband refused to cut her in. They had a shouting match on the phone a couple of nights ago. I heard her vow she wouldn't stand by and let him screw her out of millions from across the room. Afterward, I encouraged Kyle to cut his ties with her, and he finally agreed. I only wish he'd done it sooner and enjoyed some peace before he died."

The silence hung in the formerly buzzing salon, broken a moment later when the fan turned off and Mrs. Lange's nails were done. She inspected them and smiled. "Thank you, Miguel, an amazing job as always." She pointed a peachy nail at the three twenty-dollar bills laid out on the station. "I put a little extra in there for coming in on your day off to take care of me."

As she rose, did the air-kiss goodbye thing and walked out, panic gripped at Mel unrelated to the case. Oh shit, she hadn't thought to get money out to pay for the manicure and Caitlin was already applying the second coat, darkening the purple to a dramatic depth. She'd have to either ruin her nails or ask the woman to go into her purse and retrieve cash from her wallet for her. Either one was embarrassing. Then someone noisily cleared their throat behind her. She looked over and Doc Hart gestured toward the counter with her head. A twenty-dollar bill laid out in front of her.

"Rookie mistake," her friend chuckled. "So what was all that about, anyway? Why the sudden interest in the Langes?"

Clearly, she wasn't as smooth as she thought. For a moment, she considered taking the Doc into her confidence and tell her the whole story about Poppy, who she was, and the trouble she was in. If they'd been alone, she might have. But the salon had too many ears and she couldn't count on all of them being friendly. "Just trying to be a good neighbor. Kendall mentioned they own a cabin here."

"A cabin implies one room, rough-hewn walls, and

rustic furniture," the older woman scoffed. "They own an A-frame mansion with a few trees to screen it from the next mansion."

"I take it you disapprove."

"I've lived here most of my life," she explained, "and it breaks my heart to see the zillionaires from L.A., Palm Springs, and every other big city in California buy property here. They tear down the folksy cabins that have been here for years, and build monstrosities in their place. Ruins the whole vibe of the place."

While they waited for their nails to dry, she pondered if Linda Hart included her as part of the invading force. She hoped not. The O'Rourke family planned on keeping the B&B intact, having a healthy respect for preserving this new home of theirs, including the forest and brook.

Finished at the same time, Mel opened the door, taking great pains not to touch her nails to anything, and held it for the doctor to exit without risking her own nails, now sporting rose petals. Outside, she started back toward the inn when the Doc called her name. She returned to her friend's side and hoped she wasn't the reason for the scowl on her face.

"Chica, I was born in the dark, but it wasn't last night. That gun-shot wound on your friend's arm doesn't match her story." She tried to protest, but Doc put her hands up to stop her. "I'm not going to report it, but you need to watch your back. There's something not right about her."

"What do you mean?" She gulped. She knew Poppy would be found out eventually, but had counted on having a little more time to figure out who killed

Lange. So far she was hip deep in suspects, but short on hard evidence.

"You know more than you're telling, but you have to see she's hiding things from you. For starters, her accent waffles between at least three parts of London."

She jerked at the unexpected revelation. She'd been so intent on hearing lies that she never noticed anything off about her accent. "What do you mean?"

"Those guitars hanging on my walls aren't just decoration." Doc Hart pointed to her ear. "I'm a musician and I have a pretty good ear for accents. Maybe she's trying to sound more posh than she really is, beats me. But what I am sure of is she isn't what she appears to be." She laid her hand on Mel's shoulder, supportive but still protective of her nails. "I know you think you're a tough ex-cop and nothing gets past you, but you need to be careful around that one."

And with those oh so ominous words, Doc Hart walked toward her practice, leaving Mel wondering who to believe.

Chapter Nine

Back at the inn, the stack of paperwork Mel left on her desk hadn't miraculously filled itself out in her absence. Until they were turning enough of a profit, they couldn't afford a business manager. The task of doing the books, along with keeping track of their supplies, all fell to her. It was her least favorite part of the job, but someone had to do it. Thankfully, Grandma O had volunteered to man the front desk, promising to be nicer to their customers. She kept an ear out just in case. Instead of raised voices, she heard the clomping of Liam's boots long before he entered her office.

"Melly, I've got it all worked out. All I need is your approval and we can replace the wood-burning fireplaces with gas ones for a little under fifteen hundred each," he declared, clapping his hands and rubbing them together, signaling an eagerness to get to work.

"How many times have I told you not to call me that?" In grade school, Liam and his gang of hoodlums had figured out Mel rhymed with smell and she became "Smelly Melly" until she'd beaten him silly. She'd gotten detention, but it was totally worth it. No one ever called her that again, except once in a while her family would throw it out there to annoy her. Why in the name of all that's holy would he use the annoying nickname when he was trying to sweet talk her into doing things his way? "And no, we are not converting the fireplaces."

"But—"

"But nothing," she spoke over his objection. "One, we don't have the money in our budget and two, I like wood-burning fireplaces. They sound and smell…woodsy, comforting."

"Oh yeah? *Real* smoke almost killed you. What if that had happened to a guest?" He crossed his arms over his chest, stubbornly refusing to budge.

"Sweet Jesus, this again?" She rubbed her hand over her forehead before standing to meet him toe to toe. "It was a one off, an attack meant for me, not some malfunction of the fireplace."

"Hey, eejits," their grandmother barked from the doorway. "Pipe down, you're scaring off the customers."

In the O'Rourke household, their decibel level would have counted as a discussion, but a more sensitive type would have called it a shouting match. They both mumbled an apology and the old woman harrumphed back to the lobby.

"Let me convert just one. I'll install a timer so the guests can go to sleep with a cheery fire that turns itself off and not worry about burning to death. If you don't like it, I'll switch it back, no problem."

Mel had too many things on her mind right now, but her brother was doing her a huge favor spending the week fixing the myriad of little things that kept popping up so how could she say no? "All right, one fireplace," she sighed in defeat. "And I promise to keep an open mind and give the gas fire a chance before I tell you to change it back."

He shot her a confident grin before rushing off to start on his miraculous transition. She settled in to finish the paperwork, but her mind kept circling back to the Lange case. She retrieved the notebook she'd been jotting notes in from the desk drawer. It seemed like everyone who knew him loved him, but also had a reason to kill him.

Mullins was his number one fan-boy, but Lange excluded him from his latest project. Leigh Pemberton had worked with him for years, acquiring zero friends along the way. If Mrs. Lange was right and her husband had decided to split with his partner, had he told her yet? Of the two people who could answer that question, one is dead, and the other has every motive to lie. And while Heather seemed fond of her late husband, peach isn't exactly a nail color you wear when you're in mourning.

And then there was the stolen note she could practically hear thumping away in the drawer like a stationery telltale heart. Returning the notebook to the drawer, her fingertips brushed against the heavy envelope, and she thought back to the conversation she had yesterday with Gregg when he asked for her help with the case. Or had he been acting officially as Deputy Marks? She had a hard time telling when she was talking to her friend versus the cop. He was keen to get a promotion and here she was, sitting on solid evidence. Driven by guilt, she called him.

"Gregg, it's Mel," she said when he answered. In a split second decision, she'd decided to go the friend route. "You're not going to like what I have to say, but let me finish before you yell at me." She blurted out her confession to stealing the note. Then, more confidently, she laid out her case why each of the people she'd talked to so far had a better motive to murder Kyle Lange than the mysterious burglar the Palm Springs PD was focusing on.

The waves of his laughter broke over her like the crush of the tide, making her regret her choice of friend over cop. At least Deputy Marks would be professional enough not to cackle in her ear. Any hope she had of him taking her information seriously disappeared with his amused sigh.

"Oh, *ex-officer* Emmeline," he taunted, stressing her retired status and using her full name. He'd discovered her dirty little secret when he'd run her through official channels after they first met and argued over the dead body in her lobby. She ground her teeth as he continued to be a condescending ass. "How adorable, you're trying to help me solve the case. I get it, it's my fault for asking for your insights yesterday about this so-called 'Ghost,' but I don't need your assistance with this or scoring points with my boss.

"In fact, I'm following a lead on the burglar's location as we speak. PSPD pulled the video from the garage and identified a vehicle entering and exiting in the right time frame for the murder. It's not registered to anyone in the building, so the car has to belong to our suspect. We've got a BOLO out now. It's only a matter of time before we nail them."

"An all agency alert to be on the lookout for one car?" she asked, wincing at the whiny tone in her voice.

"Don't worry, we'll find it. Thanks for trying, I do appreciate your intentions, but it's best if you stick to running your inn and leave the policing to the professionals."

The fury at his dismissal of her faded into fear. She looked out the window at Poppy's red sports car and wondered how long before Marks spotted it.

Squelching her rising panic, she pulled out her cell phone to call Poppy and realized she'd never gotten her number. More proof of how what they had between them wasn't really a friendship, but leaving her at a loss at just how to describe it.

\*\*\*\*

She found Poppy exiting cabin three, the spacious three-story cabin, whistling a happy tune. Mel grabbed the other woman's arm and she stopped yet kept her lips pursed like she had put the song on pause.

"Get rid of your car," she warned, keeping her voice low so none of the guests passing by heard. "The cops have video of you entering and leaving the office building's parking garage."

"Oh poppet," the Brit said with a sparkling laugh. "I don't use my own car on jobs, I steal one and then put it back when I'm done. All they have is an SUV with darkened windows so they can't even identify the driver from the video. And when they run the plates, they'll find the car belongs to one of their own."

"You stole a car from a cop?" Mel asked incredulously.

She shrugged. "Well sure. If I stole one from a regular Joe, that might make trouble for an innocent person. What if they had a record or something? This way, they believe it straight away when the owner says 'it wasn't me, I swear'."

She had to admit the plan was kind of genius. Ballsy as hell, dangerous, but genius.

The Brit paused for a moment before adding, "But

thanks for telling me. It couldn't have been easy, breaking the old moral code and all."

Weirdly, she hadn't even stopped to think she was using the information Marks had given her to aid and abet a criminal to continue to evade arrest. It should have been a decision she had to wrestle with, but she hadn't given it a second thought. What did that say about her?

"So how goes the investigation? Find out anything at the nail salon?" The cheerful question shook her out of her reverie and back to the present. She debated with herself the wisdom of sharing what she'd found out about the Lange's marriage and Leigh Pemberton, but decided she needed all the help she could get if she was going to solve this case before the cops closed in on the wrong person. Because no matter what Doc said about Poppy hiding something, her gut told her while the thief was many things, a killer wasn't one of them.

"Well then, there's only one thing to do. Go down to Palm Springs and track down this Pemberton woman." Determined, Poppy marched toward the parking lot of the B&B until Mel, still favoring her rebuilt ankle, dashed in front of her.

"I agree, but you can't come with me. According to Marks, the Palm Springs PD has put out an all-points bulletin on you."

"Then I'll go in disguise," the self-professed erstwhile thief replied with a huff.

"There's no amount of disguise you can do to dim all that." She gestured vaguely at the other woman. "I need your help investigating, and you're no good to me in jail."

"So you're going alone? Isn't that dangerous

confronting a possible killer?"

While her concern was touching, she was sure even if Pemberton was the killer she wouldn't murder her for asking a few questions. Not yet, anyway, not until she got some proof. No, the real risk was driving down the mountain. Just thinking about all those cliffs, tight turns, and barely-there guardrails made her shudder.

When she first moved to Pine Cove, she'd made the trip by the skin of her teeth, driving at dangerously slow speeds that frustrated other drivers to pass her in no-passing zones. To make matters worse, the latest snowfall dropped four more inches, turning to ice on the roads overnight. Being an L.A. cop prepared her for a lot of things, but driving in snow wasn't one of them.

She'd have to get someone to drive her and Liam was the obvious choice, but she didn't want him to see how much heights even from the car bothered her. He already blamed Poppy for her issues. He'd go ballistic if he understood how deep they really ran. Which left only one person, and she already owed him one for nearly getting him killed last Christmas. With a heavy sigh, she pulled out her cell phone and dialed.

*****

When Jackson breezed into the lobby, a happy tingle of delight quivered through Mel at the sight of him. Had she really missed not seeing him for one whole day?

"Nice nails," he commented, taking her hand in his to draw it near for a closer inspection. Heat bloomed deep inside her at his touch. "I never would have put you down as a manicure person. I like it."

She jerked her hand out of his, heat rising to her cheeks, and mumbled, "thanks," staring at her violet nails before forcing herself to lift her gaze to meet his. "Where were you earlier? I stopped by for coffee but the Puppy was closed."

His hesitation spoke volumes and none of it was good. She'd never known Jackson not to at least have a grin or quip. "It's a long story I'll tell you about later. Ready to go?"

They hadn't gone five miles before bile rose in the back of Mel's throat as his truck navigated the twisty road. They took the highway on the opposite side of the mountain than the one she drove to get from L.A. to Pine Cove, but the sharp switchbacks looked identical. Beyond the tiny excuse for a guardrail, snow-coated terra firma plummeted down dramatic, rocky cliffs a few feet off to her right. How was she going to make it to Palm Springs without barfing?

She balled her hands into tight fists until they cramped and stared hard at the radio in his dashboard to avoid the view zipping past her window, addressing Jackson without taking her eyes off the digital readout.

"I appreciate you taking the time out of your day to do this. I just didn't want my brother to see me be so…freaky."

If she hadn't shifted her gaze from the radio to his face, she would have missed the darkness creep into his usually sparkling aqua eyes.

"No worries, I was glad when y'all called, gave me a good excuse to get away for a bit."

After checking to be sure the door was locked, the unreasonable fear it would open and she'd be tossed out to the rocks far below suddenly overwhelming, she twisted her body to face him. "Y'all? Why do you sound so Southern fried all of a sudden? I've known you for three months and I've never heard you use the word 'y'all' before."

He gave a mirthless chuckle. "Okay, you got me. My mother's been here less than a day and her Louisiana is rubbing off on me already. That's the reason we were closed earlier. I had to pick her up from the airport."

She nodded, having guessed as much. "I'm sorry, I didn't mean to drag you away from your mom the first day she's here."

"Don't worry, your timing couldn't have been more perfect. Hey," he paused and huffed a sigh, "you wouldn't happen to have a cabin or room available, do you? I don't think it's going to work out having her stay with us. Things were already a little tense between my parents, but then *somebody* used one of her shoes as a chew toy. Hint, the culprit wasn't me or my dad."

Her instincts said that pushing his mother out of their home was a bad call. How could they mend fences or build bridges or whatever the woman hoped to accomplish if they couldn't be in the same house? But from the set of his jaw, there was no talking him out of this course of action. "Sure, no problem. I'll have Grandma O give her one of the nicer cabins with the view of the creek."

"As much as she upset Dad and Chewbarka, you can give her a bed *in* the creek for all I care," he muttered.

"So things are going that good?" she asked wryly. "Anything I can help with?"

He exhaled a bitter laugh. "The woman had no time for me most of my life. When we lived together, she was always too busy for ball games and such. Once they split up and we moved here, I think she called to see how I was doing a half-dozen times at most, aside from my birthday and Christmas. Then I left for college and grad school, and the calls became cards twice a year. Which was fine with me, honestly."

She didn't want to interrupt his rant since he finally opened up to her by pointing out when you have to add the word "honestly" at the end of a sentence, the opposite is true.

"If for nothing else than Dad's sake, I was glad she made herself scarce. Every time she'd call, he'd be blue for days pining over her. But he had me, and we were happy together. And then I moved back here to open the restaurant and I can't remember seeing him more contented."

"You said 'were happy'," Mel asked, "has something happened?"

"Just Hurricane Julia, stirring things up as usual." He gritted his jaw so hard the muscles jumped on the side of his face, but she waited for him to finish on his own time.

"She came all the way out here to tell me her friend, Chef Adèle—"

"*The* Chef Adèle?" she squawked. Far from a foodie, even she recognized the name of the chef so famous she only went by her first name. "I thought your mom was in the military. How'd she make friends with her?"

He shook his head. "I have no idea, but she told her about me and The Hungry Puppy and claims she's offering me a chance to come work for her in New Orleans."

The bombshell announcement shocked Mel into

silence. She should be happy for him. An opportunity to work for a world-renowned chef in their flagship three Michelin star restaurant almost never comes along, no matter how good you are. And yet, it felt like a giant chasm split open under her feet. She'd only known Jackson for a few months, so why was she having such a strong reaction to the possibility of him leaving?

"That's great," she squeaked out in a voice she barely recognized as her own. "Your dad must be thrilled for you."

"He says he is. He keeps going on and on about how being a chef in New Orleans is a dream job I'd be a fool to pass up on, but…"

"But what? What's really bothering you about this?" His hesitation had to be about more than the thought of moving. Having gone through a similar situation herself, she understood the idea of moving to a new place could be scary, but not so much the fear should hold him back. Unless there was something—or someone—he couldn't bear the idea of leaving behind? Her heart skipped a beat, hoping it was true and yet dreading the notion he'd turn down this once in a lifetime opportunity on the chance they might have a spark between them.

"I get it. This is a golden ticket, but something just feels wrong. Is she really trying to help me, or screw my dad over yet again?" His voice vibrated with rage. "What, she can't be happy hurting us once? She has to come back and destroy us all over again, all too aware this *is* too good to pass up? It's like she's luring me away from Dad, but why? She never cared about me before."

"Maybe she wants to give her only child an

amazing opportunity? The same way my family supported me by investing in the B&B?"

"That seems…" he searched for the right word, the storm in his eyes betraying his turbulent emotions, "unlikely. And if Chef Adèle is so interested, why'd she send my mother to make the offer instead of calling herself? Something doesn't add up."

He made a good point. Why wasn't Adèle Guidry's proposal at the very least on paper? They drove the rest of the way to Palm Springs in silence. In fact, after calling to arrange a cabin for his mother, she was so engrossed in wondering what her feelings for Jackson were, she barely registered anything about the drive until they entered the city. Great, one cure for her acrophobia was to put her world at such a tilt she didn't notice the vertigo inducing fear. *Yippee.* Before she knew it, the GPS announced they'd arrived at Leigh Pemberton's home.

**\*\*\*\***

Life had been too busy for Mel to make the trip to Palm Springs since moving to Pine Cove a few months ago. The dramatic change from snowy mountaintop, through ice-melt slicked rocks to harsh, bright desert background was jarring.

She'd been to the city before as a kid on a family vacation. The former getaway destination for the Rat Pack and other Hollywood elite had become a popular holiday spot for the working stiff as well. She'd seen the giant Marilyn Monroe statue before it had left town for a bit, but hadn't been there since its return in 2021. Rumor had it that the statue, striking the famous pose from *Some Like it Hot,* offended many people who thought Marilyn was mooning the art museum she stood in front of in the busy tourist section of town. Some people aren't happy unless they're pissed off at something, she speculated.

Far beyond the touristy downtown sat Leigh Pemberton's Spartan neighborhood made up of one-story, rectangular homes packed in like sardines. It didn't give the impression of old money, but real estate in this area fetched a price tag of a million dollars or more. She didn't find the view of the squat city stretching out below enticing in the least. Pine Cove had gotten under her skin more than she'd realized.

Jackson stopped in front of what looked like a white cinderblock house. She assumed the building material was something fancier. It had to be, right? The driveway was empty, but there was a one-car garage off to the side so possibly, unlike everyone she knew in California, Ms. Pemberton actually kept her car inside. Even though it was mid-January, they'd already hit a record high of seventy-eight degrees. Who wants to burn their butt on leather upholstery if you don't have to?

She opened the car door just as Jackson, who leaped out practically before he put the truck in park, moved to open it for her. With a sheepish grin and a shrug of his shoulder, he waved for her to continue on to the house ahead of him. "Ladies first," he drawled. Mel inhaled and was disappointed to smell exhaust and asphalt, none of the pine she had come to take for granted.

Three sharp knocks to the oversized door elicited no response. "You sure she's home?" he shifted around to peer in the window but the view was barricaded by some kind of sage with nasty looking thorns.

"When I called Badger Corps, they said she was taking the week off to mourn." She lifted a shoulder and let it drop. "I guess she got over the loss earlier than she thought?" Since being nosy was part of her stock-in-trade as a cop, she sidled along the house to the tall gate blocking the path to the backyard.

Made of metal bars and frosted safety-glass, there was no way to check if Leigh Pemberton was out back, but the sound of running water confirmed she had a pool or a fountain. Only a rich idiot—no, strike that, you don't have to be smart to realize what was happening to the planet. Only a rich narcissist would see the desert landscape and think, "You know what this needs? A giant water suckage that doesn't contribute to anything except my personal status." Another thing in Pine Cove's favor; all the residents she'd met respected the natural space around them.

Surveying the house and the street, she noticed today must be trash day, as evidenced by the wheelie bins at the curb in front of most homes. Plenty of investigations had been closed by a legal search of a suspect's garbage. She shot Jackson a cock-eyed grin. Searching a private trash can without a warrant might be a problem for a cop, but there was no law against a citizen taking a peek inside.

Curious, she opened the lid and was disappointed to see the usual array of garbage bags topped by several used cans of spray paint. Weird, but not illegal. Using her phone she took a picture, just in case.

"What now, boss?" Jackson asked as they headed to his truck.

They'd driven all the way down there to catch Ms. Pemberton off-guard. Determined to succeed, Mel had figured out her plan B before leaving home and tossing a duffle bag with supplies in the backseat. "Let's pay the oil-mongers at Badger Corps a visit."

\*\*\*\*

On the way there, Mel pulled the equipment she needed out of the bag, earning a curious look from Jackson.

"What have you got in there?"

"When I was a kid, one of my favorite things to do instead of homework was watch old re-runs of a TV show about a PI," she explained as she pulled a lanyard over her head. It sported an official-looking press pass complete with her picture and the name of a fictional newspaper. "He did the coolest stuff, like keeping a tiny printer in his car. Whenever he needed to get information out of some putz, he'd print out a fake business card to lull them into talking. Thank goodness computers make creating faux credentials so much easier."

She slipped a matching cord around Jackson's neck as he navigated his truck through the entry to Badger Corps parking lot.

"Where did you get this picture?" he asked in horror. He had every right to his dismay. There were dozens online to choose from between his days at Stanford or from The Hungry Puppy's grand opening. However, he looked like a Jimmy Olsen knock-off in the photo from his high school reunion last year. She had a hard time imagining a bad picture of someone as photogenic as Jackson, but the timing was spectacularly bad. His eyes were half-closed and his mouth gaped open, as if he was in the middle of saying, "Don't take my picture."

"My grandmother, the tech whiz. Who'd have thought it?" she said as a way of not answering his question. Once he'd wedged the truck in a spot, she handed him the final piece of his disguise—an ancient camera with a crazy-looking neck strap reminiscent of something a hippy would have worn in the sixties.

"What is this?" His expression of abject horror grew into downright disgust. She laughed for the first time since the news about his job offer.

"It's a camera, duh."

He pursed his lips and tilted his head down, scowling at her through not just his thick long lashes but a stray lock of his curly dark hair as well. "Yeah, thanks, I saw one like it in a museum once. I mean why are you giving it to me?"

"Oh, didn't I tell you that part?" She hoped she sounded innocent, but the truth was she was sure he wouldn't have agreed if she'd told him sooner. "You're part of my cover for this whole reporter disguise. You're my photographer, here to help me do a follow up on the Lange story."

"A story you're not really writing."

"And you're not really taking pictures because as far as I know, there's no film in that thing." She flashed him the sweetest smile she could conjure, confident he'd help her when his scowl turned into an amused grin.

"This is a digital camera," he explained, showing her the memory card.

"Whatever. I borrowed it from the Doc."

"Explains the strap," he joked. "What am I supposed to be photographing?"

"Does it matter?" They squeezed out of the truck.

"Considering the crappy pictures you took the last time we tried this, I won't be able to recognize anything, anyway."

A month ago, when one of her guests met with a fatal accident on the mountain, she'd needed him to take pictures of the scene, since her fear of heights made it impossible for her to do so. His photography skills were so bad she'd suspected he'd botched the job on purpose to conceal his guilt in the murder.

Thank goodness he hadn't held her doubts against her, she didn't know what she'd do without him. Was she about to find out? She fought the urge to chip away at her nail polish. Could be this is why she never got her nails done. All she needed was to develop another bad habit, like picking at her nails. And on that cheerful note, she marched toward the entry to the office building, Jackson following in her wake.

****

In the few short months she'd lived in Pine Cove, Mel had gotten used to the quirky, rustic buildings, each marching to the beat of their own drummer. From the Victorian to the bungalow cabins, they all exuded a warmth, an individual personality she'd come to appreciate and tried to carry through in the inn as they continued to work on improvements.

To be fair, Los Angeles was also a melting pot of styles, from Spanish to modern, that had an eclectic appeal. By contrast, the icy chill of the sterile lobby of the Nichols Oil building, home to Badger Corp, practically burned her retinas. White walls, gleaming chrome fixtures and white leather furniture smacked of the cold, clinical precision of…well, an engineering company, she supposed. Still, would a plant or two have killed them?

"Excuse me." She approached the prissy receptionist with her best won't-take-no-for-an-answer polite tone honed by years of dealing with hostile witnesses. "Can you let Leigh Pemberton know Martha Washington from the *Suntimespicayunedaily* is here?" She slurred the name of the fake newspaper while flashing her press pass.

After a poke in the ribs, Jackson presented his ID as well, sputtering "Martha Washington?" under his breath.

The woman pursed her fuchsia lips together, the slash of color standing out in stark contrast to her porcelain skin. From her expression, Mel could see the gears turning in her head.

"I'm sorry, Ms. Pemberton isn't in today. She took a week of bereavement leave and won't be back until Monday."

"Are you sure? Her car is in her parking spot." She'd taken a wild guess: a place like this would have assigned spots for the executives and Pemberton would be arrogant enough to use hers even when she told the staff to lie about her being in. The receptionist's furtive glance at the security guard in the corner of the lobby confirmed her hunch. Pemberton was there. "We're doing a piece on Kyle Lange," she continued, "highlighting his legacy, how much he gave back to the community. It would be really helpful to get his partner's perspective."

The receptionist hesitated, eyes flicking back and forth between Jackson and the guard. *Really? You're looking to the man for confirmation? So much for sisterhood.* She gave Jackson another poke in the ribs.

He leaned in a little closer to the receptionist, almost shutting Mel out of her view altogether.

"I'd hate to have lugged this big ol' camera over here for nothing," he said, pouring on the, "aw, shucks" Louisiana charm. He put the viewfinder to his eye, took a picture of the puzzled young woman, then gave her a dazzling smile. "Well, almost nothing. It's never a waste of time to photograph a pretty woman. But it would be mighty nice, Sugar, if we could talk to Ms. Pemberton or at least take a gander at Mr. Lange's lab. You know, see where all the magic happened?"

*Sugar?* Mel threw up a little in the back of her throat. Convinced he'd overplayed his hand, she mentally rifled through their other options when the receptionist, her cheeks now almost as pink as her lipstick, pouted seductively. "I guess it wouldn't hurt to check with Ms. Pemberton to see if she's available."

A brief phone call was all it took. Once she uttered the words "photographer" and "newspaper" the screechy shriek on the other end of the line ordered they be sent right up.

Alone in the elevator, she muttered, "Sugar?" She kept her voice down, aware there was probably a surveillance camera in the elevator that recorded sound as well.

"My mama taught me to use all my gifts," he drawled. Laying the accent on thick, his voice held the promise of steamy sex. What was it about accents—Southern, British or otherwise—that made people go soft in the head? Because the receptionist wasn't the only one who would have done anything he'd asked if he used that voice.

\*\*\*\*

The elevator doors opened to an imperious grande dame, arms crossed, tapping her foot impatiently. "Did you stop for coffee on the way?" she snarled as she spun on her heel and marched toward an open door near the end of the otherwise deserted hallway. Although no invitation was offered, Mel assumed they were meant to follow her, so she did, dragging Jackson along in her wake.

The picture on the company's website didn't do Leigh Pemberton justice, Mel thought, as they hustled to catch up. In fact, despite what her grandmother thought, the photo was far too kind. An expert had enhanced the image because, as unappealing as it was, in person the impression was worse.

She hated when people, usually men, touted how much prettier a woman when be if she'd smile. There might be some truth to that, but no one ever said such condescending bullshit to a man. In this case, however, not wearing such an ugly sneer would be a step in the right direction.

The room she led them into had one wall lined with filing cabinets someone had torn through like a rabid animal in search of its next meal. Manila folders with papers and charts spilling out were strewn across the floor. From Pemberton's disheveled state, Mel made the leap of logic she was the guilty party. But why would she need to rummage through them so violently if she and Lange worked together on everything, and what was she searching for?

"Forgive the mess," Leigh Pemberton uttered in a tone that wasn't contrite in the least. She tried to pat her magenta colored hair into some order as she explained. "We suffered a terrible loss with Kyle's death and are still trying to pick up the pieces of his work." Her frustration showed. From the disarray of her permed curls, she might have literally been pulling her hair out in her hunt for… *what?*

She strutted over to another side of the large room, this one lined with what Mel assumed were scientific gadgets. She recognized the microscope, but other than that had no idea. From their undisturbed state, she'd bank on Pemberton not having a clue either. Whatever their partnership was, clearly she brought no technical expertise to the table.

"How about this?" She struck a game show model pose, waving toward some sort of scale with beakers and tubes running through them. She raised a glass jar so tentatively it was obvious she was unfamiliar with the liquid inside and more than a little afraid of getting splashed.

"Perfect," Mel said, clearing her throat to snap Jackson out of his stupor. He obliged, faking his way through taking photos from several angles. The scene made her lips twitch, fighting off a laugh. A phony photographer pretending to take pictures of a bogus scientist. The whole scenario would have been hilarious if not for the fact she suspected Pemberton of murder.

The entire time she was posing, Leigh Pemberton's eyes continued to scan the room, searching for something. Whatever it was, it must have been all-consuming, because her gaze didn't linger on Jackson for even a moment. Very few women don't notice his handsome features, especially when he smiled and turned on his dimple power.

She plunged ahead, repeating the same cover story about working for a local paper and writing a tribute to

Kyle Lange. "I understand you've been his partner and close friend for several years now."

"Yes, and?"

*Wow, cranky much?* She shot Jackson a look meant to communicate *bereavement leave my ass* and he must have gotten the gist. His smile broadened, and he made a noise as if he had to swallow back a laugh.

"I was hoping you could tell me about him. I mean, word is you recently went your separate ways, but you were partners for a long time. If anyone knows the man behind the man, it would be you."

"Our separate ways? Don't be ridiculous. Who told you that? Mullins? Oh wait, let me guess, his gold-digging wife? I assure you, nothing was further from the truth."

*Sure, that would explain why you're re-decorating your lab to resemble a college freshman dorm room.* "Terrific." Mel plastered a bright smile on her face. "Then you can tell us about this latest project he was working on before his untimely death? I understand from his assistant, Mr. Mullins, it will change the world."

Pemberton sneered as she plopped her very padded butt down on top of the desk strewn with papers and files. "Mullins," she spat out like a swear word. "Kiss ass thought everything Kyle did would change the world." Her *tsk* was full of disdain and a bit too much saliva. "*We* were working on a project related to the oil industry, but I'm not at liberty to discuss the details." She put a lot of emphasis on the word "we," but if they were collaborating so closely, why was the woman ransacking the lab?

"I got the impression from Mrs. Lange he'd opted

to go it alone on this project?"

She gave an exaggerated roll of her eyes and barked out an ugly laugh. "Yes, I admit we'd come to an impasse in our negotiations over the profit split, but I'm confident I could have changed Kyle's mind."

"So, will you carry on without him?" She doubted it, suspecting that of the duo, Ms. Pemberton handled the financials more than the Bunsen burner. Which might give her even more motive. What if she wasn't searching for evidence to prove their work, but to destroy proof she was stealing money from the company?

"Carry on? What a good idea, I wish I'd thought of that," she snapped, a storm of emotions raging across her face in unattractive red splotches.

"Is there a reason you can't, ma'am?" Jackson asked, working the drawl for all he was worth. Mel was grateful he stepped in. She wasn't sure what her response would have been, but it wouldn't have been as polite or effective. Pemberton deflated a little and fluttered her hands at the mess around her.

"Kyle normally kept his notes on projects he's developing under lock and key in these file cabinets, but either they've gone missing or he's hidden them somewhere. Even the computer files are empty. With him dead and his formula gone, I own one hundred percent of zilch. Whoever killed him might as well have killed me too," she bemoaned.

Mel thought her act was over the top, but she hadn't delved into the woman's financials. Being deep in debt would be a pretty good motive. Using her reporter steno pad prop, she made a note to check. "Do you have any idea who would have wanted Mr. Lange dead? Did he have any enemies?"

"Other than EcoWarrior?" she spat, back to the puffy, angry, red-faced beast.

"Sorry?" she asked, as if her grandmother hadn't told her about the eco-savior or terrorist, depending on your point of view.

"Some tree hugger named Oliver Brown who goes by the social media handle of @EcoWarrior69. He's been after Badger Corp and Kyle personally for years over environmental crap."

"Oh? Have there been issues in the past?"

Ms. Pemberton's beady little eyes latched on to her pen, poised over her notebook. "Don't you dare write that down or I will sue your paper. These eco pricks whine about the environment while driving around in their SUVs and drinking bottled water."

"Yes ma'am," Jackson chimed in with a sympathetic nod, "that must be upsetting."

His soothing voice calmed her down a notch. "You have no idea. The last six months, he'd been escalating his attacks and actually sued Kyle over some creek or something. Since he kept my name off any of the formulas *we* created, the legal issues didn't involve me, so I didn't pay much attention. But Kyle could afford the best legal defense money could buy, so this so-called EcoWarrior didn't have a snowball's chance in hell. He seems pretty unhinged. I wouldn't be surprised if he found a more permanent solution."

It wasn't the worst theory she'd ever heard, so she noted down Oliver Brown's name as she casually floated out the question, "Where were you the night Kyle Lange was murdered, if you don't mind me asking?"

She'd braced herself for the woman to launch herself at her, hissing and spitting with her claws out. Instead, she deflated into such a sad, miserable lump Mel felt a little sorry for her. "Home, alone, and no, there is no one to corroborate that. As usual," she added scurrying out the door before she could thank her for her time.

Chapter Ten

"Poppy says your mom got checked in okay." Mel scrolled through her texts as they left Badger Corps' parking lot.

"Dandy." The spark of humor dancing in his eyes after meeting the blustery Ms. Pemberton drained away.

"So, what do you think of the gear in their lab?" She hoped changing topics would put him in a better mood, having woefully underestimated how grumpy news of his mother would make him.

Gaze fixed on the road, he shrugged. "It reminded me of a filtration system. I worked on fixing the flavor of food. This oil engineering stuff is out of my wheelhouse, but most engineers I know don't have labs. We work in offices, like everybody else."

"That explains why Ms. Pemberton was acting so weird around the equipment. But then why would Lange have all those beakers and things in the first place?"

He answered with another non-committal shrug. Mel got the hint he wasn't in the mood for chatting and stopped trying. For almost two whole minutes. She broke under the heavy silence caused by the elephant sitting between them.

"Thinking about the job offer?"

He took his eyes off the road only long enough to give her an uncharacteristic raise of an eyebrow accompanied by a silent *duh, what do you think?* glower. She wished she had the right words to take the confused frown off his face. Working with Chef Adèle in a three star restaurant in New Orleans *was* a great opportunity for him. He should be elated for this once in a lifetime chance that had to be every chef's dream. Surely his mom was trying to help him, not screw with him?

On the other hand, Jackson hadn't dreamed of being a chef. He'd trained to be a chemical engineer and had only left the field when he realized the products the company he worked for were doing more harm than good. He'd returned to Pine Cove and moved back in with his dad to regroup and reinvent himself. Would any of it—the restaurant, the acclaim—mean anything without Hugo Thibodeaux there by his side? From the way he talked, his dad would eat ground glass before even considering moving back to New Orleans and live in the same town as his ex-wife.

She jumped when the ding of her phone broke the heavy silence that had settled between them. She read the text and muttered a curse under her breath, but said nothing. Moments later, Jackson heaved a put-upon sigh.

"You don't get to swear to yourself and then not tell me why."

Oh, *now* he wants to talk, when it's *her* life spinning out of control? Well, at least it shook him out of his pissy mood. "I got a text from Poppy instructing me to hurry home, she has a surprise for me."

One side of his mouth twitched upward in amusement. "You want me to drive faster?"

"God no!" she yipped when he pushed on the

accelerator. They'd just begun the serious uphill, zigzagging return trip to Pine Cove and her fear, as well as her dread of whatever Poppy had planned, caused her voice to become a high-pitched squeal. With a chuckle, he slowed down.

"Don't worry, I told you I got you." And he did, driving a careful speed and using every turn out along the way so he didn't hold up the drivers behind him. That was Jackson, sweet and thoughtful. How would she feel if he took the job? Sometimes he pissed her off, but most of the time she loved hanging out with him. Who else would go to the kooky movie theatre in Pine Cove with its mismatched chairs for seating and watch old black and white movies with her?

They were friends, but were they becoming something more? Mel stole a glance at him, at his lips with their perfect cupid bow. The idea of what it would be like to kiss them popped into her mind. She was still sorting out what that meant when they pulled into the parking lot and found Poppy waiting on the steps of the B&B.

"It's about bloody time," her beaming smile contrasting with her words. "Get a move on, your first knitting class is in ten. You can tell me all about whatever you discovered on the way."

"Wait, what class? I have to go inside and check on—"

"Yes, yes, yes, Jackson's mum settled in just fine, stop worrying." She shoved the bag of supplies they bought earlier into Mel's hands and, giving Jackson a brief wave, propelled her toward the store.

****

The backroom of the Yarn Barn where Dortha Jo

held classes got real cozy once all eight knitters, including Mel and Poppy, gathered around a long wooden worktable. A little too cozy for Mel's taste. Especially once Mrs. Oberdingle arrived with her bug-eyed, black and white dog hitching a ride in her purse. The animal bothered her less than the cloud of perfume the woman wore.

And seeing Kendall out of her usual suit wearing torn jeans, knitting what appeared to be baby booties, was downright weird. She didn't look pregnant, but she was finding out this town had more secrets than the CIA. The ambitious realtor sidled next to Mel, a knowing grin splitting her face.

"I understand you met Mrs. Lange while you were getting a..." her gaze dropped to her chipped nails and she frowned. "Manicure?" She shook off her repulsion at the damage Mel had done and leaned in closer. "What did you make of her? Do you think the rumors about her having a lover in Pine Cove are true?"

Stunned by the revelation, she sputtered, "*She's* having an affair?" It certainly explained coming all the way up here for a manicure. Kendall opened her mouth to respond when Dortha Jo cut her off.

"Alright gentle beings, everyone take their seats." The din of chatter lowered to a hushed murmur as the others sat in what appeared to be their usual places. That left Mel and Poppy the empty chairs at the far end of the room. With the precision of a drill team, they pulled out their assorted projects and began to knit.

She realized knitting might help her get over her fear of heights, but for the wrong reason. Far from being bored, the skein of yarn in front of her intimidated her more than the climbing wall. Almost.

Great, she wasn't getting over old issues, she was uncovering new ones. Even Poppy was fast at work, already two rows into her project.

"Son of a bitch," Mel muttered to her, "you're a ringer."

"What? I didn't say *I* didn't know how to knit," her eyes wide in an innocent expression. "But I'm rubbish at teaching people anything, hence the reason we're here."

Panic must have been writ large on her face because after kicking off the so-called class, which was more like a knitting circle of friends getting out of the house once a week to exchange gossip, Dortha Jo sat down by her.

"Let's get you cast on, dear." Her gentle tone didn't take away any of Mel's confusion or frustration. She tried to wind the yarn between the two needles, but kept twisting it instead, pulling so tight she struggled to shove the left one through the next loop.

After twenty minutes, she wondered if her competitive nature made knitting the best hobby for her. She was so busy measuring her crude beginner's work against everyone else's she almost forgot about Kendall's remark about an affair. The woman's squeal of delight as she finished a tiny baby booty reminded her.

"That's lovely, Kendall. Are they for you?" Mel asked to ease her way into the conversation.

"Did you think I was…" the woman glanced down at her plump belly and laughed. "Oh no, they're for Mr. Mittens, my cat. Until we get the heated floor installed, his wittle paws get so cold on our tile floor in the winter time."

Even as a professional schooled at not revealing her emotions, Mel had to work hard to master her reaction. "How sweet. I'm sure he'll love them." She edged closer, dropping her voice to a murmur. "So, what's this about Heather Lange having an affair?"

The other woman leaned toward her, a gleam in her eye. "Well, I heard she doesn't come all the way to Pine Cove to have Miguel just do her nails, if you catch my drift."

"Nonsense." Mrs. Oberdingle barked, abandoning the topic of who is breaking the water restrictions to chime in. "Kendall, you should know better than to spread gossip," said the biggest gossip in town. "An upstanding woman like Heather Lange would never have an affair. I understand she's working with the officials at Mount San Esteban's animal sanctuary.

"You, on the other hand," she narrowed her eyes at Mel, peering over a mountain of midnight black yarn, "what's this about offering some sort of sex package at your B&B for the Valentine's Day weekend?"

Jaw clenched, she gave Poppy a heavy dose of side-eye. The annoying brunette shrugged and smiled. "We're toying with a promo for the inn, but I can assure you there's nothing illicit about it."

"Oh, really?" the tiny woman sniffed as her fingers flew, adding another row of complicated stitches. "Because according to your web page, you're not only offering special room rates, but a romantic dinner as well."

"Are we now?" She glared at Poppy while forcing her plastered on smile to broaden.

"I had some free time while you were in Palm Springs and brainstormed with Grandma and Gemma.

Gran wanted to throw a key party, but we talked her down from that."

"You're licensed as a bed-and-*breakfast*. The city council would have to approve you serving any other additional meal." The mayor's wife barked as if that were an indisputable fact. Mel scrubbed her tired eyes. She'd have to check tomorrow.

Right now, her problems included her fingers cramping, her knitting resembling a garter snake more than the simple garter stitch Dortha Jo tried to teach her, and the search for a killer before an innocent woman was charged. That the suspect was a con artist and champion knitter, as evidenced by her half-finished colorful striped scarf, added to her annoyance. Was there nothing Poppy wasn't good at? Knitting might not be her own forte but solving at least two of those three problems was within Mel's grasp.

Getting to her feet and collecting her wandering skein of yarn, she announced, "This has been lovely, thank you for an educational evening, but *we've* got an early day tomorrow." She put a special emphasis on the "we" and her chef/assistant/marketing genius got the hint. She gathered her yarn as well, cooing how great it was to meet everyone.

"Same time next week?" Dortha Jo asked, but then she had a vested interest. Not so much the profit from the class, but presumably the yarn she'd sell if she got Mel hooked.

"Of course, see you then," she lied through her teeth. The chances of her becoming a knitter were slim to none at best.

Once out the door, Poppy admitted defeat. "Okay, so knitting wasn't for you. I see my mistake now. You don't like group activities. Or people. Which makes running an inn an interesting occupational choice, but who am I to judge?"

"I like people," she protested. "Just not so many in such a small space." Especially when she was the odd man out.

"Oh, well, in that case, there's a pottery studio in town that gives private lessons."

Groaning, she argued against the idea the rest of the way back to the B & B.

\*\*\*\*

The sun had barely peeked through the pine trees when the smell of coffee and bacon lured Mel out of her living quarters and into the Great Room. She had to remind herself not to get used to Poppy being there. As soon as they cleared her name, she'd be gone. However, her stomach nagged she might as well enjoy her delicious breakfasts in the meantime.

At this time of day, she'd expected to have the room to herself, so it surprised her to see an elegant Black woman seated near the glass doors. She thought at first she was enjoying the view of the brook down the hill, but the woman's cold, distant stare told her whatever she was thinking about wasn't making her happy at all. Deciding to veer away and give her privacy, she stopped dead in her tracks when the woman said, "Are you Mel O'Rourke? I'm Julia Landry. My son Jackson has told me quite a lot about you. Please, join me."

Despite the word "please" being included, the commanding tone made it clear she wasn't asking. Never fond of taking orders even from her superior officers, her natural inclination was to ignore her. But

Jackson was her friend and the least she could do was be polite to his mother. Besides, she was also a guest. Time to think like a hotel owner and not a cop. She took a centering breath and steeled herself to be gracious.

"Of course," she nodded, adding, "can I get you a cup of coffee?"

"No, thank you," the woman snorted. "Caffeine ages your skin, among other things. A cup of warm water with lemon is the smart way to start your day." She hefted her mug in a toast.

Mel suppressed her shudder and said nothing as she poured milk and then the evil coffee into her own mug. She toasted back without engaging in a debate over breakfast drinks. *You do you, my skin is just fine.*

She'd questioned Poppy last night about what Julia Landry was like, but all she would say was, "You have to see for yourself". Now she understood why. So far, based on their brief encounter, the words cold, commanding, and scary came to mind. However, years on the force taught her first impressions were unreliable.

She took a seat across from the woman, whose ramrod straight posture screamed ex-military even if Jackson hadn't already told her. "Did you sleep well, Ms. Landry?"

"This woodsy little hamlet is far too quiet to be restful, but I didn't ask you to join me for small talk."

She was a little blunt, even by Mel's standards. "Okay, why did you ask me to join you?"

"I assume my son told you about the offer from Adèle Guidry?"

She sipped her coffee, stalling for time as she

pondered the best answer. Pretend she had no idea what she was talking about, or be honest? Poppy poked her head out of the kitchen and shot Mel a questioning look. Taking advantage of the distraction, she replied, "He mentioned something about it. Would you care for some breakfast? Smells like blueberry pancakes are on the menu."

"No, thank you," she gave a dismissive wave. Poppy shrugged and retreated back into the kitchen. So much for a save from this uncomfortable little chat. "I can tell you have a lot of influence over my son."

"Me?" The idea surprised her. "I mean, we're friends, sure, but I don't hold any sway over him."

Her narrowed gaze and pursed lips said Julia Landry disagreed. "We both know you're more than just a friend to him. I'd be grateful if you'd encourage him to accept the offer." A millimeter at a time, her face softened as she continued, "My motives aren't entirely altruistic. I've missed out on so much of his life because of my career and then the divorce.

"I want to get to know him again. If he'd let me do this one thing for him, we might…" She went back to staring out the window, shutting down as if she'd already revealed too much. Maybe she isn't as manipulative as Jackson thought. Could she just be a mother wanting to love her son?

"I can't imagine how difficult that must have been for you, being separated by such a distance. I'm having a hard time adjusting, and my family is only a few hours away. But if it helps you at all, he's happy here, passionate about his job for the first time in his life." His happiness had to count for something, right? At least it should, but apparently not enough for his mother.

"He may be happy now, but there's no future for him in this one-horse town with no one to appreciate his gifts. These people wouldn't recognize world-class cuisine from poutine." The woman shifted her gaze from the window back to Mel. "No offense," she added.

*Right, because adding "no offense" gave you license to be an asshole.* She sighed with relief when the couple who'd arrived yesterday wandered in. "I'm sorry, duty calls," she nodded toward the newcomers. Rising, she gave the woman one last glance. "I don't think I hold any power over Jackson one way or the other, but I promise you I'll be here for him, ready to listen if he asks for my advice."

Julia Landry's grunt of disapproval followed her all the way into the kitchen.

****

There was enough of a breakfast rush that even Liam pitched in, scowling every time he exited the kitchen, grumbling about Poppy. Mel didn't understand why she rubbed her brother the wrong way. God knows everyone else loved her. But he was helping out doing repairs, so who was she to complain? With any luck, they'd start making a decent profit soon and she wouldn't have to worry about the stupid branding thing at all. But she'd agreed to try, so after the guests had left, she sat down to eat with Grandma, Liam and Poppy and asked for their help.

"I don't get why this is so hard for you," her brother answered. "Your brand is just...you. You can't get it wrong."

She wanted to bang her head on the table in frustration. Because the problem was, the more the workbook asked her to describe her mission and her vision and all that bullshit, the more she realized she had no idea. The only thing she'd ever wanted to be was a cop and beyond that, she was drawing a blank.

"If you don't mind me asking," Poppy touched her hand, "why did you buy this place?"

She was about to blow off the question with a joke about it seeming like a good idea at the time when she noticed Liam and Grandma O also studying her curiously. Swallowing down the last of her lukewarm coffee, she paused before admitting, "When I was a kid, we vacationed in Pine Cove during the summer. Once or twice, we even stayed at this inn."

"Oh yeah, I remember those trips now that you mention it," Liam agreed. "How did this not come up before now?"

"Because you all were so worried about me after my accident, when I suggested buying the place, nobody asked. And to your point," she nodded to Poppy, "I wasn't dying to run any old motel. I needed Pine Cove. Compared with the noise and" she hesitated, searching for the right word before settling on, "intensity of Los Angeles, this place was magical. Peaceful. Clean.

"And the people who ran this inn were so helpful, making sure everyone enjoyed themselves. The hiking maps in the lobby, the games and books on the shelves in the Great Room, they reveled in taking care of their guests. I guess I wanted to do the same, to serve and protect in the only way I have left."

Poppy's gaze darted between Mel and her brother as if she wanted to help but didn't want to piss him off any more than the fact she breathed the same air already did. "Okay, let's start with an easy question," she opened the branding workbook. "Here's one—name your favorite colors."

She shot her an undeserved scowl and replied, "Black and white."

"Nah," her grandmother chimed in, "those aren't colors, that's your outlook on life. Always has been. While this one" — she patted Liam's cheek — "likes to color outside the lines, you were a strictly by the book little bugger. Stop fretting and let it come to you naturally. And if that doesn't work, have some edibles for some inspiration."

The table erupted in gasps. Liam and Mel in shock while Poppy in delighted amusement. He turned his attention back to his plate, noisily going after the last morsel despite the fact his mortal enemy had prepared the food. The fork scraping across china was like nails on a chalkboard. Mel winced. "Do you want me to shoot you right now?"

He grumbled something about the problem with a family full of cops is everyone else has a gun, but he put his fork down.

"I don't have a gun," Poppy purred, batting her lashes at him. He made a disgusted sound and threw his napkin on the table. The mention of a gun reminded Mel about a part of the investigation she was missing.

"Dammit, this is when I miss being a cop." She leaned back in her chair and gnawed on her thumbnail until the polish flaked off in her mouth. *Yuck.* "Somebody owns the gun that shot at you," she nodded toward Poppy. "Used to be I'd just log onto the system at the cop shop and see if any of our suspects had a gun permit. I guess I can ask Dad to have one of his friends check it out."

"Oh, no need," Liam pulled out his phone. "Whole-Truth.com. I used the site to check out all the guys you dated."

"You what now?" Mel's voice took on a shrieky pitch.

"Oh yeah. That's how I found out the jerk Gemma was dating was already married. In fact, maybe I should look up your bakery boy."

"Shut right the eff up. He's not mine and there will be no background checks done on him." She gave him a hard stare, willing her brother to take her seriously or she would have to hurt him.

"Yeah, fine, whatever. So, who do you want me to check out?"

She recited the list of suspects, starting with Mullins and ending with Leigh Pemberton.

"Huh. Nope, no gun permits. Doesn't mean they don't own one, though."

Thinking about it, she moved to chew on her thumbnail again, but caught herself in time. "None of them strike me as the type to even know how to buy a weapon off the street, least of all Ms. Pemberton." Which was too bad because if she was a betting woman, her money would have been on her.

Liam rose to his feet. "Daylights burning and I'm almost done swapping out the wood stove that almost killed you with a clean, gas one, like we agreed." He glared at her, daring her to argue with him. She opened her mouth to complain when Poppy beat her to the punch.

"'ang on, a fireplace nearly did you in?" She gave an amused chuckle. "How is your life in this peaceful haven so much more exciting than it ever was in L.A.?"

For the first time, Liam grinned at Poppy. "I know, right?" Then, as if he remembered the role she played in Mel's fall, he reverted to scowling before turning his attention back to his sister. "I'm waiting for a part to finish the project, so this morning I'll take a look at the hot tub in cabin six you told me isn't working."

"Cabin six," Grandma snorted. "While you're busy with that branding nonsense, can you come up with something better than the Dewey decimal system to name the cabins?"

Mel sunk her head into her hands with a groan. She didn't have *time* for this bullshit. Liam gave her shoulder a gentle squeeze.

"Grandma's right, you're over thinking this brand thing. Who else could you be but you?" He kissed the top of their grandmother's head with the directive, "And you, stay out of trouble," before heading out the door.

"Bossy little shit," the old woman muttered, her beaming smile betraying how fond she was of her grandson. "So now that Mr. Grumpy Pants has left, want to see what else I found on @EcoWarrior69?"

She opted first to clear the table and tidy the kitchen. Twenty minutes later, the three gathered in the office, keeping an ear out in case a guest came knocking in need of assistance. Mel carried in cups of coffee plus a tea for Poppy, Julia Landry's theories about caffeine be damned. Then she settled in to find out what her grandmother had learned.

Gnarled fingers dancing over the keyboard, the older woman pulled up the Tweedle feed for @EcoWarrior69. "The boy is doing all right for himself, with just under ten thousand followers on Tweedle and the same on Graffer. A few less on SpinChat but then he doesn't post there as much. Bless his heart, he keeps a NewsMage profile as well. I mean, his personal account only has fourteen friends, but still."

Mel peered over her grandmother's shoulder at the computer screen to read about @EcoWarrior69, aka Oliver Brown. From his posts, Oliver seemed an earnest guy dedicated to eco-activism. His battle with Kyle Lange wasn't the only war he was waging against a company he thought was killing the environment, but it was the most heated and personal one.

"Look," Poppy showed them her phone where she played a video on Brown's environmentalist group's NewsMage Live account. "He's currently staging a tree-sitting to save an old California Oak from being cut down in Hemet. Is that close by?"

Mel grew dizzy as the blood drained from her face, knowing a trip to Hemet meant going back down the mountain. She'd barely recovered from yesterday's little jaunt. "It's not far, but I have a business to run. I can't keep taking days off to question suspects." At Poppy's offended gasp, she added, "I'll call Deputy Marks and tell him what we found. He'll interview the man and if he has any information that clears your name, the cops will have gotten it on their own. Mission accomplished," she finished weakly.

The scowl on Poppy's face testified to her unhappiness with this game plan. Mel wasn't sold on the idea either, but her breakfast threatened to make a return appearance just thinking about the steep, curvy road to Hemet.

Grandma O took hold of the phone and held the screen closer to her face, squinting for a better view. "Christ on a cracker, that boy is hot. Emmeline, you get yourself down there and talk to him toot suite."

Brightening at having an ally in her quest, Poppy's face split into a broad smile. "I'll go with you, if Gran doesn't mind watching the front desk. We can take my car, she needs to get the dust blown out of her engines, anyway. It'll be fun," she clapped to punctuate her words.

She seriously doubted that, but before she could say "no" her coat was thrust in her arms and keys jangled from Poppy's hand. Like a piece of flotsam coursing down a whitewater rapids, she was powerless to fight the two forces of nature stacked against her, so she surrendered with a sigh.

"Oh, hey," she called to her grandmother as she was pushed out the door. "Can you find out if we're allowed to serve dinner? Not that I've agreed to your cockamamie marketing plan," she warned a giddy Poppy, "but I'll be damned if I'm going to let Mrs. Oberdingle boss me around."

Chapter Eleven

The drive down wasn't as bad as she'd expected, but it wasn't good either. Poppy drove at what Mel suspected was an uncharacteristically slow pace with the top down, claiming the fresh air blowing through her hair would make her acrophobia easier to bear. She still clung to the door handle, but breathing almost normally so...winning?

"Do you want to talk about it?" The other woman had asked her as they started down the hill but didn't press after she mutely shook her head "no". Instead, she took one hand off the wheel to fiddle with the screen on her dashboard to find a digital radio station, nearly giving Mel a heart attack. Finally with a smug grin, she settled on a Zydeco/Rock station.

"Why did you pick this music?"

"No reason, certainly not because there's a cutey from Louisiana whose got his eye on you."

"Yeah, great." The pit in her stomach opened even wider. "He's going to leave town any day now if his mother has her way."

"I wouldn't be sure about that," Poppy muttered under her breath, not at all surprised by the news. She narrowed her eyes at the thief next to her.

"How did you know about the job offer? And what makes you think he'll stay?" Had Jackson been talking to her? Or did Julia Landry mention it when she checked in?

"Poppet, surely by now you've figured out I know everything." She grinned. "And what if he does go? You aren't chained to the inn. Follow him if you fancy."

The mere idea of following him to New Orleans set panic coursing through her faster than the steep drop to her right did. "It's not like that. We're not even dating."

"So don't date him in The Big Easy. Get out there and see the world, girl. You can always come home again."

Oddly enough, her family had said the same thing when she moved to Pine Cove. They encouraged her to try small town living and get away from the stress of being a cop and the disappointment of her career ending almost before it had begun. The road goes both ways, they'd insisted, she could always come back to L.A. and do something else if she hated it. But sometime in the last month or so, Mel considered Pine Cove rather than L.A. her home. She couldn't pinpoint when or why, it just felt right.

Sure, this new career felt overwhelming at times, and she definitely needed to take some hospitality business courses. They'd all been pie-eyed optimists to think running a hotel was as simple as taking reservations and changing sheets, but she enjoyed the challenge of learning new things. Well crap, now she really was going to have to hunker down and do that stupid branding workbook.

"I'm not you," she finally responded. "I like roots, I like the earth firmly beneath my feet."

"That does sound nice." The other woman agreed with an almost wistful tone in her voice. Mel's head snapped to study her, surprised her response wasn't a derisive sneer. She'd expected her companion, who'd no doubt seen a lot of the world from one heist to the next, to be fatally allergic to staying put for too long. After all, that's when you get caught.

"You are full of surprises," she muttered.

The conversation had taken her mind off her fears and soon they reached the bottom of the hill. She took a deep breath, cursing Poppy for having gotten her in the habit, and found the air was heavier, dustier. Just off the road, she caught sight of several pieces of construction equipment and a black and white from the Hemet PD parked near a single large, old tree.

At the base swarmed a dozen protestors with signs. Around them, the brush and prickly bushes were still dense, but two hundred yards out in any direction, only stumps from recently cut trees remained. His was the only one left standing. "Oh, over there, that's got to be Oliver," she pointed out.

"Thanks, I would never have spotted all those protest signs, bulldozers, and the tree without you," Poppy remarked sarcastically. "You're a born detective, well done."

Parking in what little shade remained, she hopped out and pulled a neatly rolled car cover out of the trunk. Mel gave an impatient growl at the delay, eager to talk to Oliver Brown. "What? I just got this waxed. You could help." At the admonition, she snatched one side of the canvas and helped yank the cover over the car. In no time, they were wading through the protesters toward Oliver Brown.

After closer inspection, Mel made a mental note to get Grandma O's eyesight checked. He was in good shape, probably from living in a tree, but his face resembled a Picasso painting, a little off-centered with mismatching features. His aquiline nose was too long for his square face, accentuated by his dishwater blonde ponytail at the nape of his neck. From this distance it was hard to tell, but he appeared to be wearing eyeliner. On the other hand, sitting in an old, weathered, formerly bright red rowboat hanging twenty feet in the air was a tough look for anyone to pull off.

"You have to admire his dedication," the Brit remarked. "It can't be easy living primitive in a dory."

"It's not that primitive. His groupies deliver food and water, and the Wi-Fi is strong enough he's able to live stream video twenty-four seven and post on social media ad nauseam. He's just another influencer hungry for attention."

Poppy faced her, mouth agape. "A bit jaded, aren't we? A quid says he really does love trees."

"No, thanks. What even is that in real money?" She dismissed the idea and turned her focus back to Oliver Brown.

"Mr. Brown," she shouted over the protestors' constant chanting of slogans and less original taunts such as, "hell no, we won't go". "I'd like to talk to you about your dispute with Kyle Lange."

He cupped his ear to indicate he couldn't hear her. "Sir, can you come down for a moment?" she bellowed.

He shook his head and laughed, pointing to the nearby squad car.

Well crap, of course she'd have to climb to him. Sweat trickled down her spine despite the temperature hovering in the sixties.

"Shall I go?" Poppy murmured. She stiffened,

thinking she was mocking her, but when she turned to deliver a snappy retort saw only a concerned frown.

Did she want her to go instead? Mel had too many questions to ask him to write them all down. Besides, there was a platform suspended about ten feet off the ground by a pulley system. She just needed to climb the tree's thick, generous branches to get there.

She studied the lowest one, her palms clammy already. "No," she shook her head, "I got this. Just give me a boost, will you? It's been a dog's age since I've climbed a tree."

When Poppy's brows furrowed in confusion, she sighed. "It's a Grandma O saying. It's been a long time, okay? Boost please."

Cupping her hands as if giving her a leg up on a horse, the Brit gave an unexpected powerful heave and almost shot her past her target branch. Awkwardly, keeping her focus on the next branch, she clawed her way to the platform and collapsed in relief, schooling herself not to look down.

"Mr. Brown, I'm Mel O'Rourke. I'm doing a story about the late Kyle Lange, and I understand you had an ongoing...shall we say, difference of opinion with him over his impact on the environment. Are you glad he's dead?" It wasn't the subtlest question, but in her experience, she found sometimes being blunt surprised the truth out of suspects.

But the shoe was on the other foot when he stunned her with a sad shake of his head. "Please, call me Oliver. I was sorry to learn about Kyle's murder. Such a waste."

"A waste? In what way, I thought you two were bitter enemies?" He snorted a derisive chuckle.

155

"Bill Gates and Steve Jobs were bitter enemies. What we had was an all out war."

In her mind, a few insults over social media hardly registered as "all out war," but when she rolled her eyes, a wave of vertigo made her world slide. She grasped the ropes supporting the platform to steady herself before continuing.

"How so?"

"For years, me and my group tracked every development Lange and Badger Corp came up with. Every leak caused by their means of drilling for oil, every stream they fouled, every time wildlife was harmed by their chemicals, I blasted the news all over the internet. I even included pictures and indisputable proof of what they'd done. Lange was pretty lame at responding, but some obvious flunky would try to smack us down."

"You may have won the hashtag wars, but you never could stop him from going forward. That's got to be frustrating."

He stood and hopped effortlessly from the boat to pace along the length of a thick branch. The movement sent tremors through the platform she sat on. She clutched the ropes tighter and whispered a little prayer while he strutted.

"Oh, I finally had him. We'd slapped him with a lawsuit over the last debacle that sent oil gushing in a lake thanks to those pellets he makes to help Nichols Oil keep drilling despite the danger to the environment. Then something must have happened because Lange DM'd me, asking for a meeting."

"Did you meet?"

"Yeah, I mean, if he wanted to come to the table

for peace talks, of course we'd meet him. No idea what changed his mind, but he did a complete about face on his concern for the environment. He told me about this microorganism he was working on that would revolutionize oil clean up. It would reduce or even eliminate oil contamination to water and land but would cost the oil industry millions because then they'd be responsible for clean ups.

"What they're currently doing is way cheaper but also less effective. Lange claimed he was under a lot of pressure from the mother company and his colleagues to put an end to his research, even to the point of painting the word traitor on his car."

Mel brightened, thinking back on the cans of purple spray paint in Leigh Pemberton's garbage can. Could she have painted the graffiti on his car? And would she be stupid—or arrogant—enough to throw them away at home rather than a random dumpster?

"What color was the paint?"

He shrugged. "You got me. He was upset, he didn't go into details."

Well, shoot. Nothing about this case had been simple or straightforward. Was it asking so much to get one small break?

However, if the vandalism had been done at the office, surely there'd be security cameras that caught the culprit in the act. Even if it happened at home, they probably had cameras, but those tapes might be harder to get. Especially if his wife was the guilty party, angry about the potential loss of income.

"Did he mention where this took place?"

He smirked as if she'd said the most adorable thing. *Asshole.* "Again, he was too shaken about the fact someone had it out for him to go into specifics."

"So, why did he meet with *you*?" If he was afraid someone was out to get him, wouldn't his online enemy be the most obvious suspect? Even if he'd had a change of heart and turned over a new leaf, what did he need Brown or his environmental group for?

"Last month, a bigwig at Nichols put their foot down and refused to pay to continue his research. Credit where it's due, Lange was in the testing stage and believed he was so close he decided to raise the money himself with a crowdfunding page. He asked for my endorsement since it would mean a lot in the environmentalist community, especially for donors with deep pockets."

Wow, what did it say about the state of things when people not only funded their health care via public donations but also what sounded like a significant scientific breakthrough required the man to go door-to-door hat in hand? She was so lost in her thoughts she didn't realize she'd let go of the platform ropes. A slight shift of her weight sent the wood floor swaying, causing her to windmill her arms for balance before hugging the ropes close to her.

"You okay?" He asked, sounding concerned.

She nodded and forced out, "Did you agree to help him?"

"He showed me his results, and they were pretty convincing, so sure, I gave him my stamp of approval. I even spread the word about donating to the eco-community."

"So, he'd gotten the money and continued with his work?" It surprised her he still had an office and lab at Badger Corp after pursuing a project he'd been told to drop. That must have pissed off his partner, Leigh Pemberton. But was it reason enough to kill him?

Oliver stretched his shoulders and did some squats. Mel gasped, envious of the ease with which he moved, as if he wasn't out on a tree limb some twenty feet in the air. "I guess. I mean, we buried the hatchet, but we weren't best buds or anything. I think something was bothering him though because the last time I spoke to him, he seemed distracted."

"When was this?"

He scratched at the stubble on his chin before saying, "Maybe a month ago?" Then he gave her a crooked smile. "You kind of lose track of time up here."

"What about all the slams on social media?" For someone who had supposedly buried the hatchet, his posts sounded as if he'd like to do it literally.

"Old news." He frowned. "I guess I should post a memorial to him now that he's gone. I've been so focused on saving this tree I forgot."

It was odd that Lange's lab assistant and his partner didn't know about this oil-eating enzyme, and yet he shared the details with his former nemesis. How common was it for a scientist to keep something like that a secret from the company he worked for? From his own partner? She could ask Jackson; he might have some insights given his background. But that meant talking to him, and she wasn't sure she wanted to hear what else he had to say. She forced herself to turn her attention back to Oliver.

"Do you have any idea where Lange kept this formula? When he showed you his work, did he have a computer with him or a thumb drive?" It was a long shot, but if he was working on a project outside the company boundaries, it seemed logical he'd want to keep it with him.

Brown shook his head. "No, nothing like that. He gave me a live demo, dumping a test tube of these special microorganisms into a container of oil sludge. Within minutes, the sludge had disappeared."

She gave a low whistle. "Something so groundbreaking must be worth a fortune."

"That's what convinced me the guy was the real thing. Lange told me he planned on giving all the proceeds to environmental causes once the tests were complete."

Lange spent his life profitting from sucking every last bit of oil out of the ground, damned the effects on the environment. Now he was suddenly protecting it and giving away money to boot? None of it made any sense. "Any idea why the sudden change?"

"Wish I knew. If I did, I'd put every oil and mining jackhole through the same thing." The dark edge to his voice alerted her to the violence lingering just under the surface. He might not have had a motive to kill Lange, but she felt certain he had it in him.

Then he added with a sardonic chuckle, "But, considering our history, it's a good thing I can prove where I was at the time of the murder." He waved at the camera secured to the branches above him. "My live video feed runs 24/7 to keep the public informed of my crusade."

Thanking him for his time, Mel descended the tree in graceless fits and spurts. Finally dangling from the lowest branch, she swallowed hard before letting go. Her knees quaked when her feet hit the ground, but they held. Poppy stood close enough to have caught her if she fell but let her do it on her own. The woman clapped for her, as if she'd just done some amazing trick instead of simply climbing down a tree. She shook her head in disgust, thinking about how far she still was from the person she used to be.

****

Poppy gushed over what a brave thing Mel did climbing that tree until she brought her praise to a screeching halt with a sharp, "Stop it."

Guilt washed over her at the stunned expression on her companion's face. "I'm sorry, I shouldn't take it out on you, but seriously, I climbed a tree. Big deal, eight-year-olds everywhere accomplish this amazing feat every day. What they aren't doing is practically wetting themselves when the wind blows through the leaves." She raked her hand through her messy auburn locks before voicing her real fear. "What if I never get my old self back? How the hell am I supposed to figure out my brand when I don't even like the face staring back at me in the mirror?"

"You'll beat this fear and be back to climbing mountains in no time," Poppy assured her. For once, the tone in her voice wasn't playful. She really meant it. "I, um," she hesitated, and Mel suspected she wasn't going to like what came next. "I made an appointment for the both of us for that pottery class I told you about. Sounds like fun!"

The woman was so excited she had to ponder over her words for a minute to be sure she understood them. Pottery? Fun? First the knitting attempt and now this? "Why are you trying to help me? Because if it's out of guilt, forget it. Liam's being a jackass, none of this is

your fault. You saved my life, remember? You don't
owe me anything."

For the next mile or so, Poppy remained silent,
eyes fixed on the road before she finally glanced at her.
"To be honest, I'm not sure. I like you and I'm sorry
you're having a rough go. I don't have a clue how one
behaves in this situation. I've never had a bezzie before,
is this what it feels like?"

The idea of being friends with the thief she'd
chased for so long didn't seem as outrageous as it
should. *Huh.* Just when she thought nothing could
surprise her anymore, her easy acceptance of their
relationship did. Once you take off the uniforms—both
cop and cat burglar—they weren't so different after all.
Maybe she was so determined to clear Poppy's name
because she considered her a friend as well. Mind
thoroughly blown, she focused on easier questions to
answer.

"Okay, before we get carried away and exchange
friendship bracelets like teenage besties, we need to
solve this case." She filled Poppy in on what Oliver
Brown told her.

"Whoever painted his car might be the same person
who left the note," Poppy suggested. "I wonder if
there's video surveillance footage."

She related Oliver's story about not knowing if
someone had vandalized the car at home or the office.
"We should ask Mrs. Lange about it."

"You should also check out if his defying Nichols
Oil's orders angered his bosses. Plus, if he was giving
away the profits, his partner must have been pissed off,
not to mention the wifey. How big a dent would that put
in the Langes' lifestyle? She throws pretty swanky

parties for her charities. What happens to all of that without his money?"

"What I'm curious about," Mel observed, "is what caused Lange to have such a huge change of heart about the environment? Is there some other disaster out there Badger Corp is covering up?"

"The list of people out to get him just got a whole lot longer," Poppy said with inappropriate glee. The side-eyed glance she gave the other woman must have betrayed her thoughts. "What? Before, all we had was Mullins, Pemberton and maybe the wife. If you add every exec at Nichols Oil, not to mention all the major oil companies, suddenly I'm a lot less likely a suspect."

Mel had to admit she had a point, but at the moment, they couldn't prove any of it. She didn't want to spoil Poppy's mood, but none of what they found out was useful until they located Lange's formula, proved it works, and that he intended to give the profits away. Right now, all they have is the word of a tree-hugging nut ball.

\*\*\*\*

As soon as they got back, Mel asked Poppy to relieve Grandma O at the front desk. A big part of proving Brown's story involved confirming Lange had developed this enzyme on his own, with Nichols Oil being none the wiser. Leaving her friend—yeah, it would be a while before it wasn't too weird to think of her like that—she headed to The Hungry Puppy.

Emboldened by the tree climbing, she tried to take the shortcut across the bridge spanning the rushing waters of the brook behind the inn. She traversed ten feet across, which was nine feet further than she had on any other attempt except for the time she ran across the swaying structure to save Jackson from her murderous housekeeper, but that still left thirty feet to go. Nauseous and wobbly, she turned around oh so slowly and exited the bridge, opting for the long way around.

There were still a few dogs and their owners/servants at the tables on the café's wrap-around porch, finishing their respective lunches as she approached. Some of the dogs—and one or two of their owners—were snoozing, enjoying an hour or two of afternoon sunshine before night or clouds stole the warmth away.

She scanned the area and was disappointed not to see Jackson's dad or Chewbarka around. After having met his mom, she'd been worried about how Hugo was doing. He was one of the sweetest people she'd ever known, and his mother was so...not.

Opening the door, the café's sweet and savory smells greeted her. Bacon, onions and grilled chicken mingled with cinnamon, maple, and freshly made bread. Her stomach rumbled, reminding her she hadn't eaten since breakfast.

She glanced at the specials on the chalkboard, having the regular menu memorized by now, and ordered a BLT with avocado from the kid behind the counter. She took the number on a tall, metal stand he offered and turned to find a seat in the mostly empty restaurant when she remembered what Poppy said about talking to people. She sucked in a deep breath and re-approached the kid.

"Hey there," she tried to read the name tag on the his shirt unobtrusively but suspected she failed, "Ariel, how're you doing?"

"Fine?" he answered, puzzled by the question.

Dammit, what had she done wrong? People chatted easily with Poppy but regarded her with a more than a healthy dose of skepticism. It must be the British accent.

"So, um, what's the dessert of the day? I'd like to take one back to the B&B."

"I'd go with the peach pie," Jackson said, sneaking up behind her. The clerk looked like he might faint from relief. "Matt, please box one for Ms. O'Rourke, on the house, of course."

"Matt? I thought your name was Ariel?" she asked, pointing to the nametag on his shirt.

"I forgot mine and borrowed one from the back," he mumbled, slumping in relief when his boss chuckled.

As Jackson put his hand on the small of her back and ushered her to a table, she whispered out of the corner of her mouth, "Am I so scary to talk to?"

"Don't take all the credit," he grinned. "Poor kid had a little run in with the law a while back and he's jumpy around everyone, terrified someone will find out."

"You hired a kid with a record?" The teen didn't come across as dangerous, but hiring him seemed unlike the strait-laced restaurateur.

"To be honest, it was Dad's idea. He met Matt's parents, who asked him if he knew of anyone hiring. He'd made a dumb mistake as a kid, a prank turned into a brush fire. The fire department was able to put it out before there was any real damage. People shouldn't hold one stupid blunder against him."

Most people whose business involved flammable items would never have hired him, but Jackson knew about being judged for your past. The difference was the young firebug was guilty. He hadn't even been a member of the team that developed the faulty vaping pens that resulted in the death of three teens. People like Deputy Marks conveniently forgot that part.

A moment of unusual, awkward silence between them stretched into what seemed like hours. Neither of them addressed the bigger issue, the offer to move to New Orleans. She asked what she thought was an easier question instead.

"How's your dad? It's weird not seeing him and Chewie out on the porch with the rest of the regulars."

"He, uh," her companion fell silent as Matt delivered her order and boxed pie. After he was a good distance away, Jackson continued, "Dad took Chewie to doggie obedience school after the whole shoe incident."

"What? He's a puppy, hardly a menace to society." It wasn't like Hugo to overreact.

"Tell me about it. My mother sentenced them both to ten weeks of training or else." From his expression, he was none too pleased.

"Or else what?" Mel asked between bites of the sandwich, the homemade bread so delicious she worked hard to suppress a moan of pleasure.

"That's the thing with my mom. You don't want to find out, you just do what she demands. Anyway, it's all good." A smile reappeared on his face. "Dad's actually having a great time, getting out and meeting other dog owners. They have a playtime at the end of each session, and I think he's socializing as much as Chewie. There's a widow with a hyper Jack Russell puppy he prattles on about every time he comes back from school."

Hugo Thibodeaux had lived in Pine Cove for over ten years, but as a shy, single father raising a teenage son alone, he didn't have a full social calendar. His son's eyes gleamed with the suggestion of a little matchmaking going on.

"But you didn't come here for the food or to talk about my dad, did you?" His eyes narrowed at her even as he continued to smile. "You're still working on that case."

"Guilty as charged," she muttered.

"I don't get why. I mean the last time, sure, the guy died in your lobby, so it was kind of personal, but why do you care about this Lange fella?"

She stalled for time by taking an exaggerated inhale, her nose delighted at the rich smell of peaches, brown sugar and buttery pastry coming from inside the box. This taking time to talk to people business would not be easy on her waistline if it always involved baked goods. She couldn't tell him the whole truth, but she gave him more than she'd told anyone else. "An old friend asked me to look into the situation, that's all."

"Next thing you know, you'll be hanging a P.I. shingle under your vacancy sign," he teased her with a lazy smile.

"No, thank you," she exclaimed. "I have enough on my hands learning on the fly how to run a bed-and-breakfast." *Besides, would he be around to care?*

"So, how can I help you?"

"According to the vic's nemesis turned bestie, Lange continued to work on a project even after Nichols Oil told him not to. Legally, is that possible?"

Jackson sat back, frowning. This was a part of his life he rarely talked about, but he was the only scientist she knew. After giving her question a good deal of thought, he gave her a definitive, "Maybe?" Reacting to her growl of frustration, he added, "It depends on the structure of his contract with them, if it gives him any wiggle room. From my personal experience, no. I couldn't go off on my own and create a product without the company claiming ownership. But if he formed a dummy corporation or put the patent under someone else's name, it's theoretically possible."

She hadn't thought about the contract angle. "What about the money to carry out research? How much does something like that cost? Because allegedly all he had going was a crowdfunding page."

"The price tag would depend on what he was working on."

"Some kind of oil-eating enzyme, I think." Jackson snapped forward; his eyes so keen with interest, Mel instinctively leaned away. "From what I was told, he was trying to atone for helping oil companies destroy the planet by creating some new way to eliminate the results of oil spills without harming the environment."

"There's a group of scientist in Canada who have been working on engineering micro-organisms to remove oil spills, but I don't know if anyone has figured it out. That would be a game changer. Most of the time, oil companies get away with doing the bare minimum because there's no sure-fire cure at any cost."

"Or he was lying to Oliver Brown to get him off his back and stop spotlighting him, Nichols Oil, and Badger Corp in social media." Mel thought that sounded a lot more likely than Lange risking getting his pants sued off for breach of contract. "Thanks for the info and the pie," she rose, keeping the cardboard box full of decadent goodness level so as not to crush the dessert.

\*\*\*\*

Mel was manning the front desk when Liam clomped through the front door. "I'm happy to report the Jacuzzi tub in cabin number six is working again." He melodramatically checked an item off the to do list he kept on a folded piece of paper.

"Great." Genuinely grateful for his help, she craned her neck to read his list as Grandma O exited the office and joined them. "How many more tasks left?"

"A few. But I should get the parts to upgrade that faulty fireplace in a couple of days, and that's the biggest job. The other repairs won't take long."

She wanted to remind him the fireplace wasn't faulty. The cabin filled with smoke because her evil housekeeper stuffed a sweatshirt in the chimney to block the flue. But if swapping the wood-burning one for a gas fireplace made him happy, who was she to complain? She'd just make him swap it back when he saw how much uglier gas fires were than the real thing.

"This calls for a celebration," Poppy cooed as she entered from the Great Room, perky and adorable somehow despite the rubber gloves on her hands. "How about drinks at that cute little wine bar? You know, the one across from the big wooden carved thingy in the center of town?"

Mel smirked behind her computer, waiting for her brother to pooh-pooh her suggestion. He was a beer guy who wouldn't be caught dead swirling grape juice in a fancy glass. Instead, he surprised her with his reply of, "Um, sure, sounds great." She wondered what that was about, but already had one mystery on her hands and no time to ponder his sudden change of heart.

Since all the guests they'd been expecting had already checked in, she forwarded the phones to her cell, left a note on the door telling visitors where to find them, and the four of them made the short trek through the crisp evening air to Poppy's "big wooden thingy".

The massive wooden carving represented the wildlife native to the mountain and included a bear, a mountain lion, and an eagle, as well as some smaller animals. It was the centerpiece for the shopping and restaurant area a few blocks down the hill from the inn, including the cheery bright red building that housed On Cloud Wine. This was the first time she'd left the B&B unattended, and a squadron of massive butterflies roiled in her stomach, but since they could see the front door from inside the bar, she relaxed a little.

The early evening air had gotten nippy, and it was the middle of the week, so it didn't shock her to see only a couple of other patrons in the brightly lit eclectic wine bar. A large, rectangular bar dominated the small space, with a dozen tables strategically placed throughout. Each table was distinctive, with a unique set of chairs around each one. Two walls were floor to ceiling windows but on the others hung mismatched paintings. Some were small watercolors of flowers, while others were larger oils of mountain scenes. From the variety of styles, Mel guessed they'd been painted by different artists.

"It's good for you, dear, to get out once in a while," Grandma O chided as they sat down.

"Out once in a while?" Liam scoffed. "Between running around Palm Springs and getting her nails done, she's hardly ever *in*. The place would fall apart if we weren't there."

Heat rose to her cheeks. His tone said her pain in the ass brother was kidding, but he had a point. She had been relying on him and their grandmother an awful lot. "Ha, ha, very funny. If you're almost finished, when are you planning on heading back?" Please stay a little longer, she prayed silently, and not just because of their help. Their somewhat unexpected arrival had driven home how much she missed having family around.

"Hopefully by the end of the week?" Liam sounded uncertain, which was unusual for him. An independent contractor in high demand, he was booked well in advance and stuck to a tight schedule to make sure he kept his clients happy. She'd scheduled his trip to do the repairs a month ago because of his workload, so surely he had customers waiting?

"Enough business talk," Poppy chirped. "Let's do a wine tasting." She waved the server over, apparently in a hurry to get her drink on.

"It's fermented grape juice, what's to taste?" Grandma grumbled in a not soft voice. "If I had my druthers, we'd do whiskey tasting. Now *there's* a drink with a million different nuances."

Who were these people and what had they done with her family, Mel wondered.

The server Poppy flagged down turned out to be Geoff, the manager of On Cloud Wine, who wasted no time apprising them of the merits of several local wineries. He gave them all menus of their interesting albeit limited food choices and chatted with them about their likes and dislikes of flavors in general before retreating behind the bar.

He soon returned bearing a rack with four test

171

tubes for each of them filled with a variety of wines, their types and names written on a piece of paper. Impressed, and delighted at the novelty of the test tubes instead of wine glasses, she reached for her first sip of a red when Geoff loudly cleared his throat. She glanced up and he discreetly pointed to the test tube on the far left-hand side containing a light white wine, indicating she should start there. Chagrinned, she followed his silent instruction.

He took their food order and gave them interesting details about the winemakers and the different varietals and blends before leaving them to their tasting. Mel wished she had enough of a palate to discern notes of grass from notes of bullshit, but, like her grandmother, all the fancy descriptions were lost on her. She knew wine she liked from ones she didn't, but heck if she understood all the flavors he'd rattled off.

She pulled out the little notebook she'd been jotting notes in and addressed the group. "I spent the afternoon on the phone talking to a few more of Lange's co-workers at Nichols Oil. One of them turned me on to a friend of Lange's at the golf club, who said I should talk to the woman in charge of some dog charity Lange and his wife were active in."

She flipped through the pages of notes as she spoke, sorting out important information from what she now knew was irrelevant. "Bottom line, the only people with a real motive to kill Lange are his wife, Heather, his business partner, Leigh Pemberton, and Peter Mullins."

"But what about the other executives at the company?" Poppy leaned in; eyes wide in desperation. "And the money they'd lose if he gave away the profits from his oil-eating enzyme? Somebody painted traitor on his car. Why couldn't it be one of them?"

Liam and her grandmother exchanged curious glances, clearly confused why she wanted more suspects rather than narrowing their focus. Only Mel understood what was at stake for her and regretted not having any better news.

"Lange and Pemberton, as partners, were the sole recipients of the company profits. The other scientists and executives work for Nichols Oil and don't have any real stake in the matter." Seeing Poppy's shoulders slump in defeat, she reached out to comfort her when Liam beat her to it. Her little brother always had a soft heart for damsels in distress.

"What about this EcoWarrior guy?" Grandma asked after draining one of her test tubes and smacking her lips with a satisfied "ah." She closed her eyes, hoping her grandmother wouldn't embarrass her so much she'd never be able to come in again.

Pine Cove only had a handful of restaurants, and this was one of the few, other than The Hungry Puppy, that didn't include quinoa as a main ingredient in half their foods. She was relieved when Geoff re-appeared at their table with their order, a broad smile lighting his face. If Grandma's manners offended him, he hid it well.

"Your Gran is right," Poppy said after they'd dug into their food, "we can't forget about Oliver Brown just because he says he and Lange had kissed and made up."

"I would agree normally," Mel nodded. "But remember, he has a live feed running for his adoring tree hugging fans twenty-four/seven on his social media pages. He can't be in two places at once."

"I might have unearthed the reason that dufus Lange changed his mind about oil spills being bad for business." Grandma smiled and drained the last of her test tube of wine. "A year ago, an oil pipeline cracked near Huntington Beach. They had to close the beaches, businesses lost money and thousands of animals died. It could have been worse, but once a bunch of wealthy hot shots in Orange County saw oil on their beaches, suddenly the pitchforks and torches came out looking for someone to blame and found Badger Corp. Could be seeing his own kind up in arms changed his tune."

"Or he lied to the tree-sitting weirdo," Liam offered.

Geoff brought them all a glass of sparkling wine as a freebie to taste as he cleared away their dishes. Soon Mel's head was buzzing, though whether from the wine tasting or getting nowhere on the investigation she wasn't sure. She paid the tab, and they were about to leave when Poppy returned to the bar, chatted with the manager for a few minutes and gave him a business card. When she rejoined the group, Mel asked, "What was all that about?"

"We need champagne and wine with your Valentine's Day special, and Geoff seemed like the man to talk to. He'll give us a discount if we order by the case and include a brochure about On Cloud Wine."

"We?" she choked out in surprise.

"'ang on, I haven't gotten to the good part yet," the Brit gushed, ignoring Mel's dig. "On a whim, I asked him if he knew Kyle Lange. He says the bloke was here having a romantic dinner a couple of weeks ago." She waggled her eyebrows during a dramatic pause. "With another chap."

"Way to bury the lead, Einstein," Mel huffed. Who cares about getting a deal on wine when they had a murder to solve? "Can he identify the other man?"

"No, he'd never seen him before."

She wanted to question him herself, but a party of six sat down and Geoff was busy delivering the same warm welcome, get-to-know-you-chat he'd given them. She'd have to come back another time to talk to him about the mystery suspect and the odd twist he'd just thrown into the mix. Heather Lange suspected her husband was having an affair, but could it be with a man?

## Chapter Twelve

"Oh my God, how are you getting worse? Have you been practicing at all?" Doc Hart groused at Mel over their weekly guitar lesson slash coffee klatch. They sat in the doctor's cozy living room decorated with rock 'n roll paraphernalia alongside framed needlepoint pictures. Somehow, the two sides of her personality blended beautifully.

Mel had long ago come to the same conclusion Poppy had—she needed a hobby that would take her mind off her fear of heights while living on top of a freaking mountain. Her answer had been to learn to play the guitar. Inspired by the instruments hanging on Doc's wall, she'd asked and her friend had been more than happy to oblige. The lessons had been going pretty well until now.

"I can't practice, not with those three clowns hovering around me." She set aside the guitar and reached for the slice of homemade coffee cake instead. "Dammit, how are you so good at so many things? You can bake, play guitar, and save lives. I have one cookie I've sort of mastered and it's so easy Vin's children can make them." She'd baked her way through pounds of butter last Christmas to figure out why her Starlight Mint Surprises were so terrible, only to find Grandma O, that sneaky so-and-so, had left out an important ingredient to ensure no one made them as tasty as hers. "And apparently, I'm not much of a detective. How did I sit here with you for weeks learning *All Through the Night* and never notice those nails?"

Doc put her hand out to admire her manicure, now sporting little hearts instead of flowers. "I imagine the same way you've avoided going to physical therapy for your ankle that you still limp on once in a while. I'm sure you were a great cop, but you have a habit of ignoring inconvenient truths. Like grandmother's sometimes lie, shattered bones don't heal themselves, and fun, perky friends aren't always what they seem to be."

"Don't forget, I can barely climb a flight of stairs without fainting," she bemoaned. "I really am a hot mess."

"I wouldn't say 'hot'," her friend chuckled, getting her to break out of her gloomy mood before adding, "but you need to be more careful."

"I take it you're talking about Poppy and not my ankle."

Doc Hart picked up the guitar and strummed a tune, avoiding her gaze. "There's something else going on there, and I don't mean the part you already know and aren't telling me."

"So, you mentioned before." She stared at her ruined manicure, remembering the conversation they'd had outside the nail salon. "You're not wrong about her, but my gut tells me I can trust her. Not around knitting needles or pottery wheels, but other than that..." She shrugged.

"Pottery wheels?"

Thinking back to the class they took together and

the wet blob of mud flying off Poppy's wheel and splatting into Mel's hair, she shook her head. "Don't ask."

Her gut had been wrong once or twice, but she'd learned it was better to go with her instincts than constantly doubt herself. She just wished she could crack this Lange case. Once Poppy was in the clear, whatever she did next would reveal the real woman behind the facade. Until then, she'd rather steer clear of the topic, so she grabbed on to one even less fun to talk about. "You heard about Jackson?"

"You mean the offer of a lifetime to work at a Michelin starred restaurant in NOLA? A town this small, it's all anyone's talking about. How does that make you feel?"

The corner of Mel's lips curved into a smirk. "Really? I didn't know you were that kind of doctor, too. How does it make me *feel?* Like everyone else, I'm happy for him. His mother is a piece of work, though."

"Tell me about it." Her gentle strumming became violent. "She stopped by to ask for medical advice and when she didn't like what I had to say, she told me I was a quack."

"Don't take it personally, I don't think she's impressed with our little town as a whole."

Her friend gave her a sly smile, no doubt wondering the same thing Mel did as soon as she said it. When had Pine Cove become *her* town? Doc let it go, asking instead, "What are you going to do about it?"

"What can I do?" She shrugged. "I'd never stand in the way of him reaching for that brass ring."

"I think you're looking at this from the wrong angle," her friend said, her voice laced with an "*I'm about to say something very wise "* vibe.

"What do you mean?"

She faced her. "The real question you should be asking is what will he be giving up if he leaves?"

Mel scrubbed her hands over her face, grunting in frustration. *What was that supposed to mean?* "Thanks. Mind thoroughly messed with, if this disastrous lesson is over, I'm heading back to the inn to see what else I can botch today." But as she grabbed her jacket, a thought struck Mel. What if she was looking at the murder investigation from the wrong angle? She'd hit a dead end trying to figure out who killed Lange, but what if she focused on who hired Poppy to steal the necklace? After all, they were the ones who arranged for her to be in the office just after he'd been shot. It was a reasonable assumption they either were the killer or were connected somehow, otherwise why the attempt to frame her?

The only clue they had, however, was the message sent to Poppy via Salutations. The message disappeared after thirty seconds, but she wondered if her phone records would show who sent it. Even if it came from a burner phone, they might get lucky and discover at least what city it originated in. Who knows, the knucklehead might have bought the phone with a credit card? Stranger things had happened. And even if they never found the phone itself, having the number on her records at least backed up her story. Her mood brightened at having a do-able task to sink her teeth into. Sort of. She cringed as she considered her next step.

****

Back at the B&B, she sat at her desk and stared at

her cell phone. The last conversation she's had with Deputy Marks, when she'd called to tell him about the note they'd stolen from the Langes' so-called cabin, hadn't ended well. Was he still mad at her, pissy because he thought she was telling him how to do his job? There was only one way to find out. She opened his name in her contacts, swiped at his work number, and waited for him to answer.

"Deputy Gregg Marks," the voice at the other end of the phone rattled off.

"Hey Gregg." Mel tried for the flirty approach, fluttering her eyelashes even though he couldn't see them. "I hate to bug you, but I was wondering if you—"

"Stop right there," he growled. "Whatever information you're fishing for, report the crime and let us do our job. That goes double if this has anything to do with the Lange murder. Stay out of it."

"Sheesh, I was just asking." She hadn't expected him to be happy to help, but biting her head off was over the top, even for him.

"Sorry," he muttered, his tone softening, "the Sheriff is up my ass about catching Lange's killer." As if that excused his current mood. At least he'd dialed back the harshness of his voice a couple of notches.

"What about the lead you told me about, the car in the video?" She crossed her fingers as she tried to innocently ask the question, hoping her acting ability had improved since she tried lying to her mom as a teenager about who really put the dent in the station wagon.

"Turned out to be a bust. The car belongs to the Palm Spring's Chief of Police. Their PD is pissed as hell right now. They dusted it for prints—"

"But didn't find any," she murmured along with him. Damn, she had to give Poppy credit, she was good. And ballsy, because the Chief of Police's parking spot was marked as such. She knew exactly whose nose she was tweaking.

"Why are you so insistent on meddling in the Lange case?" Deputy Marks had taken over for her friend Gregg, and the grumpy was back in full force. "You didn't even know the guy, so for everyone's sake just stay out of it."

"I'm not meddling, Deputy, sir," she snarled at him.

"Oh yeah? What about breaking into his house? And don't give me that load of crap about buying it. Do not make me regret letting you off by screwing my chance for promotion."

"Right, I'm so all powerful I can control your promotion fast track." This time, no acting chops were required to sound hurt. She couldn't believe he'd think she'd purposefully mess around with another cop's career when she'd gone through the pain of losing her badge herself.

"We've got a couple of leads from the BOLO Palm Springs PD put out that will hopefully lead to the killer. Do not start stirring the pot when we're so close to catching them."

The crashing down of his phone rattled her less than that last tidbit. What are the chances someone saw Poppy and recognized her?

She shook off the clenching of her gut and dialed a more familiar number.

"If you found another dead body, my advice is to bury it this time," her father's rich voice rumbled, laced with humor. "Especially if my mom doesn't have an alibi."

"Dad, you're being mean," she laughed back at him. "Grandma O is doing a great job. She's being very helpful. Do I even want to know what she did to drive Mom to exile her here?"

"No sweetheart, you really don't." He heaved a sigh she often heard whenever the two women in his life, his mother and his wife, butted heads. She almost pitied him, except their battle of wills was so entertaining.

"Hey, is your friend still working in the Cyber Crimes Division? I've got a phone number I need to run down."

\*\*\*\*

"Do you have someone who can help us with our bags?" asked a portly gentleman with a thinning crop of hair. He was checking in with two women Mel assumed were his wife and daughter from their ages and resemblance to each other.

"Of course, dear," Grandma peered at him over her glasses, "if you need a seventy-two-year-old woman to schlep your suitcases up one step and into your cabin, I'm happy to oblige."

Mel stepped out of the kitchen with an afternoon snack and froze. *Shit.* That was it, no more front desk duty for her grandmother. Then the man *and* his family laughed out loud and informed her no, he's got this. If she'd said that, the guy would have handed over the bags, thanked her, and given her a dollar tip for her troubles. Somehow, Grandma turned being old and cranky into a superpower. Cantankerous must be the new quirky. Her grandmother wore a big smile as well.

Clearly, being busy doing things rather than sitting around the house was good for her.

Giving her grandmother a wave, she continued on to the office and did the one thing she hated more than her branding homework—balancing the books. The inn's business had been picking up, and this month was the first one they'd be operating off the profits rather than dipping into the savings the family had set aside for emergencies to pay the bills.

However, their finances were still too close for comfort, especially after Liam discovered a leaky pipe in cabin eight. Since the whole place had been built back in the 1950s, he warned her they'd be in for more pipes breaking in the future. If one broke and flooded a cabin, damaging the structure, it would be a disaster.

She'd asked him to keep the leak to himself for now, but she didn't like hiding information from her family about their investment. She spent the rest of the day calling around for quotes on pipes and plumbers. Liam had his own business to get back to, after all. Getting a ballpark figure, she weighed the possibility of shifting money around to cover the expense and suddenly the Valentine's weekend special was more like a necessity rather than a crazy notion.

By the end of a long day, she wasn't in the mood for her brother's complaints about the spot she'd put him in by asking him to lie to the family by omission. Instead, she sent him off to listen to a local musician Doc Hart had recommended who was playing at the pub in town. Poppy and Grandma O "skedaddled," as her gran would say, to the tiny theatre down the street for a movie. Even the guests had all settled in and, for the first time in days, Mel had the place to herself.

She snuggled in the big cozy chair by the fireplace in her private living quarters, opened a book, and reveled in the peace and tranquility for about forty seconds until the front door creaked on its hinges. It was just after seven, which meant the lobby was technically still open, but she wasn't expecting any new arrivals. She got up to go see who it was and found Gregg Marks there. Not the deputy, he must have left him in grumpy prison, but the charming friend, dressed in a sweater that set off the blue of his eyes and worn, black jeans. He had flowers in one hand, a bottle of wine in the other, and an apologetic look on his face.

"Can I come in?"

"What are you, a vampire now? You can't enter unless you're invited?" She wore a stern expression until he gaped at her in blind panic and she couldn't hold her laughter anymore. "I'm kidding. Of course you can come on in, unless you're going to yell at me again."

"I'm sorry for being a complete jerk on the phone with you this morning."

"Yes, you were," she agreed. If she read the flowers and wine right, his apology was sincere. She waved him into the lobby and led him through the office to her living quarters.

"I know it's no excuse, but my boss is putting the screws to all of us. He wants us to find the killer and get credit for solving the murder before the Palm Springs cops do," he explained, as he followed her. Once they got to her living room, he handed off the flowers and wine to her while he started to build a fire.

They had an easy, natural rhythm to their movements since he'd come over once or twice to check on her after she'd re-injured her ankle kicking the shit out of her kill-happy maid. He surprised her by revealing he was a secret wine drinker, only swilling beer when other people were present. She found his dedication to maintaining his image hilarious and a little sad.

"I don't understand," she said as she opened and poured the wine. Her apartment had an open plan, with an island counter separating the kitchen from the living room. The bedroom was tucked away behind the floor-to-ceiling stone wall with a double-sided fireplace, allowing her to enjoy the fire from either room. "Aren't we all supposed to be one big brotherhood in blue? Although I guess in your case, it's beige."

"We prefer khaki, and it's an election year so…"

"Ah," she nodded in understanding as she handed him a glass of wine. "Your boss wants to keep his job, which means he needs votes, and the media circus of catching a killer would help."

They sat down on the couch facing the fire. He sipped his wine and the tension in his shoulders melted a little, but there was still a hardness in his eyes.

"I like the guy, he's a good boss, but he's pushing the whole department way too hard. Everyone is doing overtime to keep our people on the mountain safe and solve a murder. This is the first night I've had off since Lange was killed."

Okay, on the one hand, the murder was just five days ago, but still, the fact he'd chosen to spend his time off with her was touching. Jackson might be leaving, but Gregg was here. Was the universe sending her some sort of message?

"Do you want to talk about it?" She enjoyed

talking to people as much as the next person, despite what Poppy might think. Topics like work, sports, or movies she could chat about at length. But feelings? Yuck. He gave an involuntary shudder, appearing to share her dislike for delving too deep.

"I've already given the job too much of my time this week," he shook his head. "Have you seen that new action movie about the art heist and the spies? It's on one of the streaming services."

"No, but the reviews are great." She grabbed the TV remote, found the movie, and then settled back to enjoy. She hadn't watched a movie with someone else in a long time and scooted a little closer to Gregg, happy to share this with him. She had to roll her eyes when he did the "arm on the back of the couch slipping down to her shoulder" move but didn't object.

They laughed over the opening stunt and made fun of the usual "gathering of the team" section. Relaxing and being herself was easy around him. When he wasn't being a jackass, that is. The main character pulled off an impossible stunt and when she asked if he thought the scene was as ridiculous as she did, she got a soft snore in reply. She turned to see Gregg's eyes were closed, his head lolled back, and mouth slightly open.

"Gregg?" She shook his shoulder. His head rolled to one side instead of straight back, but nothing else changed, including his snoring. *Way to go Mel, you really know how to show a man a good time.* The poor guy was too exhausted to kick out into the cold night. She rose, pulled his legs up on the couch, and put an extra pillow under his head. The fire warmed the room, but she laid one of her mom's soft, timeworn quilts over him for when the flames died to embers and the room cooled.

Taking her glass of wine with her, she changed into the flannel pants and hockey sweater that served as her pajamas and climbed into bed. Just before dozing off, she smiled at the memory of how adorable big, tough Deputy Marks looked sacked out on her couch.

****

"Here," she handed a sheepish Gregg Marks a to-go cup. He'd woken up before she got dressed, but she'd thrown on her robe to make him coffee. His drive home wasn't long, but she couldn't even think straight before her first cup of the day. "Just in case you have to get to work early."

He took the cup, sipped cautiously, and grimaced. "It's a mystery how you manage to brew coffee that's even worse than the stuff from the vending machine, but I appreciate the gesture all the same." His eyes danced with laughter, however, and he took another, deeper drink to prove his gratitude. The moment between them lingered until she wasn't sure what to do next. Give him a kiss on the cheek? Pat him on the head?

"What's this now?" a voice croaked behind her. Mel closed her eyes and swore. What was her grandmother doing up so early? Dear God, she prayed, let her be wearing something other than her flannel gown. And Marks had the nerve to laugh.

"Bye," he waved to them both as he hurried out the door.

She turned around and was relieved to see Grandma O fully dressed, silver curls in place, ready for the day.

"I like your style, kid. Make the man do the walk

187

of shame." She patted her cheek and continued on her way to the kitchen.

"Nothing happened. The poor guy fell asleep on my couch," she called out after the retreating cardigan sweater-clad woman. "And don't drink the coffee," she warned. "I made it instead of Poppy."

"Yeah, no kidding," she replied, followed by the sound of liquid being dumped down the sink. Just her luck, she passed Poppy as she fled to her living quarters to get dressed and re-start the day. The other woman gave her a smirk but said nothing.

"Shut up," she muttered despite the Brit's silence. "Just please don't tell Liam."

"Tell me what?" her brother asked as he walked in.

For once Poppy mutely shrugged and Grandma re-appeared to mime her lips being locked and throwing away the key. Heaving a put upon sigh, he stomped into the Great Room, grunting about being tired of women outnumbering him.

"You should be used to being the minority by now," Mel called and took the opportunity to go get dressed.

****

After the breakfast rush was over, Mel returned to her office and the *How to Find Your Brand* workbook. It asked her to imagine her target customer. She rolled her eyes at first—duh, people who needed a place to sleep? Then she thought back to what she'd confessed to Poppy, Liam and Grandma earlier. The memories of their family trips to Pine Cove had inspired her to make the move.

Families were one target, she realized, reminding herself to dust off the games on the shelves in the Great

Room and shop for newer, popular ones to add to the collection. But also for people like her, who needed a break from the hectic world. And yes, Poppy and Gemma might have a point. There is something romantic about the starlit sky at night and cerulean clear sunny days. At least in the summer, as she recalled. This morning the clouds refused to relinquish their cold, gray grip. She typed furiously, filling in the blanks when her cell phone rang. A glance at the screen made her smile.

"That was fast, Dad, what have you got for me?" In the background, there were squeals of delight as Vinnie ordered her children to calm down or else. The noise grew louder, but Mel never found out what the "or else" was. Her father must have retreated into his office and shut the door because there was a *click* and sudden silence.

"I thought having grandkids would be quieter than this," he muttered, followed by the familiar creak of his desk chair as he sank into it. Seamus O'Rourke was built like Liam. Tall, broad shoulders and well muscled, but some had gone soft over the years. "Russell Woods from Cyber crimes says hello, by the way. Claims the force is duller now without his favorite fiery redhead to liven things up."

"Yeah right," she blushed, "he always was a smooth talker. Was he able to trace that Salutations text thing?" she bungled the name of the message device. Tech stuff was never her strong suit, but it made her father chuckle so score one for Mel.

"Took a little doing, but he got it. Are you sitting down, honey? 'Cause this is weird."

She was already seated, but figured it was more of

a rhetorical question. How much weirder can this case get? "Go on."

"You said the person who sent the message hired your thief to steal the necklace, right?"

"That's what she told me." She couldn't quite bring herself to assert anything Poppy told her as an absolute fact. Yet.

"Then I'm glad it's you and not me unraveling this case, because the message was sent via a cheap phone bought with a credit card by Kyle Lange. Not exactly a master criminal, was he?"

"The murder victim arranged for his own robbery?" She hadn't seen that coming.

"Or someone using his phone. The only other person contacted was a Leigh Pemberton the night of the murder. They talked for about twenty minutes."

"What time was that?"

"Started at eight seventeen, ended at eight forty-two." Depending on where she was when she took the call, Pemberton had plenty of time to drive to the office to kill him. She would have seemed a hell of a lot less guilty if she'd told Mel about the call when she was fake interviewing her.

"Just be careful, sweetheart," her father warned in a serious tone. "You, of all people, know how dangerous investigating a murder without a badge can be."

That might be true, although she'd done okay for herself the last time. This time was different. Unless she was willing to see someone go to jail for the one crime they didn't commit, she was going to have to continue poking around.

Chapter Thirteen

Confused, she set off in search of Poppy and found her in her room knitting a riotously colorful striped long scarf. If she didn't know better, she'd swear a shadow of fear crossed her face when she opened her door until she saw it was only Mel. But did she really know her well enough to dismiss the possibility that the thought of being arrested terrified her?

"Can I come in?"

The other woman, appearing more waiflike without her fake eyelashes and makeup, waved her inside. She told her what her father found out, adding, "Are you telling me you had no idea Kyle Lange hired you to steal his own necklace?"

Her eyes widened, startled but not shocked. "I've heard of wankers hiding assets from wives so they don't have to split them in the divorce proceeding, but if they were happily married, why pinch his own shite?"

"Not a clue, I feel like I'm going around in circles." She scrubbed her face with her hand and realized she hadn't seen this infamous piece of jewelry. She'd been avoiding the thing because she didn't want to think about having a stolen object in her possession. However, there might be some clue in the stones or the setting. The cat burglar was the jewelry expert, but she wanted to examine the piece for herself. "Show me the necklace."

"Your loss," she shrugged, "it's an ugly trinket you won't be able to unsee." She opened the top desk drawer and pulled out a padded envelope.

"You're keeping stolen property in a drawer?" Mel squawked.

"Where'd you expect me to keep my valuables? This room is sweet, but there's no safe. Which might be a nice upgrade, something to think about."

Her palm covered her face as she muttered through her fingers, "I don't know, I assumed you had it in a waterproof bag in the toilet tank or taped to the underside of the desk or something."

"Somebody's been watching too many movies," she laughed, holding out the padded envelope.

With a sigh of resignation, Mel took her offering. After examining the plain manila surface for any clues and finding none, she pulled the necklace out. The cold of the metal and stones in her hands surprised her, then she scoffed at herself. Was she expecting the mysterious piece of jewelry to be radiating heat? Pulsing with a telltale heartbeat? Pushing aside her fanciful thoughts, she switched to cop mode.

The first thing she noted was how rough some stones were, while others were smooth. The colors were an unattractive combination of muted tan baubles, a shiny dark orange carnelian and an array of opalescent rocks, the only consistently sized beads. The setting was equally unattractive. The links between stones were larger than a woman's necklace usually were and in a cheap metal rather than quality gold or silver.

"The only reason I'd hide this from my spouse would be to keep them from finding out I spent money on something so ugly," she muttered.

"Maybe that's why he hired me? To keep his dirty little secret and collect on the insurance money while selling the thing to some other old coot with poor eyesight."

Examining the piece more carefully, Mel turned the necklace and studied it vertically, then flipped it back horizontally but from the other direction. The small opal stones formed a pattern, but if they spelled out a message, the meaning was lost on her. She didn't recognize enough of the gemstones to know their names—could the first letters of each spell out a word? If the necklace wasn't valuable for the rocks or setting, it might be some kind of code related to this enzyme.

Using her phone, she took pictures of the necklace from several angles to study the patterns later. There must be an expert to ask, but who specializes in hideous jewelry? "Let's assume Oliver Brown is right, Lange defied Nichols Oil and was working on a new enzyme to eradicate oil spills. Considering how many accidents happen, if they were forced to use this enzyme, the oil companies stood to lose millions in profit."

"Maybe even billions," Poppy suggested.

"Certainly worth enough to kill over. If his files are missing, did Lange get rid of them himself and had this made as a kind of life insurance?"

"But even if it's a code for his formula, why pay me to steal it?"

Mel could make an educated guess, but she had the advantage of having met Leigh Pemberton, who had both a means and a motive. She liked Heather, but she wasn't too devastated by his death to get a manicure. There's a reason the spouse and business partner are always the first one you suspect, after all.

"Because he didn't trust anyone close to him. The safe wasn't much of a secret, anyone might have tried to crack it. He needed to be sure the formula was someplace secure." Only now his formula might be so safe it's lost to the world forever.

****

Mel stepped out of Poppy's room into the crisp, clear, sunny afternoon and down the old wooden stairs to the pine needle strewn ground below. She was so deep in thought about the formula she didn't notice she was taking the stairs like a normal person instead of one at a time, with a pause between each. She smiled for a moment and then scowled. *Really? You're proud of that?*

A loud *woof* caught her attention, and she glanced up to see a small, chestnut, furry pony rocketing towards her. Chewie hit her full force, front paws on her shoulders, nearly knocking her over.

"Hey big guy," she cooed, rubbing behind his ears, "what are you doing out here all by yourself? Did you escape again?" Pushing him off her chest and back to the ground, she scouted the area for Hugo or Jackson, but there was no one around except the usual tourists. Then she spotted Jackson skulking in the shadows, swiveling his head before creeping toward her.

He'd been familiar with the concept of an oil-eating enzyme. Maybe if she showed him pictures of the necklace, he could make sense of what the stones and settings meant? Brightened at the thought of possibly getting a break in the case, she was about to ask him, but the miserable expression on his face and changed her mind. His normally bright aqua eyes were dimmer somehow, with dark smudges underneath them.

Even his silky, dark brown curls hung limp.

"Hey, are you okay?"

He answered with his customary curl of his lips, but the grin never made it to his eyes. "I'm just peachy," he mumbled, scanning his surroundings like a thief on the run. Momentarily puzzled, she gawked at him until the reason for his odd behavior dawned on her.

"Are you hiding from your mother?"

A look of terror flitted behind his gaze. *Oh my God, he* is *hiding.* Then she surprised herself by making a choice she never would have back when she was in uniform. The case could wait; her friend needed her.

"C'mon," she hooked her elbow through his, "you could use a little pick me up. Did you know Pastry Village has great chai apple crullers?" It was late morning, the gap between breakfast and lunch, so his crew could handle the stragglers at his café. They continued down the street, sticking to the shadows with Chewbarka trotting by their side, tongue lolling out in pure pleasure.

****

The coterie of coffee drinkers had thinned out since the earlier rush, so Mel, Jackson and Chewie had no problem grabbing one of the few outdoor tables under the green awning of Pastry Village. The wrought-iron table and chairs weren't as comfortable as the wooden ones inside, but the seat cushions helped and the warmth of the late morning sun breaking out from behind the clouds warmed Mel's face.

"Thanks, Amy," she said as the young, freckle-faced woman with bright purple pigtails cascading from the crown of her head deposited coffee and pastries in front of them.

She must have been trying too hard because the woman gave her a strange look through her round, owl-eyed glasses. "You're welcome, Mel," putting extra emphasis on her name. She had to admit if she'd said her name like that, it did sound weird. The barista gave a friendly smile and said, "Jackson," before returning to her place behind the counter.

"I didn't realize you and Amy were friends?" he commented as he blew on his *café au lait* to cool it off.

"I'm getting to know lots of people." His laughter told her that sounded weirder than she meant. Way too defensive.

"Thanks for the rescue." He sunk into his chair, more defeated than relaxed. "I needed an excuse to get out. Mom keeps stopping in to taste some dish or another off the menu and sending texts to her chef friend in New Orleans."

"So, are you going to accept her offer?" And leave Pine Cove forever. A knot twisted in her chest at the thought.

He ran a hand through his thick, dark curls with a frustrated grunt. "Why couldn't she have come to me with this after the whole vape pen thing hit the news and my reputation was trashed? When I needed motherly support? Why did she wait until now when things," he peered at Mel with an intense gaze, "when everything is going so well?"

"I'll take that as a 'no' then, you haven't decided." Her heart leaped a little. Then she remembered how she spent last night with Gregg on the couch and hated herself for playing both sides. What was wrong with her? She should make a choice, but what if her heart voted for Jackson and he left anyway?

He closed his eyes and groaned, sinking even deeper into his chair. She turned around and saw Julia Landry stomping up the porch steps toward them. "Oh, there you are. And with Ms. O'Rourke. Again."

He stood and offered his mother a seat, but she shook her head. "Time is short, Jackson. I was talking with Adèle and she won't wait forever. You're going to have to give your answer soon one way or the other and honestly, I don't understand what there is to think about. Your talent is wasted in this hick town."

Finding her comment to be downright rude, Mel rose to his defense. "But he runs the most popular diner in Pine Cove, what will we do without him?" She hoped he understood she meant for more than just his food.

"There's no glory in being a big fish in a plastic baggie of water," Julia replied with a sneer. But whose glory was she talking about, hers or Jackson's? Was she more interested in the place in society given to the mother of an apprentice at a Michelin starred restaurant in a town famous for good food? Mel was certain he'd succeed, but would it make him happy?

"Pine Cove isn't a plastic—" His defense of their home stopped as he took in a deep breath, stood taller to face her, "Why now? Why this sudden interest in my career? I don't mean that unkindly, Mother," he added as she paled in shock. "I just mean you never took much interest when I left chemical engineering to own a café."

Julia Landry sank into the chair she'd previously refused. "You used to call me 'ma mère'. Do you remember?" Her voice lost all of its command, taking on a wistful tone. Jackson's frown as he sat back down told Mel this was not normal. Something was definitely wrong.

His mother straightened her shoulders, as if she'd made a decision and was determined to carry on full steam ahead. "I've made some changes in my life recently I'd like you to be a part of."

"Changes?" Her statement didn't ease his concerned expression. In fact, it deepened. If Mel could have commanded the ground to swallow her so she wasn't present for this uncomfortable mother and son moment, she would have.

"The truth is, Chef Adèle and I are a couple. Things are serious enough that I'd like her to get to know my son."

His furrowed brows skyrocketed, a smile twitching at the corner of his mouth. "You and Chef Adèle are a thing?"

"I don't see what's so amusing about that," she railed.

"No, um, *ma mère*, I didn't mean—" The shrill ring of Mel's cell phone interrupted his riposte. She recognized the number as the B&B and rose to step away from the table to take the call.

"Hello?" She wasn't sure between Grandma or Poppy, who would be on the other end. The one person she didn't expect was Liam.

"You've got to get back over here. Now." It should have annoyed her that he blurted out his cryptic message and hung up, but the panic in her unflappable brother's voice overrode everything else. Did that pipe burst before she had a chance to call a plumber? How screwed were they? She spun, sprinting all the way to the Babbling Brook, aching ankle be damned.

Chapter Fourteen

Mel took the steps of the inn two at a time and burst through the lobby door, out of breath from the short run and grateful she'd started jogging again. It would have been humiliating to collapse on the floor at the feet of a very pissed off Deputy Gregg Marks.

"Listen here, you little twerp," Grandma O raged at the cop, her bony finger poking on his firm chest Mel had been leaning into less than twenty-four hours ago. "You can't bust into a private business and arrest a person." Liam scowled at the deputy as well, arms crossed and looking infuriated, though for the life of her, she couldn't figure out why. Then she had the panic-stricken thought the deputy was there to arrest Grandma. That would explain Liam's outrage, anyway.

"What's going on?" she demanded, coming to her grandmother's side.

Marks bent to pick up a piece of paper and slapped it down on the front desk, parking his large hand on top while Grandma O tried to tug the document away. No doubt she was the reason it had ended up on the floor.

"I have here an arrest warrant for Agnes Mary Noble." Holding the document, he glared at Mel. Guilty and confused, she shrank under the heat of his anger. "Did you enjoy making a fool of me last night? Inviting me in, drinking my wine, letting me think…" he shook his head. "You know what I thought. And the whole time your were harboring a fugitive. I don't know about down in L.A., but here, that's a criminal offense."

"How dare you risk everything we put into this place over her?" Liam demanded.

Finally, she snapped out of her stupor and snarled, "Who the hell is Agnes Mary Noble?"

"Oh really? That's what you're going with?" Deputy Marks' voice dripped with disdain as he showed her the other paper in his hand. Poppy's mug shot from when she'd been arrested after saving Mel from a fall to her death. The charges had been dropped, so she'd forgotten all about the records. But more to the point, she didn't know Poppy was an alias. Was every word she said a lie? "I told you we put a BOLO out for your cat burglar. Old Bart, who owns the pottery studio, is a retired state trooper. He reported seeing her with you. Do you deny it? Is there any reason I shouldn't haul you in as well for aiding and abetting?"

Rocked to the core, she went on the offensive.

"First off, Deputy, you did not have a warrant for her arrest at the time. You told me she was a person of interest, in which case I have no legal responsibility to tell you jack shit. Of course, now that you've served your warrant, we'll cooperate." A dark glare shut down Grandma O's squawk of protest. "Look around the premises all you want. We, however, are under no obligation to help you track down your suspect. In L.A. we follow the letter of the law, fella, not just bend it to our will."

She hoped like hell her jibe would send him storming out and give her time to think. If Poppy didn't trust her enough to be honest about her real name, then how much of her story was true? Doc had warned her, but she had no idea how far the lies went. She needed time to figure out what to do, so of course when the deputy stormed through the lobby and yanked the door open, he nearly pulled Poppy off her feet.

"Shit," Mel swore under her breath, shoulders slumped in defeat.

"Agnes Mary Noble, from Cleveland, Ohio, by the way, I'm putting you under arrest for the murder of Kyle Lange," Marks barked, turning the woman around in a flash, putting the cuffs on her and reciting her rights before Poppy or Agnes or whoever she was let out so much as a squeak. She glanced over her shoulder at the O'Rourkes, huge brown eyes imploring them for help. Liam took a step forward, but Mel put out a hand to stop him.

"What evidence do you have other than the climbing equipment you can't tie to her besides the fact that she's used similar gear in the past?"

Marks grunted an ugly chuckle and shook his head. "It's all I need to arrest her. Convicting her isn't my problem. You'd better call a big shot L.A. lawyer to get her out of this, but why you'd even try after the way she played you, I have no idea."

"Mel, wait, it's not like that! I..." the faux Brit tried to explain while keeping the pretense of her posh accent, but her gaze met Mel's and she stuttered. The cold, unexpected emptiness from her betrayal must have been written all over her face. When had the other woman become a close friend? Because only someone you cared about could cut you so deep.

"I'm willing to bet when we search her room and vehicle, we'll find the stolen necklace and money. Stay out of this Mel, you're skating dangerously close to being hauled in as an accessory."

He turned Poppy toward the door and pushed her forward, but she used the momentum in her favor and continued the spin until she faced Mel again. Her dark eyes were haunted and desperate. "It's not how it looks, I didn't—" But Marks regained control of his prisoner and this time succeeded in shoving her outside. The whole way, until he stuffed her in the back of a squad car, she shouted her protests.

Once in the car, she searched through the window until she found Mel's face, continuing to shake her head "no," tears trailing down her cheek. Their gaze met briefly before Mel broke their contact. She didn't know what to think, a condition she was unused to and didn't much care for.

The remaining officers tromped up the steps leading to Poppy's room.

"Should we call Uncle Colm?" Liam asked.

The mention of the uncle who used his connections to get Poppy off before made her purse her lips. "And help her again? No, not this time."

It wasn't long before the search team streamed back down the stairs. Even through the window of the Great Room, she could see the plain, padded envelope that contained the necklace in one evidence bag. The other bag contained a stack of money in a baggie with duct tape around it. Son of a bitch, she *had* hidden something in the toilet tank after all.

****

"That's so..." Grandma O hesitated.

"Hideous?" Mel grumbled.

Her brother threw his hands up in disgust, bristling at the critique of the new gas logs he'd installed in cabin one. "You can't tell them from the real ones."

"Maybe, if you're visually impaired or have never actually seen a real fire before." She crossed her arms, itching to get into a fight.

"What bug crawled up your," he glanced over at their grandmother and altered his word choice, "derriere today? You'd think you'd be happy with that woman behind bars."

"Shut the f—," she caught her Grandma twitch an eyebrow at her. Did they have such potty mouths they couldn't have one argument without swearing? "Front door, you don't know what you're talking about."

The old woman patted her shoulder. "Now, now dear, you have to admit you've been a pain in the ass ever since that pushy deputy took Poppy away."

She put her hands on her hips, ready to take on both of them before she realized they were right. But who could blame her? Gregg was mad at her, Jackson was probably leaving, and the only friend she'd made in Pine Cove other than Doc Hart was a fraud. She lied about her entire life and odds on was faking it when she acted as though she cared. And now Mel was behaving like a grade school kid. Great.

"I'm sorry. Between the Lange case, figuring out this Valentine's thing, being short-handed again, it's all been a bit much. When you get the part for the timer, we'll give the fireplace a try and let the guests vote on if they prefer gas or the real thing. Fair enough?"

Her little brother wrapped one arm around her shoulders and gave her a hug. She had no idea how close she was to breaking, and how much she depended on the pair of them until they sandwiched her between them.

"It's going to be fine," he assured her. "Admitting you're wrong is the first step on the road to wisdom."

All three of them laughed. His antics were exactly what she needed to lighten her mood. Then her cell rang, the call coming from an unknown number. Huh. Concerned a guest might need help, she answered it.

"Oh good, you picked up, love. I was worried you wou—"

She disconnected the call, her newly acquired good-humor shattered. A moment later, the phone rang again with a call from the same number. She stabbed at the button on the side to ignore the call.

"Who was that?" her grandmother asked.

"Who knows? It's been half a day, she probably changed her name by now."

The phone rang again, and again she silenced it, earning a scowl from her grandmother. "Emmeline Rose, I may not think much of your mother at the moment, but I know she raised you better than that. If the woman wants to explain herself, the least you can do is listen."

Thoroughly chastised, her face flushed. When Grandma O used your whole name, you were in trouble. However, as the minutes ticked by and no call came, it seemed like a moot point. Liam and their grandmother waited with her, the tension in the room a palpable force, though for the life of her she couldn't figure out why her family was so invested in the call. Finally, the phone rang again.

"What?" Grandma O pursed her lips at her terse greeting, but she didn't care.

"Please don't 'ang up, let me explain."

She rolled her eyes. "Why are you still using that

stupid fake accent? The jig is up, Aggie from Cleveland. And how are you calling me, anyway? Prisoners only get to make collect calls."

"Oh, that," she gushed. "One of the other ladies has a secret phone. When I told her about our little row, she offered to let me borrow it."

She scrubbed her hand over her eyes. "You're calling me on an illegal phone? Are you trying to get thrown into solitary?"

The other woman's voice became more serious, although she sustained the British pretense. "It would be worth it if it meant I got to set the record straight with you. Yes, I lied about my past, but you have to understand I'm not like you, Mel. I don't have a loving family. The only thing my mum ever gave me was a terrible name."

"You want to compare terrible names?" she muttered, but against her better judgment, her attitude towards the liar and thief softened. A bitter chuckle cackled at the other end of the line.

"But that's my point. Yours stuck around to make things right. Mine buggered off when I was five, left me to foster care."

"Is this the part where I take out my hankie to wipe away my tears?" She'd meant the words to be sarcastic and mean, so why did they sound almost sympathetic?

"No, Officer O'Rourke, I don't expect your compassion, just your ear for a moment longer. I didn't have a single person in my life who cared about me, but I also figured out early on that meant I could be anyone I wanted. It took me a while to get there, but this person, British Poppy Phillips, is who I want to be. I'm not limited by a birth certificate or defined by a name. I create my reality.

"In case we never speak again, I wanted to tell you to do the same. Don't let your past or your fears define you. You go out there and create the Mel you want to be. You don't need to figure out your brand, you need to invent it."

She blinked rapidly for a moment, willing the moisture in her eyes to go away, dammit. "You risked getting busted to make an illegal phone call to tell me that?"

"Well, that and I didn't kill Kyle Lange, but mostly that. Hell, the bloody killer saw me and is framing me."

"Oh, now I see what this is about." She shook off the dewey-eyed demeanor. "You call with this poor neglected little girl fairytale, which I bet isn't even true, to get me to keep working on proving your innocence. Yeah right, good luck with that, Agnes." She ended the call and took the extra step of turning the phone off. No more calls, no more lies, enough was enough.

"What did she say?" Liam asked with uncharacteristic interest.

"Oh boo hoo, poor me, you go out and have a good life, Mel. Forget about me going to jail for something I didn't do. You know, the usual lying bullshit." Her grandmother frowned and cleared her throat. "Sorry, Grandma, I get it. You like her, but come on, talk about having some nerve. I'm still not exactly off the hook for aiding and abetting if Gregg decides to be a by the book kind of guy, and now she's calling from jail asking me again to clear her name?"

"Is that what she said, dear? Because something got you rattled for a moment." Her brother and grandmother exchanged a suspicious glance. Dammit, why did everyone in this family have to be so observant?

"Not precisely, but she's sticking with her claim that the real killer shot her and is framing her." Then she remembered Poppy's story about her daring escape. She didn't think she'd left a blood trail, but if she could go back to the Nichols Oil building and examine the scene, she'd find out the truth once and for all. Granted, the lack of a bloodstain only meant some fastidious cleaning crew got there first, but if there was even a smudge of blood, it would confirm her gut hadn't led her astray when it told her to trust the thief.

"We gotta go." She grabbed Liam's arm and dragged him toward the door. "You're in charge, Grandma O," was a statement she never thought she'd make, but desperate times, desperate measures. She just hoped her mother never found out.

****

"You want me to go out and check?" Liam asked as Mel stood next to him, frozen in place except for the quaking that shook her entire body. She couldn't even shake her head to tell him no.

The drive down the hill had been uneventful. They chatted about family gossip and laughed over memories of the trouble they'd gotten into as kids. It all felt so normal she hadn't thought about the steep drop off inches outside of the door of Liam's truck.

Once they got to the Badger Corp building, the receptionist remembered Mel from her last trip and accepted her claim Peter Mullins was expecting her without question. Which she thought was a little lazy as the woman called the elevator for them, but who was she to complain?

Thankfully, he was nowhere to be seen when they stepped off on his floor and searched for Kyle Lange's office. No one noticed them at all as the few employees worked in hushed silence, apparently still stunned by the violence that had taken place there. Or slogging away for a big oil company bent on destroying the planet took its toll, one of the two.

The large, lavish office where the murder occurred wasn't hard to find. The police tape was long gone, but the hall outside it was as quiet as the proverbial tomb. People walking past the door sporting his name gave it a wide berth. Location noted, the O'Rourkes made their way to the floor below and two offices over.

The door was propped open with "Finance Department" printed on the frosted panel. She peered inside and saw several desks in an open floor layout. She weighed her options of how to get on the balcony when a young man with thinning hair asked if he could help them.

"We're from the insurance company, filling out paperwork regarding the burglary on the floor above. Can we take a look at your balcony?" The story tumbled out of her mouth almost on its own. She must have been hanging out with Poppy too much, as lying came more naturally to her now.

The confidently told fib did the trick and moments later they were at the door to the balcony. Mel made the mistake of glancing down and became a human stalagmite, rooted to the floor.

"You okay?" The concern in Liam's voice splintered the icy control fear had over her. As much as she wanted to back away from the balcony, her pride wouldn't let her. This stupid phobia was so embarrassing and if she didn't go out there right now, he'd probably re-tell this story at every family occasion for the next ten years. *Hey, did I ever tell the story about Smelly Melly peeing herself just looking out the window? I have? Well, let me tell it again.* She nodded her head in a jerking motion.

"I'm fine," she growled, then squared her shoulders and slid the door to the balcony open. The chill of the late winter air bit her cheeks. Several voices in the office behind her grumbled in protest about the cold air coming in. She needed to get out there now or risk an angry mob closing the door against the cold, her investigation, and getting over her fear forever. Sucking in air as if diving into a deep pool, Mel stepped out onto the balcony and closed the door behind her.

The railing was about four feet away, the balcony more of a decoration and source of light than a place to hang out, but the concrete deck was the longest four feet she'd ever had to cross. Because she could see a dark smudge on the railing off to the left, but she'd have to get closer to confirm if it was blood.

She forced her feet forward, body thrumming with terror, until she stood close enough to touch the stain. A wave of vertigo hit her, but she didn't put her hand out to catch herself, certain the Palm Springs police would have to treat this as a crime scene and dust for prints as well as sample the blood to see if it's a match for Agnes Mary Noble.

A test wasn't necessary for Mel. This was all the proof she needed that Agnes or Poppy or whatever she called herself was at least telling the truth about Lange. If she had murdered him, there were plenty of better ways to leave a crime scene that didn't involve shooting herself and then leaping across the outside of a building.

With trembling hands, she took out her phone and photographed the stain. She tried to turn around to head back to the door, but another bout of vertigo smashed into her. Instead, she backed away until the dizziness receded enough to allow her to face the door. Her brother slid it open, worry still etched on his face as he guided her to a nearby chair. When she plunked down into the lumpy, rolling desk chair, her knees no longer up to the task of standing, they both breathed a sigh of relief.

He disappeared for a minute and returned with a glass of water. She accepted the cup, her hands shaking less now than they had been when he left, and drank most of the cool, slightly chemical tasting liquid down in one gulp.

"Walking four feet is thirsty business," she quipped, handing him back the glass.

"Conquering your fear is a thirsty business," he corrected. "I'm proud of you."

"Well, you might not be so happy in a few hours," she told him as she texted the photo to Deputy Marks with a strongly worded message demanding he get the proof to Palm Springs PD, or she would. "This should be evidence enough to clear your frenemy of all charges. For now, at least."

"Okay, so if she didn't kill the guy, what about the stolen necklace?"

Mel told her brother what Detective Russell Woods in the Cyber Crimes Division shared with her about Kyle Lange being the one who sent the Salutations to Poppy. "I can't prove what it said, although I bet a search warrant would find a record of the message, but the fact we can prove he contacted her should back up her story. If he hired her to steal his own necklace, she has no motive to kill him. I don't think they can charge her." Unless, of course, they wanted to be dicks. Knowing how badly every police department in the state yearned to nail "The Ghost" for anything right down to jay-walking, they might have to call Uncle Colm after all.

"I hope you're right," Liam said cautiously.

She narrowed her eyes at him. "Wait, you *hope* the cops will let her out of jail? I thought you were pissed at me for helping her out?"

"You could have gotten yourself and the inn *we* all own in a lot of trouble. But if she stays in jail, that means you'll be cooking breakfast." He gave an exaggerated shudder.

She laughed as she rose to her feet. "Shut up, brat. Help me secure the scene until the cops arrive."

****

By the time the siblings returned to the Babbling Brook, lunchtime had come and gone. To their surprise, their grandmother had a plate of sandwiches with all the fixings, including chips and soda, waiting for them.

"You made us lunch? What's the occasion?" Liam asked as they ate standing at the island in the middle of the kitchen. It wasn't ideal, but this way they could eat while still keeping an ear out for the front desk.

"Don't be silly, dear, I ordered from that food delivery app Mel has used quite a lot since moving here."

She cringed, realizing she'd have to be more careful about what she left open on her computer as

212

long as her tech savvy grandmother was staying here. Then a thought struck her. "Wait a minute, did you pay for this using the credit card I have on file with them?"

"Do I look like that bald knucklehead with enough money to buy a rocket? I'm an old lady on a fixed income. Of course I used your credit card."

Liam and Mel caught each other's suspicious gazes at the same time. She loved her grandmother, but she wasn't the doting type. At no time in recent memory had she ever made them a meal, so why now?

"Alright, out with it. What did you do that you're trying to soften the blow? And don't *tsk* at me," she interrupted her grandmother as she made a clucking sound.

The old woman stole one of the homemade potato chips off her plate with a scowl. Her expression couldn't have anything to do with the chip, they were delicious. Mel braced for the worst.

"I did a little research like you asked and that blowhard Mrs. Mayor was right. We can't serve any other meal except breakfast. The most a B&B this size can do is a snack, like cheese and crackers. The good news is we can serve booze, but only to people staying here."

*Dammit.* She hadn't been thrilled at the prospect of doing some sort of holiday special, but with the threat of plumbing repairs right around the corner, the idea of boosting the business had become critical. Plus, poor Gemma had worked so hard on promoting the event on a shoestring budget over their social media accounts.

She pushed the sandwich aside, no longer hungry. Grandma O pulled the plate closer and helped herself to more of the potato chips. Food in the O'Rourke household rarely went abandoned for long. The amused curl of Mel's lips grew into a full-blown grin when Jackson, bundled against the winter chill, crossed the bridge connecting their two sides of town.

In his arms was a plastic box, held high to prevent Chewbarka, dancing circles and leaping around him, from helping himself to the culinary delights inside. Because it was a given he was delivering some delicious treat.

Despite her worries about repairs, their promotional Valentine's dinner being thwarted, and whatever she felt about Poppy lying to her, seeing the lanky man making his way toward her lightened her dark mood like the sun coming out from behind a cloud.

The happy anticipation sparking inside had nothing to do with the promise of a sweet or savory morsel. Well, not one hundred percent anyway. She strode through to the Great Room and opened the sliding glass door to let them both in. When they'd opened the Babbling Brook, they'd made the place pet friendly. The big Labradoodle puppy wasn't the first furry guest to come through.

"Chewie, chill," Jackson commanded, not bothering to suppress a grin. Semi-miraculously, the dog stopped running in circles and threatening to knock over every piece of furniture he bumped into. He didn't drop into a submissive position, but he did indeed chill, focusing those huge brown eyes on his person.

"Chill?" Mel laughed as her grandmother and brother joined them at an empty table. "Only someone from New Orleans would train their dog to answer to that." Even as she made the remark, a stinging pain zinged through her at the reminder he might be leaving.

"No," he drawled, "A true NOLA native like my mother would use a Cajun or French word. 'Chill' is something Dad and Chewie learned in dog obedience school. I hate to admit it, but my mother was right about a little training being good for him." He set the box in his hands down in front of them, his smile fading. "I've seen happier folks at a funeral. What's going on?"

"Oh, nothing," she said with a wave of her hand. "My cousin suggested we have a Valentine's Day special and include a romantic dinner with the cost of the room, but as usual Mrs. Mayor rained all over our parade. She's taking the 'breakfast' in B&B very literally."

"We're not licensed to serve lunch or dinner," Liam clarified.

"Well shoot, if that's the problem, you can have it at The Hungry Puppy."

"You would do that for us?" she asked, flooded with relief and not just over the Valentine special being back on. Surely this meant he was planning on staying in Pine Cove, right?

"It'd be my pleasure, gives me a chance to experiment with a menu I've been thinking about."

"Enough chattering, what's in the box?" Grandma demanded, inhaling deeply. "Smells like sugar and sin."

Jackson laughed at her description. "You're close. My mother demanded I work on my beignets in case I decide to go back to New Orleans with her. I noticed you all were just now getting around to lunch, so I thought I'd bring some by for a taste test."

Her brother tensed next to her, brows knitted and

eyes flashing. "Are you stalking my sister?"

A bark of laughter escaped Jackson's lips. His gaze dropped to the now open box of powdered sugar covered confections as her grandmother helped herself. Then he turned his aqua colored eyes, sparkling in amusement, back to Mel. "No sir, but there's only one food delivery person in a town this small and Stephanie loves to stop by and talk about who's ordering what."

Heat crept up Mel's cheeks, unaware she'd been ordering from the town crier. Every pizza, Chinese dinner and liquor store delivery were now apparently a part of the public record. Great.

Eager to change the subject, she remembered her earlier attempt to ask Jackson about the stones in the necklace got de-railed by his glum attitude earlier and his mother's astonishing revelation about the new woman in her life. Now would be the perfect time to talk about anything else other than her dependency on food delivery for her existence. She pulled her phone out of her pocket and showed him the pictures.

"Hey, do you have any idea what any of these stones are or what their significance is?"

He took the phone she offered and zoomed in on the photos. Killing time, she popped one of his beignets in her mouth and let out a soft moan of pleasure.

"You said it, sister," her grandmother agreed as she grabbed another. "If this is what they eat in New Orleans, sign me up. I thought it was all crawfish and fruity drinks, but Christ on a cracker, this is good."

Still casting a suspicious glare at Jackson, Liam took a sugary rectangle of fried dough as well. His eyes sort of rolled back in his head and without a word, he picked up another one. He took a little more time to chew this one and gave Jackson a slight tilt of his chin. She sighed inside, relieved. The bro-nod was the highest form of approval her brother gave a man who wasn't his friend or relative. Maybe she wouldn't have to threaten bodily harm to stop him from running a background check on her neighbor.

Studying the picture of the necklace, he scrunched his nose as if the so-called jewelry smelled as bad as it looked. "Is this a prop or costume? Like from a horror movie?"

She laughed before admitting with a sigh, "We were hoping the stones might be some kind of code."

"Sorry, these don't mean anything to me right off the bat, but text me the pictures and I'll see what I can find. Is this connected to that murder case you were telling me about?" He handed her back her phone.

"Yes, but don't tell Deputy Marks or he'll lose his nut."

He jutted out his lower lip in a mock pout. "Shoot, I was going to call my high-school bestie and rat you out." The two men had gone to school together and their rocky relationship hadn't improved after they became adults. She punched him playfully in the arm and they both laughed.

"Do you...um...have a few minutes to go for a walk?" He stumbled through the question, pink coloring his mocha cheeks. His dog perked up at the word "walk" and her grandmother shot her brother an evil smirk. Embarrassed, Mel would have buried her face in her hands at their antics but didn't want Jackson to take the gesture as a comment about him.

"Sure, I need to walk off your beignet, anyway. Let me grab my coat, I'll be right back." Glaring her family into silence, she hurried to her room, fear gnawing at her gut and turning the delicious pastry into a heavy lump. Clearly something was on his mind and she didn't have to be a psychic to know what. The question was would she like what he had to say, and could she be a supportive friend if she didn't?

****

Bundled in her parka, scarf, and leather gloves to guard her L.A. acclimated body against the dropping temperature, Mel rescued Jackson and Chewie from her meddlesome family moments later. The three of them exited through the sliding glass doors into the soft orange glow of the setting sun. As elevations go, Pine Cove wasn't as high as the ski resorts like Big Bear or Mammoth Lakes, but for a lowlander like Mel it was cold enough.

He guided her along a path she'd seen but never taken before, Chewie capering in circles around them. They ambled down a gently sloping hill to stroll beside the bank of the brook that gave her bed-and-breakfast its name. The narrow trail led away from town into a woodsy area she hadn't taken the time to explore in all the hustle and bustle of re-opening the inn.

"I hear your friend got hauled off to the hoosegow by the almighty Deputy Gregg Marks this morning." Jackson commented without casting a glance her way, staring off instead at the rushing waters as they shambled alongside Blueberry Creek.

"Hoosegow?" She chuckled at the old timey expression. "You make it sound like he threw her over the back of his horse. It was all a misunderstanding. Sort of. I think she's going to be released but not in time for breakfast tomorrow so expect a rush coming your way."

"Ooh, back to your rubbery eggs and burnt toast? I'll be sure to bake and extra batch of—ow!" He laughed as she jabbed him in the arm and then cringed. Was her go-to flirtatious move to punch the guy she liked? *What was wrong with her?* She needed to work on her game. His laugh faded away, and they continued on in silence.

Keeping her mouth shut and waiting for someone else to say what was on their mind didn't come naturally to Mel. In her defense, peace was a rare commodity in the O'Rourke household, where there was no shortage of people eager to voice their opinions. But as a cop, she'd had to learn to embrace the quiet. Silence gave the perp an opening to speak their mind when pushing for answers might have driven them to refuse to talk. So while it was hard walking with Jackson and not pressing him for answers about New Orleans or argue why he should stay, she forced herself to give him the space he needed.

They passed a big fallen pine tree whose bare limbs testified to the fact it lost its battle with the elements long ago when he cleared his throat. "So, pretty weird about my mom and her girlfriend, huh?"

"Did you have any clue?"

"Never in a million years would I have guessed," he said, shaking his head. "My mother swears their relationship has nothing to do with the job offer. I called Chef Adèle to talk, but the call went to voicemail."

She cocked her head toward him to study his expression. "You don't sound so sure."

He pursed his lips and threw a stick for Chewie

before saying, "There's just something off about this whole thing. I mean, I'm glad my mom has found someone to love, and this is a huge opportunity I'd be a fool to pass up, but there's more going on here that she's not telling me, I'm sure of it."

Her heart thudded dully at the way he said "huge opportunity," but she stayed quiet and waited for him to get whatever he wanted to say off his chest. "I told my mother I'd give her my answer after I talked to Chef Adèle, but honestly I don't know what I'm going to say. I mean, I'm flattered, but this is a big change."

"What is your heart telling you?" she asked in a voice barely above a whisper.

He gave a mirthless laugh. "It's as confused as my head." Heaving a sigh, he added, "I love my dad, but it's been just the two of us since high school. Even earlier, what with my mom being deployed to Germany for a while before they finally split. It might be good for me to spend some time with her, get reacquainted?"

From what little she'd dealt with Julia Landry, spending time with her seemed like a scary proposition. Her impression was that the woman was relentless about getting what she wanted. Like water over stone, she'd wear you down until she shaped you in her image, but this wasn't about Mel. "Sounds reasonable."

"I have relatives down there I've barely spoken to. I go back once or twice a year, but it's not enough time to get to know people. And my cousin had a baby last fall I haven't even seen yet." She understood the argument, the three-hour drive to L.A. being the farthest she'd ever been from her immediate family. However, the unspoken "but" in his debate weighed heavily in the air. She had to bite her lip to hold back, but he needed to be heard, not lectured to.

"On the other hand, I've worked hard to build what I have here. And I love the mountain, Deputy Marks aside. Look at that sky." He gestured to the expanse of stars starting to come into view overhead. "I can't imagine seeing a sky so clear in New Orleans. I left Pine Cove to spread my wings after high school and came back because this is my home." He stopped walking and turned to her, aqua eyes meeting hers. "The people I care about most live here."

Her commitment to staying quiet and listening to him shattered. She took his face in her hands and kissed him, then deepened the caress before breaking off. Both of them stared at each other for a moment, astonished at what just happened.

*Oh shit.* Obviously when he said "people I care about most" he was talking about his father, not her. Her humiliation ran so deep that she decided if he didn't move to New Orleans she would, because she couldn't bear to be in the same city as him after what she just did.

Then Jackson closed the gap between them, taking her in his arms and gave her a kiss that sent a bolt of molten heat all the way down to her toes. She ran her hands through his dark curls and pulled him closer. At the sound of Chewie's urgent barking, they broke apart, breathless. Mel's thoughts spun. Had kissing him been the right thing to do? The worst? He must have shared her dilemma because neither of them could look each other in the eye.

"We'd better go see what my dog has gotten in to," he murmured, taking her hand to investigate.

In the soft glow of twilight, they picked their way

along the shrouded, uneven path in silence, following the dog's loud, insistent barks. She grappled with what to say, how to explain away what just happened, or if she even should. The woods thinned out, and cars racing along the road occasionally broke the quiet at the top of the slope to their left.

Chewie ran back to them, still barking and jumping up and down. He put his hand on the big dog, petting his head. "Enough, buddy. Nobody wants to hear about the squirrel you...stop," he laughed as the dog rubbed his muzzle into his owner's hand. "You're getting me all wet. Did you go in the water, you goof?"

But Mel caught the faint scent of something more suited to a crime scene than a pine forest. Blood. "Hang on to Chewie's collar for a second," she told him. "Don't let him rub on you anymore."

"What's up?" he asked even as he obeyed her command.

She hoped she was wrong, but she pulled out her cell phone and turned on the flashlight app to be sure. It was hard to distinguish on the dog's chestnut coat, but the dark stain on his muzzle definitely wasn't water. "Stay here and don't let him go."

She crept along the path, guessing whatever Chewie continued to bark at was how he got his muzzle covered in blood. She hated to think about the animal carcass she was going to find. It had likely been hit by a car speeding on the nearby road and was in a broken, bloody, and hopefully dead heap. Her phone's flashlight was no match for the growing darkness so it took her longer than she thought before she found the body and gasped.

Jackson must have heard her because he crashed

through the woods to stand behind her, one hand still wrapped around his dog's collar. She slammed her phone against her leg, dousing the light. He didn't need to add to the trauma he'd already been through from her kiss by seeing Leigh Pemberton's mutilated corpse.

With an exaggerated sigh, she hit redial and called the last person on the planet she wanted to talk to. "Deputy Marks we have a situation that requires your expertise."

"What now, Mel? Did you find some other piece of random evidence to make my life harder?" His tone said he was as happy to talk to her as she had been to make the call.

"Far be it from me to tell you how to do your job, deputy, but in my limited, amateur opinion there's a dead body on the banks of Blueberry Creek about a half a mile from my inn. And since you're still holding her prisoner, you can't blame Poppy Phillips for this one." She ended the call without listening to his reply, not looking forward to the long night ahead.

Chapter Fifteen

The morning was as terrible as Mel expected it
would be. Last night she'd been stuck waiting for the
sheriff's office to send someone out to her location.
Thankfully, the responding officer wasn't Deputy
Marks, but she'd had to stand around for an hour while
the cop took her and Jackson's statements. An
unexpected snow flurry was icing on the cake. On the
other hand, the night had gone much worse for Leigh
Pemberton.

When she finally returned home and collapsed into
her soft, warm bed, sleep evaded her. Images of the
woman's body kept popping up just when she'd drift
off. Her wounds indicated she'd been attacked by a bear
hours before they found her, but the idea seemed
improbable. Jackson confirmed there were bears in the
area, but they rarely ventured this close to town and
he'd never heard of one attacking a person before.
There were also no tracks in the mud other than
Chewie's, but something tore into her torso and neck
with long claws.

And then there was that kiss...

The lack of sleep did nothing for her culinary skills
the next morning. As she predicted, her disgruntled
guests, disappointed by the offer of rubbery eggs and
cold toast, beat a track to The Hungry Puppy instead.
Even her own family followed suit, leaving her alone to

rehash how stupid it had been to throw herself at Jackson last night. Hopefully, his breakfast rush will keep him from thinking about their kiss. Embarrassed by the memory, she wanted to bang her head on the table. He was a terrific kisser, so no regrets there, but now she realized her actions complicated an already bumpy situation.

"Hey, anybody home?" Doc Hart called out from the doorway, two to-go cups in her hands.

"Doc, come on in. You didn't have to bring coffee. This is a bed-and-breakfast, you know." Mel stood and pulled out a chair.

"True, but I could tell from the line outside Jackson's place you were the chef today. Hence, stopping for this," she slid one cup toward her. "You're a sweet kid, but you make the worst coffee."

She wanted to argue, but her friend was right. So she accepted the offering and added a splash of milk from the pitcher on the table before taking a sip. Flavorful but not overpowering; she really needed to learn how to brew a decent cup of coffee. They sat in amicable silence, staring out the patio doors as last night's dusting of snow melted in the warm morning sun. Doc scrutinized her over the top of her glasses.

"You okay? I mean, you're a tough big city cop and all, but word has it this crime scene was pretty gruesome."

"You've been talking to Gregg Marks, I assume." She shook her head, still amazed at how fast news spread in a town this size. The doctor nodded.

"I saw him at the bakery while I was getting coffee. That boy likes to chatter, mostly about you."

Somehow, that figured. She blew out a frustrated

breath at the idea of being in Deputy Marks' crosshairs. "It wasn't the worst crime scene I've been called to, but it was pretty awful," she confirmed with a shudder. "Somebody went to a lot of trouble to make her death appear to have been the result of an animal attack."

"It happens from time to time. Bears around here don't hibernate, so one might have been foraging for food and thought she was a tasty snack."

Unconvinced, Mel shook her head. "There wasn't enough blood in the area. Not to mention Pemberton wasn't dressed for a hike. I think the perp killed her somewhere else and dumped her here." She chewed on her almost bare thumbnail, thinking out loud, "Most likely scenario is somebody transported her body in a car, stopped on Center Drive at a dark spot where they didn't have to worry about being seen and just rolled her down the hill."

"Did you tell that to Gregg?"

She gave a rude snort. "We aren't exactly playing well with each other. The last thing he's interested in is hearing my theories about his new case. If he blames her death on a bear, I'll have to tell him, but hopefully he's bright enough to figure it out."

"So what kept you up all night if it wasn't the dead body?" her friend asked. She protested, but Doc Hart wagged a finger at her. "You don't need a medical degree, although I happen to have one, to see the bags under your eyes."

Mel succumbed to the desire to talk to someone and confessed, "I think kissing Jackson left me reeling more than finding that horrible little woman torn to shreds."

The utter silence tore her gaze away from the

woods beyond her patio to Doc Hart. "Back up for us old people." She put her coffee cup down as if she might drop it. "You and Jackson were making out by the brook? Is that what you were doing when you found the body?"

"No," she said, her voice sounding like a petulant, guilty teen. "Not exactly making out. He was debating the move to New Orleans, and talked about all the things he'd miss about Pine Cove, including the people he cared about." She stopped, too embarrassed by her own dumb-assery to continue.

"And?" her friend urged.

"He looked at me with that lost, earnest, puppy dog thing he does."

"Oh yeah," the corner of the older woman's mouth rose, "I know the one you're talking about. I mean, not at me, but at you. Damn."

"I know, right? So it's not entirely my fault I…kissed him."

Doc Hart winced. "Ouch. Did he walk away? Is that when you found the body?"

"No, he kissed me back. Like kissed-kissed, not a brush on the cheek, sorry you mistook my signals consolation prize."

"Oh." The doctor's countenance brightened at the news.

"No, not 'oh.' More like 'uh oh' because then Chewie started barking his head off. He stepped away with this, I don't know, horrified expression on his face?"

Her friend chuckled and put a hand on top of hers. "I've known that boy since he was in junior high. I doubt one kiss horrified him. He's no monk, but he's selective about who he swaps spit with."

"Delightful," she muttered. The lobby door opened and Jackson's mother entered, dragging her suitcase behind her. "Crap," she forced a smile on her face as she waved at the woman.

Julia Landry altered her path from the front desk to the table where they sat. Putting her key down in front of Mel, she said, "Ladies, it's been a pleasure, but considering the crime rate around here, I can't say I'm sad to be returning to the relative safety of New Orleans."

"Oh? Are you leaving today?" Mel's insides turned to ice. Did this mean Jackson was leaving too? Or had he turned the job down and his mother was beating a swift retreat?

"I didn't know myself until my son called me this morning and said he'd come to his senses and would join me ASAP to accept Adèle's offer. I feared I was losing him, and I can't help but think I have you to thank for talking sense into him."

*Jackson was leaving?* All the air left her lungs. She made a wheezing sound, and Doc frowned at her in concern.

"Me?" she squeaked out. "What did I do?" she asked, but knew damn well what she'd done to scare him into running away as fast as he could. Why had she kissed him so impulsively? But then, he kissed her back, so maybe his leaving had nothing to do with her?

"He speaks so highly of you, I just assumed he turned to you for advice. Anyway, shall I put the key on the desk in the lobby? I did the auto checkout on the TV, so I'm all set, just waiting for Jackson to drive me to the airport."

"I'll take the key for you," she all but moaned. Had he even planned on saying goodbye before he left?

"The two weeks he'll need to wrap things up here will be just enough time for me to find him a suitable apartment in the Quarter. Not too close to me but not too far," she beamed.

"Oh, he's not leaving with you today?" Doc asked when she couldn't bring herself to talk.

The woman had the temerity to frown. "That wouldn't be very responsible of him, would it? I just hope he can avoid getting mauled by a bear until he leaves." A familiar pickup truck swung down her street. Mel glanced away, experiencing a rush of guilt like she'd been caught peeping through someone's window. "Oh, there he is now." Was there a touch of gloating in her voice? "*Au revoir.*"

The three women stood and moved to the porch. Julia rolled her bag to the truck before Jackson, who had already hopped out, could get it for her. Without so much as a glance in her direction, he helped his mother in and drove off.

"Girl," the doc's voice snapped Mel's attention back to her, "you've got two weeks to change his mind. What are you going to do?"

And that was the million-dollar question. She wanted him to be happy, but had no idea if that meant going to New Orleans or staying in Pine Cove.

\*\*\*\*

"What's with the cabins having numbers, anyway?" Grandma O demanded as she and Mel browsed through the bookings for the coming week.

After the events of the last twenty-four hours, she wasn't in the mood for more branding debate. "How do you want us to label them so guests can find their rooms?"

"Christ on a cracker, I don't know. Name them trees, like the Sycamore cabin, or the Pine loft? Or what about after birds? You're Irish dear. You're supposed to be more poetic than 'cabin four', for Pete's sake."

She opened her mouth to argue about stereotypes when there was the crunch of tires on the gravel parking lot. A quick glance at the clock on the wall told her it probably wasn't the family they were expecting to check in this evening, it was way too early. Curious, she crossed to the window as a tan Sheriff's Department SUV pulled in. The passenger door opened, and a very relieved Poppy sprang out. She dashed up the steps and burst through the lobby door.

"Hullo, mates. Miss me?"

Mel couldn't help but return her infectious smile. Even her grandmother bore an uncharacteristic uptick of the corners of her mouth when the brunette hugged her. Then she remembered the lies she'd told and got angry all over again.

"You don't have to carry on with the accent, mate," she spat out the last word, earning her a *tsk* from Grandma O.

"Love, I told you before I might not have been born in England, but in spirit, I'm as British as tea time and crumpets. Don't even know how to talk like I'm from Cleveland, if I'm being honest."

She wanted to continue arguing about the lies when heavier footsteps on the porch drew Mel's attention. Sheepish, with his hat literally in hand, stood Deputy Gregg Marks.

"Ms. Phillips has been cleared of all charges. Even

the sheriff had to agree that Pemberton was murdered, despite the killer's attempt to make her death seem like an animal attack. "

Mel breathed a sigh of relief at the news as he continued on. "In light of that, he had to admit the idea of a second, unrelated killer was pretty far-fetched. Don't get me wrong, if it were up to him, she'd still be in jail for robbery except Mrs. Lange dropped the charges. There's a chance he'll reconsider and even go after you for aiding and abetting, so I'm begging you, can you two please stay out of trouble?"

"Wait, what did you say?"

"Oh, don't be so offended, Ms. O'Rourke. You keep poking your nose in this case, you'll be lucky if the two of you don't occupy adjoining cells," he huffed out in a humorless dig.

"No, I meant the part where Mrs. Lange dropped the robbery charge. Why would she do that?" Her husband had been killed, and the necklace had to be tied to his death somehow. If she were in her place, Mel would have wanted to keep Poppy in jail until they sorted out the murder.

"On the condition we return the necklace to her immediately. She claims it has some sentimental value, and she didn't want it held as evidence while the court case dragged on."

Her brows furrowed, not buying her story. Who could get sentimental about such an ugly piece of jewelry? On the other hand, an emotional connection would have to be its only value. It certainly wasn't the stones or the setting. "What about the money?"

Marks and Poppy packed a lot of emotion in one simple glance. Haughty triumph on her part, a jaded, weary expression from him.

"As it was only one of the missing ten thousand dollars, we all agreed it was best to donate it to the Police Benevolence Fund." She crossed her arms and arched an eyebrow at Marks as if waiting for a grateful response. If she was, she'd be waiting a long time.

"Yes, 'The Ghost's' reputation of being some kind of kind-hearted antihero remains intact." His words carried an exasperated edge. "Congrats," he muttered before heading toward the door.

"Thanks for the chauffer service," Mel called after him.

"It was on my way," he sighed as if he hated her pointing out he was a nice guy.

"Any leads on Pemberton's cause of death?" She raised her hands defensively before his mood swung back to grumpy a-hole. "Just curious, don't care, since I don't have to worry about proving my friend didn't kill her."

Before answering, he gave her grandmother an abashed grimace. She cackled in reply. "Don't worry about offending my delicate sensibilities, boyo. It'd curl your hair to hear half the things I've seen." Mel didn't know if that was true or not and made a mental note to ask her dad the next time they talked.

He paused for a moment and let out a huff of breath he'd been holding, admitting, "The ME's finding shows she wasn't killed where you found her. Also, since all of her parts are there, we can rule out animal mauling. But there's no tire tracks or drag marks to tell us where she might have come from."

She studied her chipped nail polish, hesitating to say anything and ruin their delicate détente. "Can I make a suggestion?"

Rubbing a hand across his exhausted face, he replied, "Can I stop you?"

She ignored him. "When Jackson and I were walking down there, before we found the body, I heard the cars on Center Drive. There aren't a lot of places to turn off until farther down the hill, so maybe a traffic cam caught a vehicle. A shot of the plates, if you're lucky. There aren't many cars travelling at that time of night, so scanning the video might narrow the suspects."

He nodded in approval. "That's a good idea. I'll get someone to check it out." He paused. She sensed something else on his mind, and bided her time until he filled the uncomfortable silence with, "Can I make a suggestion of my own?"

"Um, sure." She was fairly certain she didn't want to hear whatever he was about to say.

"I've accepted you're going to keep poking around in this case." He shook his head at the start of her protest. "You're a dog with a bone, you can't change who you are. But have you considered why the killer dumped the victim's body in your backyard instead of an anonymous hole somewhere?"

The thought had been niggling at the back of her mind, but she refused to believe the body was some kind of message, especially for her. Why would anyone want to warn her off? She was too clueless to be much of a threat. "A couple of theories come to mind."

He smirked at her despite the serious tone of his warning. "Oh really? Do tell?"

"One, the Langes own a house here. It could be a message to Heather Lange to hand over that formula they're all chasing?"

Gregg shook his head, unconvinced. "Seems like a long way to go to send a vague message."

"Or this was a convenient place to dump her. Sure, a hole in the middle of the desert would take longer to find, but whoever killed her might not have had a lot of time. What if they needed to get it done quick?"

He scowled to show his displeasure with her theory. "Pretty damn convenient wherever they were coming from or going to took them right past your inn. All I'm saying is whoever killed Leigh Pemberton isn't messing around. Not to be too graphic, but the killer used some kind of sharp instrument to rip her open while she was still alive to throw us off. Just be careful. All of you," he said, swiveling his attention to her grandmother and Poppy for a moment before returning his gaze to her. "Life would be dull without you around."

The thought of a killer out there chilled Mel. Also, were they back to being friends or was there a glint of romance in his eyes? He offered no clues as he put on his hat, touched his finger to the brim, and left. She grew concerned over what he wasn't telling her.

Poppy glanced at her, an uncharacteristically serious expression on her face. "I was sitting there in handcuffs as Gregg and his boss argued over what to do with me. Mel, he faced down his boss, really put his neck out there to get me released because it was the right thing to do."

She frowned. "The sheriff wanted to keep you locked up even after Mrs. Lange dropped the charges?"

"It was bullshit, but he stuck with the idea despite the blood confirming my story. Ta for that, mate, by the way. It didn't prove beyond a shadow of a doubt I didn't kill the bugger."

"But he knows for sure you couldn't have killed Leigh Pemberton. Does he believe there are two killers out there knocking off Badger Corp employees?" She crossed her arms in annoyance. "I'm never sure if Gregg is as smart as he thinks he is, but he's definitely brighter than his boss."

The faux Brit put a hand to her shoulder, her brown eyes conveying wisdom beyond her years. "Poppet, I know the two of you have your differences, but don't be so quick to judge. There's more to Deputy Marks than meets the eye. Now, what's for lunch? I'm starved." And with that one hundred and eighty degree change of topic, she flounced toward the kitchen.

Mel and her grandmother followed when her cell phone rang. Jackson's name appeared on the screen. Ugh, she did not need more drama. Instead, she sent the call to voicemail. Grandma O pursed her lips and glared at her over her glasses.

"You're going to have to talk to him sometime. He's supposed to be hosting the Valentine dinner, remember?"

*Shit.* With everything going on today, she completely forgot about his offer and they'd already booked some cabins for the special. "We'll figure something out," she said, though whether to reassure her grandmother or herself she wasn't sure.

Chapter Sixteen

The afternoon drug on as Mel called around to other restaurants asking about a joint Valentine's Day promotion. What choice did she have? According to his mother, Jackson would be gone by then and without him, who was going to cook? She doubted Hugo would take over. She pushed the question of the fate of The Hungry Puppy down the same dark hole she shoved the thought she'd blown whatever they had with that stupid kiss. Mentally sealing the hole with an extra heavy iron door, she searched the list for the next possible partnership.

Her cell phone dinged, alerting her she had a text. The message was from Jackson.

*—We need to talk.—*

Her grandmother was right, she'd have to talk to him eventually, but she had too much on her plate to deal with him right now. At least, that's what she told herself. When her cell phone rang moments later, she almost turned the thing off, thinking it was him. The call came from an unknown number, but he's sneaky enough to borrow a phone to call her, trying to trick her into answering. However, it might be one of the restaurants she'd left a message for calling her back. Reluctantly, she answered. "Hello?"

"Is this Ms. O'Rourke from the Palm Springs Times?" a squeaky male voice asked.

She was about to say they'd reached the wrong number when she remembered that was the cover story she'd used when asking around about Lange.

"This is she," she replied, her curiosity piqued.

"This is Peter Mullins. You'd asked me to call if I thought of anything else that might be important about Kyle's murder?" The voice sounded like him, but there was no quivering on the verge of tears. This time, he sounded assertive, even a little angry. She was curious what information he had but remembered her promise to Gregg to stay out of his case from here on out.

"Mr. Mullins, I appreciate the call, but in the light of things, it's best you contact the police about any information you have. Deputy Gregg Marks is the point person on the case. I can give you his number."

"No, no police. I don't want to get involved. I'll tell you and you can do with it what you want, or we can just forget about the whole thing. It's up to you."

Well, shoot. If God laughs when we make a plan, He must be rolling on the floor hooting when you promise a cop to stay out of his case.

"If the information is so important, why didn't you tell me the first time we talked?"

"I didn't want to get involved, but after what happened to Leigh, I thought someone should know."

"All right fine, I'll bite. What's this new evidence?" She tried to keep the exasperation out of her voice, but the more she wanted to stay out of this mess, the more people kept pulling her back in. Gregg was going to kill her.

"No, not over the phone. It has to be in person, in public. Do you know Lola's Diner on Palm Canyon?"

*Christ on a cracker, these trips to Palm Springs*

*were becoming a pain in the ass.* Not just forcing her to handle her agoraphobia, they also meant she was falling behind on running her business, as well as turning into Grandma in her head. *Great.* But there was an urgency in his voice that made her itch to find out what this new information was, so she agreed to meet him in an hour and a half.

After making sure her grandmother was okay watching the front desk, Mel grabbed her keys and headed out the door, nearly colliding with Poppy, who shoved the last bite of something wonderful smelling in her mouth.

"What were you eating?"

"A turkey and melted brie sandwich," she answered between licking her fingers. "A little pepper jelly to add some zing."

In ninety seconds, the woman could create a meal out of ingredients she didn't even know they had *and* polish it off. She had to give her begrudging admiration. Mel's go-to meal was noodles in a cup.

"Where are you off to?" She spotted the keys in her hand. "See, I'm aces at this detecting stuff." She punctuated her statement with a wink.

"I'm going down to meet Lange's lab assistant, Peter Mullins. He says he has new information. I doubt it's anything but…" She shrugged.

Which was met with a cocked eyebrow and a menacing frown. "I thought you promised Gregg to steer clear?"

"What can I say? The guy refuses to talk to the police. I'll pass on whatever I find out and then stay out of *his* case for good."

Poppy stared at her for a moment before reaching

some kind of decision and springing into action. Grabbing the coat she'd left on a chair in the Great Room, she returned to the lobby in a flash. "Fine, then I'm going with you. I heard what Deputy Marks said about the killer being dangerous, and I'm not letting you go anywhere alone as long as you're poking around."

****

Lola's Diner boasted a prime location on a busy corner of Palm Springs' main drag, but since tourists were scarce this time of year, it was practically deserted. Designed with people watching in mind with plenty of patio seating, the diner featured lots of chrome and gleaming white tile floors.

The dining room was almost empty. There was only the sporadic clatter of dishes and she smelled coffee, not food, as she waited for Mullins to arrive. Poppy hung out at a booth inside, sipping on a giant milk shake, ready to spring into action if the meeting took a dangerous turn. Based on his picture on the company website, she doubted that would happen, but underestimating someone is a great way to get killed.

Because she was going off the photo, she was taken aback when a reedy man with thin wisps of pale hair approached her table. "Ms. O'Rourke?"

She choked on her iced tea. His picture must have been over twenty-years old, showing a slightly chubby man with a full head of glorious blonde waves. The refined face was too distinctive to be anyone else, even if there were a few more wrinkles. He was still handsome in that bookish way she always associated with Ivy League brainiacs. However, he needed to work on his undercover skills. Nothing screams "look at me" like wearing a trench coat in a resort town like Palm Springs.

"Peter Mullins, I assume?" She gestured for him to take a seat. He swiveled his head around, narrowed eyes searching for any ears listening in. *Again, congrats on not appearing too suspicious—not.*

"Thank you for meeting me on such short notice. After what happened to Kyle and Pemberton, I'm leaving tonight for…" He scrutinized her, and she must have cratered on his trustworthy scale because all he'd say was, "Leaving town."

"Kind of extreme, don't you think? You told me you weren't on the team for this latest product." She left the description vague, unsure if he'd figured out Lange had created an oil-eating enzyme. "If that's what the killer is after, you should be safe."

"Yes, but they don't know that, do they? And what if the motive is something else? That's why I wanted to meet in person. Our offices have too many ears. For all I know, they bugged the phones." As he spoke, he continued to sweep the diner for threats, never making eye contact with her for more than a moment.

Mel sighed, because none of what he said made any sense. If the killer bugged the offices, then they know he isn't involved. He didn't seem all that bright, but then again, having someone you work with, even if you despise them, torn to shreds, could rattle anyone.

"No problem, sir. My office is just a few blocks away." She winged it. Who the heck knows where their local paper is located, anyway? "What did you want to talk about?"

"If you've talked to many of Kyle's associates, I'm sure you've heard the rumors he was having an affair."

He paused, so she nodded, assuming he needed a cue to continue. "It's true, but what no one knew was he was sleeping with me."

She had to admit she didn't see that coming. Not that there were types that fit in the gay box, that was a stupid assumption. It was that having an affair with your assistant was such a cliché. For a guy who invented a groundbreaking enzyme, she'd expected more from Lange.

"I was out long before Badger Corp hired me. Then, about two years ago, Kyle began to question his sexuality. He'd slept with dozens of women, most of them gorgeous. I mean, Heather's no slouch. Still, he couldn't shake the feeling that something was missing. He knew I was gay and talked to me about it, but that's all it was at first, talk. I gave him LGBTQ 101, introduced him to some friends. Honestly, he was more bi-curious at first. The more time we spent together, the more being with me spoke to his inner truth than being with Heather ever did.

"He decided to stop lying to himself about who he really was. After years of repression, it wasn't easy, but he was finally free to follow his heart and that led him to me."

"Are you saying his wife killed him over this?" Mel remained unconvinced. She liked Mrs. Lange from what little she knew of her and was confident she was more of a take 'em to the cleaners type than kill him in a jealous rage kind of woman.

"I didn't think so, until I found this." The nervous man scanned the room again for curious faces, then pulled a piece of paper out from the deep pocket of his trench coat and slid it across to her side of the table.

"This note is why I asked to meet you."

She took the stationery, stunned to see it was identical to the one they found at the Langes' cabin. Same ecru color, same linen texture with no markings to identify where it came from. Written in the same computer generated, generic font, the note was brief. *You're next.* She had to give the writer credit; they didn't waste any time ranting about their cause or their plans the way idiot villains did on TV or the movies. Of course, if they had, she would have had more to go on.

"Do you recognize the stationery?" He shook his head.

"It's not from Badger Corp, our paper is white and we have our logo emblazoned across the top."

"When did you receive this?" At least this made his sudden departure from town make sense. The poor man feared for his life. Or so she thought.

"Oh, the note wasn't sent to me. I found it in Pemberton's desk drawer. I think Heather Lange sent it."

Every time she thought she had some answers in this case, all Mel had were more questions. "Why would Mrs. Lange send this to Ms. Pemberton? What were you doing going through her desk, anyway?" The last question wasn't relevant to the case, but she couldn't believe the balls on this guy.

"I used to go through her desk all the time to spy on her for Kyle, but isn't Heather's motive obvious?" He sneered at her like she was an idiot. "She's the only person connected to both Kyle and Pemberton."

"Not to play devil's advocate or anything, but *you* have ties to them both as well. How do I know you didn't write this yourself to cover your tracks?"

"Because I have an alibi for the night of Kyle's murder. I was out celebrating our win at a local talent show with the rest of the Sonoran Desert Gay Men's Choir, and there are plenty of pictures proving it."

He slid a second, smaller piece of paper across the table to her with a neatly handwritten list of a half dozen names. "My rock solid alibi is all over social media, if you want to check." She nodded, slipping the paper into her pocket. She'd already seen the proof of his partying when they first spoke. He still could have hired someone to kill Lange for him, but the sweat beading on his brow told her his fear was real.

"When you found the note, was it in an envelope on top of her desk, or inside a drawer?" She wished he'd left it alone so the police could have found it and investigated it properly, but since she'd been party to stealing evidence herself, she couldn't throw rocks at his glass house.

He gave an impatient, jerky shake of his head. "There was no envelope. I was searching through her stuff for Kyle's enzyme thingy formula and the note was in her top desk drawer mixed in with some receipts and other junk."

*Enzyme thingy?* He may have been Kyle's assistant, but clearly he wasn't a science whiz. On the other hand, he didn't have to be a genius to steal the missing formula and profit by either selling the information to an environmental group to produce it or to an oil company so they could bury it. "Did you find it? The formula, I mean."

His delicate facial features twisted into a petulant scowl. "No, and I'm certain that bitch stole his crowning achievement. I've searched every possible place he might have stashed it and found nothing. That's the other reason I'm sure Heather killed them. If he divorced her to be with me, she had to get that formula now or stand by and watch while the two of them became millionaires."

Mel pulled a face. *Was that really his plan?* Instead, she asked, "But wasn't she the rich one in the marriage?"

"Well, you can never have too much money, can you?" He stood, pulling his coat tighter to him as if the thought chilled him to the bone. "I have to get going. Heather might assume Kyle trusted me with the formula and I don't want to end up slashed to ribbons like Pemberton." Pretty spry for a guy who spent his life behind a desk, he was at the door before she jumped to her feet, landing badly on her re-built ankle, and touched his arm.

"Sir, just one last question. What can you tell me about Mr. Lange's car being vandalized?"

"Vandalized?" He frowned. "Vandalized how?"

"I was told someone painted the word 'traitor' on the side of his car."

"He mentioned something about taking his car in to get buffed. I assumed someone had keyed it or dinged it with their door. Honestly, I wasn't listening. Now if you don't mind." He hurried out without waiting for an answer. The more she talked to Peter Mullins, the more she realized how self-centered he was. If Kyle was having an affair with him, either he was starving for attention or was as shallow as his assistant.

****

Mel sat in her car checking her watch for what seemed like the hundredth time until Poppy finally

244

opened the door and got in.

"What took you so long?" she snapped as she started the engine.

"Ice cream headaches are a real thing, love. Also, I was curious where our rabbit was headed, so I accidentally bumped into him on the street and dropped one of those chips you use to track your luggage and such into his daft trench coat pocket."

Mel mentally kicked herself. She should have thought of that. Her only excuse was she was so pre-occupied with the Jackson situation she was off her A-game. "Okay, that was actually pretty smart. Where'd he go?"

Consulting her phone, she reported, "He's on the freeway heading north. My guess would be Vegas. How convenient that the person who claimed ten thousand dollars went missing from the safe is on his way to Sin City. Hmm, where did he get the money, I wonder?"

"Point taken," she admitted, hands raised in defeat. "Although you did lie to me about not taking any money, so you can't blame me for thinking he was innocent."

Poppy waved off the idea like it was a pesky fly. "Whatever. Where to next, DC O'Rourke?"

She laughed at the police title. She knew from her favorite British mystery shows a DC was a Detective Constable. Higher than the rank she'd held in the LAPD, but not the top dog. "DC? If you're going to promote me, why not Detective Inspector or all the way to Chief Inspector?"

"Crikey, now who's got a big head?" she smirked. "Before we make you the commissioner of Scotland Yard, what *is* our next move?"

That was an excellent question. There were more loose ends with this case than on the crooked scrap of her knitting project. She narrowed her eyes as she considered the possibilities. "While we're down here, we might as well talk to Heather Lange about this note and the alleged affair with Mullins. Plus, we still don't have a lead on who wrote *traitor* on Lange's car. We find out what she knows and then hand the whole thing over to Deputy Marks." After all, she reasoned, if she gave Gregg what she had now, it was no more than rumor or gossip.

"Not to rain on your parade, mate, but why would the woman talk to us?"

Heather had already met her at Nailed It, so the reporter ruse was out. She started to chew on her thumbnail and recalled the remaining speck of polish in the nick of time. "Remember in the Lange's cabin there were all of those pictures of her with dogs?"

Her friend furrowed her brows and frowned. "Not really. I was too busy checking out the artwork. Most of which wasn't real, by the way."

"She had more photos of her with dogs than with her husband. And Mrs. Oberdingle mentioned she was working on some kind of animal rescue project. She knows I live in Pine Cove, so what if we go to her with the pretense of opening a dog shelter in town?"

With a few more taps on her phone, Poppy said dubiously, "There are a couple of highly rated ones currently up and running."

"Even better. We can approach her about our desire to open one and she can tell us all the good works already being done to save us poor fools from making a mistake." Mel grinned, liking her idea more and more.

"And we can work in a few questions about the murders."

"Like, did you hack that woman to death?" Her passenger seemed unconvinced.

"I admit, it's a fishing expedition, but you'll see. People confess to all kinds of things when their guard is down. Now we just have to find where they live."

"Then you're in luck because I happen to have the address to Lange manor."

She shook her head as her partner in crime entered the details in her phone's navigation and they were on their way. She wasn't surprised a thief would know where the richest people in town lived, but *manor*? "Do they really call their house that?"

"No," the other woman laughed. "I was running with the British vibe we had going. Although maybe they should. I only saw it once, at night." Mel gave her a side-eyed glance. "All right, the two times during the days I spent sussing out the security and what not, plus the night of the swanky charity event they threw last fall. The point is, the house is big and very well maintained. If Heather's the one with the money, then she's got a lot of it."

"Which also means she's got a lot to protect if they divorced, unless they signed a pre-nup." She was mulling the idea over when her cell phone rang. Jackson's name lit up the screen. Without hesitation, she sent the call to voicemail.

"Playing hard to get? Seems a bit underhanded for you."

"His mother told me he's leaving town in a couple of weeks, so I can't imagine what we have left to discuss." She hated the butt-hurt, teenage angsty tone in her voice. *God, what was wrong with her lately?*

"His mother told you?" Poppy frowned. "Not the most reliable news source there, mate. What are you, some bird in a romance novel? Go talk to him."

She gripped the wheel so hard out of frustration, her knuckles turned white. "If he had something to tell me, he should have come to see me himself."

"Says the person who refused to tell anyone about being injured on the job when she first arrived because she was too proud to accept help. Don't take this the wrong way, but you can be kind of prickly sometimes."

"Is there a *right* way to take that?"

The robotic voice of her phone's GPS announced they'd reached their destination, forcing them to shelve the topic for now. Unfortunately, Mel had no doubt Poppy wouldn't hesitate to bring it back up again and dammit, she might—*might*—have a point.

Chapter Seventeen

As opposed to the costly mansions in Beverly Hills, the Langes' house had no grand gate barring them from entering. A wide, short driveway led to a very large front entrance with thick double wooden doors and hard, squared edges common to a lot of homes built in the nineteen sixties. And that was as welcoming as it got. A tall, solid fence stretched from the sides to keep the riff-raff out, along with a sign proclaiming armed response could be expected.

It also stood in direct contrast with Leigh Pemberton's home, which, despite the audible water feature splashing in the backyard, at least was landscaped to match the native desert environment. The Langes lived like water was an infinite resource. They had a lush lawn most golf courses would envy, a flowering garden more typical in England than in an area in a near constant state of drought, and ivy spilling out from stone containers. Just when she thought she liked Heather, it turns out she's one of those people who said "screw the planet, I want what *I* want".

Mel parked her car off to the side of the wide driveway, in case the armed response was real and they needed to make a quick getaway. Then she and Poppy proceeded to the front door.

"Here's hoping the doorbell doesn't alert the storm troopers," she muttered as she pressed the bell. A ringing sound must have happened, but all she heard was a cacophony of barking dogs. Amidst the chaos, a fit blonde woman opened the door, greeting them with a puzzled expression as the dogs continued barking out of sight.

For some reason, Mel had imagined the Langes' staff would dress in old-fashioned stiff, black uniforms with white aprons. Instead, she wore a maroon polo shirt and khaki pants with sensible but stylish loafers. They could have been regular casual clothes except for the *L* embroidered on the upper left side.

"May I help you?" Her tone was polite, but her stance blocked the doorway. When she explained they were hoping to speak to Heather about her dog rescue charity, the woman remained skeptical but showed them in. She left them in the foyer with the instructions to wait right there while she asked Mrs. Lange if now was a good time.

She hadn't quite disappeared down the sun-drenched hall when Poppy turned to her with a gleeful, "We should get a uniform like that with a snazzy logo for the B&B."

"We?" Her eyebrows rose in amused curiosity.

"You know what I mean."

After several minutes, the woman returned to show them through so many square rooms with glass walls that Mel lost count. Each had a door that slid aside, giving the entire space an open feeling as if they were in a garden. Finally, they entered the interior courtyard, where Heather Lange was finishing her lunch.

Despite eating alone, she was dressed in a skirt and sweater set, heels, and the pre-requisite string of pearls worn by women who needed to remind everyone around them how superior they were. Or at least, that was Mel's take on the fashion accessory. On the table were the remnants of a salad on fine china and a glass of tea in cut crystal. She thought back to her usual lunch of a sandwich on a paper plate, often standing at the island in the kitchen. *Oh, how the other half lived.*

The older woman greeted them with narrowed eyes and none of the warmth she'd displayed getting her nails done, but then they were intruders in her home. "Elsa said you wanted to talk to me about my dog rescue?"

"Mrs. Lange, I'm not sure if you remember me. We met at Nailed It a few days ago? My name's Mel O'Rourke." She offered her hand, but instead of accepting the handshake in the typical way, Heather Lange took it and examined the nails.

"Of course I remember you. What a shame, Caitlin did such a beautiful job and you've ruined it."

She jerked her hand back and fought the urge to stuff both of them in her pockets and out of sight. "I've had a stressful few days."

"Tell me about it," the new widow muttered.

"Again, you have my sympathies. That's why we almost didn't stop by, but my friend and I are considering opening a dog rescue in Pine Cove. I understand you help fund shelters and someone suggested coming to talk to you about how you got started."

Most people would jump at the opportunity to humble brag, or even outright brag, about the charity work they did, but the stylish, aloof woman was distracted by Poppy. She tilted her head one way and then the other to study her before remarking, "You look familiar. Have we met?"

"What a fabulous memory you have for faces, Mrs. Lange." The petite brunette beamed as if she'd been paid a compliment, but Mel had a hunch from her frown their hostess didn't mean it in a friendly way. "In fact, I was fortunate enough to have been here for the fundraiser you held last fall."

"Funny, I handle all the details for my parties, including the invitations, and I can't put a name to your face."

"Oh, I didn't have an invite. Honestly, between the British accent and showing your security man a little cleavage, getting in was far easier than I expected."

Mel gritted her teeth. How was admitting to being a party crasher going to get them any information? When she didn't stop there, she wanted to bury her face in her hands. *So much for the softening her up by talking about animal rescues.*

"In fact, I'd come to steal your statue over there," she pointed to a blob of white marble, "but since it's a fake, I decided not to bother and enjoyed the free food and bevvies instead. Oh, and the music. Nice jazz quartet you had."

It would be a tough call on who was more shocked, Mel or Mrs. Lange, but the older woman got the power of speech back first. "You knew the statue was a fake?"

Interesting first question. Not "what do you mean you were going to steal my statue" or "how dare you accuse me of owning fake art". Which meant the woman gleaned the blob was a fake, but when? After she bought it, or did she sell the original because money wasn't as abundant as she lead everyone to believe?

"Easy to tell once you get close enough."

The other woman, whose nails were still perfect, stiffened and scowled. "I'm going to have to ask you to leave."

Before she called on the crack unit of armed responders, Mel jumped in. "Considering the fake art, imagine our surprise to discover your husband had hired my friend here to rob his own safe."

"He what?" Mrs. Lange paled.

"Oh yeah," the thief purred. "He hired me to steal the necklace. He even left instructions as to the day and time to break in. I figured he popped off someplace to give himself an alibi, so imagine my surprise when I found him there, dead."

"What's the importance of the necklace?" she probed, trying not to scare the poor woman off, but wanting to take advantage of the opening Poppy had created. "Why were you willing to drop all charges to get it back?"

"Because it isn't a necklace. It's the key for unlocking that stupid enzyme Kyle invented," the bereaved widow spat. "He loved his puzzles. Nothing was ever easy with him. He told me he was going to give the formula away as his gift to the world, the big dumb idiot."

"Is that why you killed him? To prevent him from giving away all that money?" she continued in her gentle tone. The maid behind her gasped.

"Or because he was having an affair with Peter Mullins?" Poppy chirped, sounding more amused than anything else.

"I told you before," she said to Mel, "I presumed he'd have affairs. That he was sleeping with a man was an unexpected twist, but we still loved each other."

"So then, it was about the money?"

"You've got it all wrong. The night he died, I was at a board meeting for the charity you used as an excuse to insert yourself into my private life. Elsa will show you to the door." She pivoted on her heel to leave, but the ex-cop pressed on.

"So if you didn't kill him, why were you in such a hurry to retrieve the necklace that you were willing to let the only suspect in his murder go free?"

Mrs. Lange spun around, eyes blazing in fury. "Because I'm certain Leigh Pemberton killed him. Besides, I have offers on the table now for the formula. If this case drags on through the courts, they might go away or that woman could counter sue and tie ownership up for months or years."

"Well, you won't have to worry about that, love," Poppy scoffed.

"Why? What do you mean?"

"I hate to be the bearer of bad news, but Ms. Pemberton's body was found last night, brutally murdered." Mel revealed as little as possible about the crime to her number one suspect.

"What?" Heather Lange looked aghast at first and then burst out laughing. *Nothing says guilty like laughing about a murder.*

"She was killed shortly after she got a threatening note. From you."

"Don't be ludicrous. My father was a lawyer. He taught me better than to leave a paper trail. I mean, a horrible death was never more richly deserved, but I didn't kill her."

"Where were you last night around five o'clock?" Mel pushed.

"Not that I have to answer any of your questions, but I was here from about four-thirty until a little after ten hosting my monthly sound bath and meditation circle."

"A what now?" she asked at the same moment Poppy cooed, "Ooh, brilliant." She thought she'd seen every weird woo-woo thing there was back in L.A., but what the heck was a sound bath?

"Why didn't I think of that before?" her friend exclaimed. "You should absolutely try one. It's a great way to deal with anxiety by meditating while immersing yourself in singing bowls or any repetitive sound. I took part in one once where they used a didgeridoo, but I don't recommend it. After an hour, it just sounded creepy."

*An hour?* To Mel, the instrument sounded creepy from the start. She shook her head and returned her focus to Heather Lange. "You did this sound bath thing for five hours?" She asked, more out of curiosity than testing her alibi, but the question was the last straw for the widow.

"It was three hours," she snapped. "Afterward, my friends and I had dinner, but no, I will not give you their names so you can annoy them. In fact, I'm not answering any more questions without a lawyer and someone with a badge present." She nodded toward Elsa, who waved her arm in a 'this way to the door,' gesture.

"Just one more thing, Mrs. Lange. Do you know anything about Kyle's car being vandalized? I was told someone painted 'traitor' on it."

"No idea what you're talking about. It's news to me."

Mel pushed her luck, asking, "Do you mind letting us take a peek at his car?"

The woman plastered on a huge fake smile. "Of course, I'll let you in the garage as soon as a pig flies past my window." Scowling, she huffed deeper into the house while the imposing maid gave them the bum's rush.

****

"What happened to our plan to cozy up to her and bond over dog stuff, find out what she knows?" Mel hissed out of gritted teeth when they got to her car.

"Once she recognized me, that was off the table, so I had to improvise," Poppy said with a casual wave of her hand. When she glanced over, however, her perfect lips puckered into a frown. "You're awfully pale. Do you want me to drive back?"

"I'm fine," she grumbled, claiming her spot behind the wheel. The truth was, she was getting nowhere with this case and it left her feeling as wrung out as an old dishcloth. "And why didn't you tell me you *went* to the party? I thought you hung out all cat burglar style and snuck off with whatever you were after. If I'd known, I would've had you stay in the car."

"Never mind about that, water under the bridge and all. But this sound bath idea is a winner. I wonder if anyone performs them in Pine Cove?" She pulled her phone out of her pocket and started typing away. "I bet it's just the ticket to cleanse your chakras and put you right."

Driving back to the top of the mountain in what had now become an almost daily routine, Mel took her eyes off the road for a millisecond to glower at Poppy. "I'm doing better, thanks, but as far as suspects go, we're running out of them. Heather might have motive, but her music bowl alibi sounds too kooky to be a lie."

"You mean sound bath, and I agree. Besides, while I can see her shooting her hubby, I can't imagine her risking breaking one of those gorgeous nails by using her hands to kill Leigh Pemberton. What about the person who may or may not have vandalized Lange's car? If someone hated him enough to ruin his paint job, could it have escalated to murder?"

"Yeah, but there's no witness or CCTV video to prove this alleged tagging ever happened. The only thing left is to check all the body shops in Palm Springs to see if Lange had his car repainted recently."

"That should only take a month," Poppy groused. "What about the tree-sitting chap?"

"Oliver Brown? I thought about him but I checked and his live feed confirms he's been in that tree twenty-four/seven. There's a few hundred people following him, and my guess is at least one of them works for the builder who wants to chop the tree down just to be sure he's still there. If he left, they'd jump on the chance to cut it down."

"Right, and besides, the missus confirmed what Oliver told you before. Kyle was going to give the formula away for free."

"Not quite." Mel frowned in concentration. "Oliver said Lange was going to donate the profits from micro-organism to wildlife causes. That's not the same as giving the formula away for free. Either way, with Lange dead and the formula missing, Oliver's causes could be out a lot of money."

"Giving him an anti-motive?"

"And me a headache." If she could have taken a

hand off the wheel, she would have rubbed the spot right above her eye where a dull pain thudded. "My life would be so much simpler if you had killed Lange."

Poppy patted her shoulder as she scrolled through her phone. "Don't worry, I'm going to find you a nice relaxing sound bath."

\*\*\*\*

Just her luck, Poppy found a yoga studio in Pine Cove that held sound baths. The Brit insisted the experience might be what she needed to unblock her brain and solve the case, but after she played a sample of what one of these bizzarro things sounded like on her phone, Mel doubted it. The annoying noise was akin to holiday carols produced on wine glasses filled with different levels of water. She begged off, claiming she needed to stretch her legs after the drive. It wasn't far from the truth, because her ankle was stiff.

Instead, she left Poppy to check in the guests at the Babbling Brook since Grandma O volunteered to call body shops in Palm Springs. In the meantime, Mel drove to the grocery store for supplies to prepare for the busy weekend ahead. The weather promised to be gorgeous, and the inn had a lot of new bookings that were bound to be hungry for breakfast.

\*\*\*\*

Mel took the long way around to the store, avoiding going past The Hungry Puppy. She didn't even want to imagine how much the town would miss the café, not to mention how empty her life would be.

She was still brooding on the topic as she wheeled her cart around the corner of the grocery store aisle and ran into Hugo Thibodeaux. It was as if by thinking about the son she'd conjured the father. She nodded at him awkwardly and moved to continue on her way when he stopped her.

"My son is being foolish and I blame my ex-wife. I don't know what they talked about this morning, but after their private, hush-hush meeting at the house, his mind was made up to go to New Orleans."

"This job is a great opportunity," she said with all the enthusiasm of a person getting ready for a colonoscopy. He made a rude noise in response.

"That woman is a force of nature, and not in a good way. In a 'rip your life apart like Katrina' kind of way."

A laugh escaped Mel's lips before she realized he wasn't joking.

"I'm sure she has Jackson's best interest at heart. We'll all have to muddle through without him, let him go to find his happiness." She forced a smile, struggling to take the high road.

"Happiness my Aunt Fanny's fanny," he grumbled. "For someone chasing the so-called chance of a lifetime, that boy sure is miserable."

She placed the two large cartons of eggs in her cart and gave him a sideways glance. "Well then, why is he going? Isn't he a little old to do this just to please his mother?"

"I was hoping you could tell me," he admitted. "I would have put money on him staying, but then he went over to see you last night. Did finding that body bother him so much it made him run for New Orleans?"

Something scared him off, but Mel was certain it was that damned kiss. She wanted to smack herself in the head for being so dumb. "I wish I could hit rewind and undo last night," she bemoaned.

His father gave her a candid look that made her

feel like the Cajun saw right through her. "Don't give up on him yet. For a genius, my boy can be pretty thick sometimes. He's not gone till he's gone." Giving her a mysterious smile, the man walked away.

****

Mel returned to the front desk after putting the groceries away, more confused than ever about the case, Jackson, and life in general. She longed for the simple days when all she had to worry about were the bad guys trying to shoot her. Her grandmother strolled by with a book in one hand and a steaming mug in the other. Seeing Mel, she stopped. "What's with the sour puss?"

Despite her mood, she had to crack the tiniest of smiles. "You know, most grandmothers would say something sweet like, 'are you okay' or 'how can I help'."

"Then you're lucky I'm not most grandmothers. How boring would that be?" She made a disgusted face like she'd just smelled doo doo. "So spill. What's on your mind?"

She sorted through all the things bothering her, trying to find the safest topic. Jackson? Hard pass. Grandma O loved to gossip, and in an hour the whole family would know about their relationship. Then the book in her grandmother's hand caught her eye. "The Collected Poems of W. B. Yeats? You're into Irish poetry?"

"Me? Balls, can't stand the stuff. Give me a good steamy romance any day. But your grandfather loved this book, made all kinds of handwritten notes in the margins, see?" She pointed to the faded, tightly curled cursive at the edge of the page. "Taking it out once in a while reminds me of him."

The touching, sweet sentiment came from out of left field. Her grandfather passed away a little over a year ago and while she'd always thought of them as a happy couple, she'd never call them romantic. The pain on her grandmother's face made her realize his death explained why Grandma O was getting under Mom's feet and causing trouble. She was also jealous, hoping someday to love someone so much it physically hurt when they were gone.

"Plus, I'm pretty sure that old coot has money stashed away, and this is exactly how he would have hidden it, with some dumbass word puzzle." And there was Grandma, keeping it real. Mel smiled and wrapped an arm around her boney shoulders. She expected the old woman to shrug away with a typical quip about hugging being for Protestants but instead, she patted her blue-veined hand on top of Mel's.

Thank God Liam interrupted this uncharacteristically touching moment by blowing into the lobby. She braced herself for whatever this particular storm turned out to be. She loved her brother, but he'd been moody ever since he arrived. As her grandmother might say, he was like a bear with a thorn in his butt. Come to think of it, he got this way when his love life fell apart. Getting dumped by his latest in a long string of girlfriends back in L.A. would explain so much. Like why he came here now to do some minor repairs and was in no hurry to leave.

"Come on, the renovation is done and I think you're going to love it." He grabbed her hand and tugged her out of the lobby.

"Love what? What are you talking about?" Then

she remembered giving him the go ahead to trade out a singular wood-burning fireplace with a gas one as an experiment.

Dragging her out the door, he collided with Poppy, who was passing by, loaded with fresh towels. "'Ang on love, where's the fire?" she asked with a laugh.

He clumsily helped her gather the linens, but Mel took the load out of both of their arms and put them down on the front desk.

"Those will keep for a minute. Come on and see what Liam has done. You okay waiting here, Grandma?" After all, misery loves company. She was certain she was going to hate the gas fireplace, no matter what her brother said about it being safer and cleaner, but could she tell him the truth? Especially when he was as excited as a kid at Christmas over his project.

The old woman waved them all out the door and moments later they arrived at the cabin closest to the main building but still shaded by the tall pines on three sides. Grinning, he led them inside and sat them both down on the foot of the bed.

"Kinky, but I'm not saying no," Poppy said in a playful sex kitten voice.

"What?" His face turned bright red when he figured out what she meant. "Eww, no, I'm not into—never mind. Watch." He spun the dial on the wall next to the fireplace and the cheerless gas flames danced in their organized rows. "This is a timer, not just an on-off switch, so the guests can get ready for bed, set the length they want, and fall asleep with a safe fire burning until the time runs out."

Mel bit back her first response to come up with a

more thoughtful one, although the loud ticking of the timer made thinking difficult. How would anyone sleep with that racket going on? "It's nice, Liam, but the timer is a little loud." She raised her voice in an overly dramatic fashion as if she needed to in order to be heard.

His face fell, and he twisted the dial to turn off the flames. "Fine. I was just trying to make it safer. The thought of you almost dying of smoke inhalation made me crazy. Swapping wood-burning fireplaces out for gas is the best way to be sure an accident like that doesn't happen again."

Mel stood and put her hands on his shoulders, sudden understanding dawning on her about why this was so important to him. "Listen, baby brother, it's not your job to take care of me. I do pretty good on my own."

He shot back a snarky comment when Poppy shushed them both. "Stop. Stop!" she commanded until they were quiet. "If you turned off the fireplace, why am I still hearing a ticking sound?"

Understanding dawned on all their faces as they raced out the door. Tires squealed down the street and she halted, searching for the culprit.

"Mel! Come on," Liam shouted at her just as the cabin erupted into a fireball. Something hit her hard, and she flew backwards several feet before hitting the ground with a thud. Pain exploded in her head, competing with the ache in her ribs that made breathing next to impossible.

Heat from the burning structure washed over her as she tried to sit up, but the world slid and tilted so she settled for rolling to her side instead, gasping for air. A concussion and lack of oxygen was the only explanation for what she saw when she scoured the area for Liam and Poppy.

Her brother had protectively thrown his body over the petite woman, a look of abject terror on his face as he checked to be sure she was alive. His mouth was moving, probably yelling her name, but the ringing in Mel's ears made it impossible to hear. When Poppy's eyes fluttered open and she gave him a weak smile, he sagged in relief. At first she was happy just to see the two were okay but then the realization hit her with the force of...well, a bomb. *Liam was in love with Poppy.*

*Oh, hell no* was her last thought before the world winked out again.

Chapter Eighteen

"Ow!" Mel yelped as Doctor Linda Hart stitched the cut on her forehead just inches above her right eye. "Are you using a harpoon or something?"

She gloomily surveyed the fire department, putting out the remaining blaze, leaving the half-charred remains of cabin four. Fortunately, other than the blown out part of the wall where the fireplace used to be, there didn't seem to be too much damage. As bombs go, the explosion was pretty small.

Doc crossed her arms and glared at her. "Were you always such a wuss?"

Next to her, Gregg Marks jumped on the bandwagon. "You're damn lucky you didn't lose your eye. Or worse. Now will you listen to me and stop digging in to this case?"

"I can't believe I'm saying this, but I agree with Marks." A voice with a hint of a Southern accent declared a few feet behind her. Casting a glance over her shoulder, much to Doc's irritation, she saw Jackson hurrying towards her.

*Shit, the one person she'd been avoiding.* Since The Hungry Puppy was on the other side of the brook, of course he'd heard the explosion and came running. She would have hidden her face in her hands except Doc had wised up and taken a firm hold of her jaw, tilting her head so she got a better and more stable view of the slice in her forehead, most likely from the blown window. *So much for having to worry about thinking of a clever name for that cabin.* The thought was so absurd she wondered if the doctor was right and she had a concussion to boot.

"There's no proof anyone tried to blow me up. It could have been—"

"Don't you dare finish that sentence if you're about to imply the explosion was my fault." Liam's hazel eyes flashed a darker green, fueled with righteous anger. "The fireplace was perfectly safe until someone used the timer as a detonator."

"'Fraid he's right, love," Poppy said. "Remember, we heard something ticking *after* he'd turned off the gas."

Stiches done, she was free of Doc's vice-like grip and able to see for herself that no one else had been hurt. She heaved a sigh of relief that the two of them were soot-stained and had a few minor scrapes but were okay. Then Liam took Poppy's hand, and she cringed. In hindsight, Liam's uncharacteristic grumpiness made sense. This whole time he'd been falling for the thief. How had she not seen that coming?

The shock of the explosion made this unexpected twist in their relationship a little easier to swallow. However, if her brother shot the waif-like cat burglar one more mooning, puppy love expression, they couldn't blame her for throwing up. Okay, the nausea might be the result of being thrown fifteen feet in the air and landing with a thud, but the hell if she'd admit it.

What worried her was she didn't recall any ticking. The last thing she remembered was entering the cabin.

Everything until she came to and saw Liam and Poppy in each other's arms was a fuzzy kaleidoscope. And was there any way to *unsee* them locked in an embrace?

But instead of admitting to her lapse of memory so they could hustle her off to the nearest hospital back down the damn mountain where she would spend the rest of her day being poked and prodded for nothing, she turned to the lot of them and declared, "You're right Liam, I'm sorry, this isn't your fault. But this dickhole made solving this case personal. I'm going to nail his ass, ringing ears or not."

There was a moment of stunned silence. *Oops, did I say the last part out loud?* Six different voices talked over each other all at once, demanding she go to the hospital for further tests.

"Liam, you remember the time you got knocked out at the track meet?"

The gaggle of protests turned into twitters of laughter. Mission accomplished.

"I played football for eight years and never had my bell rung," Marks scoffed. "How the hell did you get knocked out running around a track?"

Her brother shot Mel a heated glare. "I got hit by a stray shot put, it wasn't my fault!"

"How long were your ears ringing?"

He shrugged. "An hour? It wasn't a big deal. I don't remember."

Although his faulty memory didn't bolster her argument, she bulldozed over it. "Exactly my point. It's no biggie."

"Let's hope you're right," Poppy smirked, "because here comes a really big deal in her own tiny mind."

A sensible, dark grey American sedan carefully rounded the corner to lurch to a stop in the Babbling Brook's small parking lot. The door opened and out popped the diminutive Mrs. Oberdingle. She marched straight to Mel, disregarding the cut over her eye that surely was turning some spectacular colors already, and barked, "You're not having any sort of Valentine extravaganza, missy."

Waving her toned arm at the wreckage of cabin four where the fireman were focusing their efforts on the last of the dying embers, she added, "Yesterday it was a dead body in your backyard and today an explosion? This place is a public nuisance and I'm going to see to it my husband and the town council shuts you down."

She never understood why Mrs. Oberdingle had such a hard on for causing her trouble. First over the guest who died in her lobby, then the stupid Holiday Cookie Contest, and now this, but she was done. She hadn't even wanted to have any sort of Valentine's special in the first place, but now they were definitely having one.

"You know what? Suck it. You just try to stop us. Jackson, I'm booking The Hungry Puppy for the fourteenth. Poppy, call Gemma. I want hearts, balloons, pull out all the stops. Get the winery involved, all the things you talked about. Let's do this."

The mayor's wife spluttered in disbelief before harrumphing back to her car and driving off. The rest of the little group all stared at her open-mouthed like she'd lost her mind, so maybe confronting Mrs. Oberdingle wasn't the best idea.

Gregg and Jackson exchanged a look before the

latter murmured, "Why don't you go lie down until your ears stop ringing?"

The deputy bobbed his head in agreement. "You've had a pretty rough day." That was the first time they'd agreed on anything. Well, great, lucky her.

"They could have killed my grandmother. If she'd come with us or was walking by, she'd be dead. So no, I'm not napping. I'm going to find out who blew up *Innisfree* and put him in the darkest hole I can find."

Blank stares greeted her all around. Finally, Doc Hart asked, "Blew up the what now?"

"*Innisfree*." She jutted her chin out defiantly. The inspiration hit her to name the cabins and rooms references to Yeats' poetry for her grandparents' sake and that was the only one of his poems she could remember.

While the others continued to stare at her as if she'd lost her mind, Jackson asked, "Mel, can I please talk to you? It's important."

She knew what he wanted to talk about. She'd been avoiding his calls and texts all day, but she couldn't handle one more disaster. "Not now. I have a killer to catch."

If she hadn't wobbled as she pivoted on her heel and stormed back into the Babbling Brook, her exit might have kicked ass.

\*\*\*\*

The small lobby didn't prove to be the refuge she'd hoped for as Gregg Marks followed close on her heels. Only it was one hundred percent *Deputy* Marks, the cop and not her friend, who thrust his arm out to prevent her from retreating farther into her office.

"This time you're going to listen to me, Emmeline

O'Rourke, when I tell you to stay the hell out of my case. You need to accept you're not a cop anymore."

"Oh yeah? Well, you *professionals* haven't done jack shit to catch this killer."

He glared at her, muscles in his jaw twitching. "Maybe if you'd been honest from the jump, hadn't stolen evidence and covered up the identity of your little friend, we would have been looking in the right direction instead of going on some wild goose chase. We might have even made an arrest before he killed Leigh Pemberton.

"You keep recklessly poking your nose in, putting everyone around you in danger. I warned you before to back off. Are you finally going to listen, or do we have to keep finding bodies?"

Mel stared at him, wide-eyed in horror. Oh crap, was he right? Did a woman die because she kept playing at being a detective? She opened and closed her mouth a few times, but no words came out. Without another word, Marks jammed on his sheriff's department cowboy hat and left.

She stumbled to the chair behind the front desk and plopped down onto the worn cushion, all the fight knocked out of her. If her grandmother, an innocent bystander, or hotel guest was injured or killed because she kept digging into this case, she'd never forgive herself. Burying her head in her hands, she fought off the panic attack that lurked around the corner.

Then a light hand brushed across her shoulders. "C'mon love, I know just what you need."

"A cup of tea? No thanks," she ground out, still trying to scrub the image of Poppy and Liam from her mind.

"God no," the other woman said, laughter in her voice. "A stiff shot of whiskey and then a nice, soothing sound bath."

She groaned in protest, but it did no good. Her friend dragged her to her feet and out the lobby door.

\*\*\*\*

True to her word, the Brit stopped at the winery first, where they enjoyed a surprisingly decent scotch. Then she ushered her to the town center where tranquility awaited. Or so the sign to the small studio advertised, along with yoga, chanting, and breathwork. Whatever the hell that meant. And of course, sound baths.

As soon as they stepped inside, Mel was overcome by the cloud of incense filling the cramped reception area. Between the whiskey and the smell, she felt lightheaded. Or she might have to concede she had a teeny, tiny concussion.

"Ah yes, the folks who phoned earlier," the tall, willowy honey-blonde woman behind the counter greeted them after Poppy explained who they were and why they were there. "I'm Rachel, *namaste*. The bath will start in fifteen minutes. I'm running a little late, my apologies. Did you hear about the explosion this afternoon? I was one of the volunteer firefighters called to the scene. What a mess!"

Hearing her inn described as a "mess" when she'd been the victim of a bomber was more than a tad infuriating. "You don't say," she muttered, as she took in the various items for sale on the dark wood shelves draped with colorful scarves behind their host.

A display of familiar gemstones caught her eye. Unpolished and unfettered by the rustic copper wire settings of Kyle Lange's necklace, they appeared even less attractive than she remembered. Curious, she asked, "Are the rocks part of this sound thing?"

"You mean these precious and semi-precious gems?" Her words would have been snooty coming from someone like Mrs. Oberdingle, but Rachel's expression oozed kindness and warmth. "No, I sell these for healing. Gem therapy can impact both your physical and spiritual journey. Using numerology, we decide what gemstone you need to fulfill your life. Want to try it?"

A quick glance at the price tag on the rocks confirmed she was fine without them. Still emitting a Zen calm, their hostess led them into the studio and showed them where to store their shoes and bags. "Please, make yourself comfortable," she directed as she returned to the front where the dinging of an overhead bell announced more patrons had entered.

Easing her way to one of the two dozen colorful mats strewn in a semi-orderly fashion on the floor, Mel became painfully aware of every bump and bruise from this afternoon's adventure. She reconsidered the wisdom of letting Poppy talk her into this. Right now, the only bath that appealed to her was the kind with steaming hot water and lots of bubbles. She rubbed the back of her head. "Maybe I should go home and rest."

"Funny, you weren't whinging on about your boo boo when you belted down your shot of whiskey." Poppy grinned and handed her a folded blanket to cushion her head.

"Yeah, well, I can't imagine this is what the Doc meant when she said to take it easy."

"Nonsense," said a familiar voice. "This could be

just the ticket."

She bolted upright, wincing at the pain the sudden movement caused everywhere, surprised to see Doc Hart coming through the door. Grandma O and Liam had agreed with her that this was a stupid waste of time and rejected the invitation to join them in no uncertain terms, but surprisingly, the doctor had already planned on being there. The only thing she objected to was Poppy's presence after Mel told her she'd been right about the fake accent and fabricated past.

"For an ex-cop, you are way too trusting," her friend had harrumphed, and then dropped the subject when Mel remained resolute that everyone deserves a second chance.

The doctor squatted beside her on the floor and, taking her chin in her hand, checked her eyes again. "Pupils are okay, and the stitches are still in place." She continued to scrutinize her patient. "So why do you look worse than when I left you?"

"Deputy Marks gave her a right tongue lashing. Told her she was no cop and needed to stop pretending she was," Poppy answered before she could.

"Why are you still talking with that accent?" Doc asked, her sharp tone crackling with annoyance. "In fact, why are you talking at all?"

"Enough," she interrupted them. "He's right. I'm lucky nobody got hurt today. From here on out, I'm stepping back and letting him do his job." As they'd been chatting, the other patrons, bathers she supposed they were called, had been filing in, exchanging hushed greetings. The group was a mix of both men and women of a variety of ages, including the woman she recognized as the food delivery person.

Soon they were all reclined on their mats, some covering up with a blanket they either brought from home or borrowed from a set of shelves along the wall. Taking her cue from these presumably seasoned sound bath vets, Mel accepted an offered soft fuzzy throw and tried to relax, but found the whole experience disconcerting. Laying on the floor with her eyes closed among a cluster of strangers ran counter to every instinct she'd honed, not just as a cop, but also as a woman living in L.A. She felt too vulnerable. And stupid.

As soon as they'd all settled into their places, Rachel lit a few candles scattered throughout the small studio and dimmed the lights.

*She's a volunteer firefighter?* This has got to be breaking so many codes, Mel thought, unable to quiet the inner cynic.

Then their...bath leader? Sound guru? Whatever her title was, she gracefully sank down in the center of a u-shaped collection of bowls. They were a variety of shapes and sizes made of either copper or brass. There were a couple of larger crystal ones thrown in for good measure. She had no idea what any of them did until the woman started running a tiny wooden rolling pin with a suede wrapped handle around the rims of the bowls.

"For our newcomers, there's nothing you need to worry about doing except taking big breaths in and out of your nose, filling your tummy to let your body know it's safe," she said in hushed tones as she gave each bowl a test run. The thrumming each emitted was as irritating as the session Poppy had played for her on her phone. The good news was that since her ears were still ringing from the blast, the sound was muffled.

A few 'ohms' and other chants later and the noxious fumes of the incense weren't so bad after all. Or she'd gotten used to the smell. She wasn't sure when it had happened, but at some point Mel had actually blissed out. The humming of the bowls *was* soothing, mellowing her mood into peaceful serenity. Or was the incense really pot? She tried for once not to over analyze the why and enjoy this tranquil vibe.

That's when it hit her from out of the blue. She hadn't been able to remember what made her stop and turn toward the road right before the explosion, but now she did. She'd heard the squeal of tires and turned to see who was speeding away. They might have been running because they'd planted the bomb.

Then she'd paused for a split second because she realized there wasn't the usual roar of an engine that accompanied squealing tires. Right before the blast, she saw one of those odd hybrid SUVs. She remembered seeing the same two-toned car at Brown's tree rally. But did it belong to him, one of his groupies, or the company trying to cut the tree down?

She sat up with a start, cuing Poppy to ask, "Are you alright, love?"

She nodded and lay back down, needing time to think and too afraid of pissing off the other Zen-sters if she walked out in the middle of the bath. Although she closed her eyes and tried to get back into the sound bath, her racing brain made it impossible. Step away, she kept telling herself, tell Marks what you remembered and then step away.

After it was over, they put their shoes on, gathered their jackets and headed toward the door. Poppy bounded over, beaming, with the owner of the studio in tow. "You won't believe what Rachel just told me."

*Then let's skip it and move on?* She was tired and irritated at being relegated to the old and worn-out pile, but maybe it's where she belonged.

"Go on, love," she nudged the reedy woman. "Tell her what you told me."

"Well," she hesitated, giving the brunette a sidelong glance as if to say, *why am I doing this again?* "Your friend here asked about the crystals and stones in the lobby, if there was one to help with anxiety. I told her you choose the stone depending on your life path. Once we figure out your path, carrying the stone with you will help you fix the problem."

Doc Hart snorted in disbelief and she had to agree. She'd try a lot of things to overcome her sudden fear of heights, but couldn't see how a rock was going to help. However, the sound bath had been refreshing, so she didn't want to be rude to the woman. "How...interesting. How do you go about choosing your life path?"

"Oh, it's all based on numerology. We take the numbers from your birthday, add them until we get a single digit, and the stone matching the number is the one you need."

Brows furrowed as she pondered this, Mel asked, "How does knowing the number help you pick a rock?"

"Each of the nine gemstones has a number value. For instance, rose quartz is a nine. If the numbers from your birthday add up to nine, that's the stone you need." The woman gave a shy smile. "I get it. Gem therapy sounds a little odd, but the power of gems and the numbers they relate to is an ancient belief."

There was never a shortage of whacky ideologies,

she supposed. However, she didn't see what this had to do with her until a gleam flashed in her friend's eye she understood where she was going with this.

"No, absolutely not. I don't care what the sum of the stones on that necklace is or what the number represents. Talk to Deputy Marks if you're so sure this is the big clue he's been searching for." She moved toward the door but Poppy blocked her way. She pulled out her phone and showed a picture of the hideous necklace to Rachel.

"What about these stones? Do they have any meaning for you?"

"May I?" the woman asked, gesturing toward the phone. She eagerly handed it over. "Love your accent, by the way."

"Thank you," she answered with a triumphant grin. Doc made a growling noise but said nothing.

The sound guru expanded the picture to get a closer look. "Together, they aren't very harmonious. For instance, the rose quartz next to the aquamarine is, well, not the most attractive combination and work at odds. One brings you peace if you're troubled, while the other increases passion. If you're asking if there's a message in the stones, I don't see one. Sorry."

The feeling that they were on the right track was undeniable, however. This could be the key to unlocking the motive behind the two murders and the attack on her hotel. Her resolve to stay out of the case waivered. What harm was there in gathering the intel and giving it to Marks?. "What about the numbers? Can you write down the number sequence of the stones?"

Within minutes, she'd written the sequence of numbers. "I don't know what the small black stones are," she pointed to the picture, "but these are the numbers for the rest." On the paper she'd jotted down eleven numbers—5, 2, 0, 7, 5, 7, 3, 1, 2, 5, and 9.

"Maybe a combination for something?" Doc asked.

"There's too many numbers for a usual rotary safe or combination lock." Mel frowned, but agreed it looked like a combination or a passcode. She turned to Poppy. "Could this be for a digital safe where you assign the numbers?"

"Some have as many as nine, depending on the make and model, but I've never seen eleven. Eleven," she repeated in an even odder accent than normal, and waggled her eyebrows.

"What are you doing?"

"You know, 'eleven,' because it's louder?" When she got no response from anyone except a giggle from the doctor, the cat burglar shrugged. "The safe in his office was the regular old tumbler type.

She clenched her fist in frustration. They were so close, they nearly had the clue that would tie everything together, she was sure of it. This case started with the necklace and Mel felt it in her bones that's where they'd find the answer to who killed Lange and why. Then she reminded herself she only got this information to give to Marks, and that's what she was going to do. Finding out what the stones and numbers meant wasn't her problem, she thought bitterly, as she stuffed the folded paper into her jacket pocket.

"It's too bad we don't know someone who's really good at numbers." Doc snarked.

"Nope, not going to happen." Besides his science background, Jackson liked numbers. However, she'd been dodging his calls ever since she found out he was leaving. There was no way she was going to ask a favor now after she'd been such a jerk.

Decision made, she reached for the door when it flew open and an angry Jackson Thibodeaux, still wearing his apron, stood between her and escape. "I am so done with you ignoring me. You are going to listen to what I have to say and then if you never want to speak to me again, that's fine with me."

Chapter Nineteen

A dozen different thoughts bounced off each other in her already aching head, making it hard for Mel to decide what to say. When she finally made a choice, even she had to admit it wasn't the most relevant question.

"How did you know where to find me?"

"Stephanie posted about the sound bath on her social media site a half an hour ago," he answered, like it was the most obvious thing in the world.

"Who the hell is Stephanie?" Instead of things becoming clearer, his answers confused her all the more.

"Your food delivery driver? The one who likes to stop and chat?" The name rang a bell, and she remembered the familiar face in the class but hadn't put two and two together. "Everyone follows her to keep up on what's going on. Three people came into the restaurant to tell me all about your exciting day in the last twenty minutes." His explanation was laced with impatience. "We need to talk, and you're not getting out of it this time."

"This town is so weird," she muttered, unable to wrap her head around the idea that anyone even cared enough to gossip about this silly sound bath thing. "Fine, let's talk, but not here." She gave Poppy and Doc Hart a pointed glare. Both women glanced away, the pictures of innocence.

Taking in her surroundings, she spotted a bench in the little park across the street. It was too cold to comfortably sit outside, which meant they'd have to keep this short and that was okay with her. "Over there," she suggested, pointing to the park.

"And freeze my *cajones* off? Not hardly. I have a better idea." He took her hand and led her to a dark corner on the porch of The Hungry Puppy. It was a short walk, but her heart ached at the intimacy of his hand holding hers. They'd never shared such tenderness before, and this might be the last time.

He lit the portable heating tower, the orange glow from the gas flames the only light. Sitting down next to her, he clasped both of her hands in his. She fought hard to keep the tears at bay.

"My mother told you I was going to New Orleans, but she didn't tell you why."

*Because I kissed you and scared you off, forcing you to run to New Orleans?* But that wouldn't have been a smart thing to say. "To work at Chef Adèle's restaurant, I already know all of this and I'm happy for you Jackson, I really am."

"True, I will spend some time learning from Chef, but that's not the real reason. My mother has been diagnosed with lung cancer."

"Oh my God, I'm so sorry," she stammered, giving his hands a gentle squeeze.

He glanced at their joined hands, the corner of his perfect mouth curling up as he stroked his thumbs along the back of her hands. "I didn't find out until Chef Adèle told me when I called to turn down her offer. The crazy thing is, she never smoked a day in her life.

Fortunately, they caught it early." His gaze shifted to meet hers. "I'm leaving in a couple of weeks to be with her for the surgery and the recovery time after. She'll need someone around for a while and Chef can't take off work to be with her."

"I thought she had family in the area? What about them?" She hoped he didn't misconstrue her question a whiny demand. She was genuinely curious why his mother had no one else to turn to.

"They'll be there too." His smile twisted into a more cynical smirk. "I'm pretty sure my mother thinks once she gets me there, she'll convince me to stay, but she won't succeed. I will be back. This is my home now."

And that's the moment her eyes started to leak. She pulled a hand away from his to wipe away the offending drop of moisture. He put his palm to her cheek and smiled. "I'll be back," he repeated. "I promise."

A comfortable silence settled between them, as no more words were necessary.

"Ask him about the numbers," a loud British whisper demanded from behind a nearby tree.

"For the love of God," she muttered, shaking her head in embarrassment.

He took his hand away from her face and grinned. She immediately missed the warmth of his touch. "You want to tell me what this number thing is about? I don't think they're going away."

"Come on out," she directed and was startled to see not just Poppy but Doc Hart emerge as well. At least her two friends had found common ground. Jackson drew two more chairs closer to the heater, and the ladies settled in as she pulled the paper with the number code out of her pocket.

"Remember the ugly necklace I showed you a picture of?"

He gave an exaggerated shudder of horror. "Kind of hard to forget."

"We believe the stones hold the secret to Lange's enzyme I told you about the other day."

"The one that can digest oil spills?" he asked, his curiosity piqued.

"We might have found a clue to cracking the code, but I'm not sure." She handed the paper to him and turned on her cell phone flashlight to make it easier to read. Briefly recounting the number system from Rachel at the sound bath, she finished with, "It's a good theory, but we can't figure out what the numbers relate to. Do they mean anything to you? Could they be a mathematical formula?"

His cupid bow lips thinned as he studied the paper. "That's not like any kind of formula I've ever seen. Could be a phone number?"

She shook her head. "U.S. phone numbers are ten digits unless you count the 'one' to start, and this starts with a five."

He continued making guesses as he researched something on his phone. "Bank account numbers? A computer password?"

"We can check with the banks in the morning, but hiding a secret account number in a necklace seems so over the top," Poppy chimed in, her low opinion of Lange's theatrics obvious from the scowl on her face.

He chuckled at his phone. "I thought the numbers might be a location, but they're the latitude and longitude of a tiny little town in Wales called Hay-on-Wye. I think it's a solid bet your murder victim didn't go all the way to the middle of nowhere Wales to bury his secret formula."

Mel squared her shoulders, resolved to do what she should have from the start. "Ah, but he's not my murder victim, is he? He's Deputy Marks' problem." She stood, holding Jackson's gaze as he joined her. "Thank you for telling me about your mom. You take care of her. I'll keep an eye on your dad and Chewie while you're gone."

She crunched through the snow that was turning to ice in the dropping nighttime temperature, pondering whether to give Marks this information before or after a glass of wine.

**\*\*\*\***

Mel entered her office, wineglass in hand, to find her grandmother once again clacking away on the computer and smiled. "I'm going to have to get you one of your own if you stay much longer."

"What you're going to have to get me is a glass of whiskey. What kind of grandma would I be if I let you drink alone?"

Moments later she returned with the amber, peaty-smelling Scotch the old woman liked and slunk down in the chair opposite her. Grandma O stopped typing and studied her until she broke under the pressure. Running a hand through her now mussed auburn bob, she asked, "Do I have something in my hair? On my face? What are you looking at?"

"A quitter, apparently," she said, but what stung more than her words was her soft tone. She could take her grandmother being harsh—nice granny was unbearable.

"You heard Marks, and he's right. I have to learn to stay in my lane."

The old woman made a rude raspberry sound before taking a sip from her tumbler. "Did you know Colonel Sanders was sixty-five and tired of living on his pittance of a pension when he came up with his famous recipe for fried chicken?"

"You've tasted my cooking," she laughed. "I don't see a future for me in creating the next fast food mega-hit."

"No, you ninny. Don't make me come over there and smack you. I'm saying plenty of people told him he was too old, that he didn't know anything about the restaurant business, blah, friggity blah. But he believed in himself and his God-given talent and the next thing you know, there's a bucket of chicken everywhere you look. You, my dear, have a talent for unraveling mysteries, you always have. If you want to keep digging, don't let some blowhard in a cowboy hat stop you."

"But I could have gotten you, or some innocent bystander, killed."

"No deary, the person responsible for destroying *Innisfree* is the killer. Nice name, by the way."

"Thanks," she mumbled, her mind spinning. Grandma O might have a point. She wanted to solve the puzzle of the meaning of the necklace, at least. What could it hurt to work on that?

"Also, no body shops in Palm Springs repainted a car matching the description of Lange's or any vandalized vehicle. I called while you were taking your woo-woo nap."

"So either Kyle lied to Oliver, or Oliver lied to us," she reasoned out loud. Something clicked in the back of her mind, but she wasn't sure what. "Can you show me Oliver's social media friends again?"

Handing her the empty tumbler, she said, "For another whiskey, I'll show you whatever you need."

When Mel returned with a fresh refill, she found her grandmother going over all the posts and picture in his Friends group. "See anything interesting?" Grandma O asked with a cat that ate the canary smile. She leaned in to study the computer screen more closely.

"They all have the same patch on their Army jackets."

"It's called a 'crab'. All the military branches share that one particular insignia. Wanna take a guess what it means?" The woman's eyes sparkled as she took a sip of whiskey, giving Mel time to work it out. She studied the photos again. There was no way they were Special Forces. Those had different insignias, and some of these guys were downright scrawny. What did the meaning of the patch have to do with...oh.

"Bomb disposal?"

Her grandmother touched a bony finger to the end of her nose. "Bingo."

If they could defuse bombs, how big a stretch was it that Oliver also knew how to make one? "Okay, so he's got the means, but not the motive. And it doesn't change the fact he's got a rock solid alibi. His hundreds, er," she looked at the number of viewers watching at this moment, "well, dozens anyway of followers watching his live feed who can testify he was in that tree when the cabin exploded and both Lange and Pemberton were killed."

"Maybe he got help from one of his buddies?" her grandmother suggested.

"Or he's not in his tree at all," Poppy offered from the doorway, phone in her hand. "I've been watching for the last few minutes since you started talking about him and—"

"You were eavesdropping?" Mel sputtered.

"Aw, you were having such a cute bonding moment. I didn't want to disturb you. Anyway, watch this." She strode around behind the desk and enlarged the image for the tree-cam on the computer. As directed, the three of them never took their eyes off the monitor.

"There!" Mel exclaimed. A tiny glitch flitted on the screen. The threesome re-watched the scene until, after seeing the glitch repeat five times, they were certain the video wasn't live but a loop.

Should she tell Marks? Thank God she hadn't called him about the wacky gem number idea or he'd bitch about her being a nuisance caller. The video loop theory would be pretty easy to prove. If she drove to the tree now and he's not there, she'd call Marks and tell him what she found. His motive was still a big blank hole, but she'd tackle one problem at a time.

"But what if he's there, or returns to the tree by the time we get there?" Poppy asked.

"We?" Mel scowled at her.

"Granted, you made it out onto a balcony to find the blood on the railing, huzzah. There's no way you can climb that tree to prove if he's there or not by yourself. You *need* me." The tiny woman stood with her legs wide and her hands on her hips. The picture was ridiculous, but she had a point.

Marla A. White

"Alright, fine, *we'll* go visit Oliver's tree boat. Grandma, keep an eye on the video and call us the minute something changes. If we're right and the boat is empty, we'll call Marks from there. Sound good?"

"Sounds like a great way to stir up a hornet's nest, but I've got my anti-stinger salve," Grandma said, toasting them with her whiskey.

On her way out, Mel texted Liam to give him a heads up. If she'd told him in person, he would have insisted on coming. Having the two love birds staring dreamily at each other was enough to make her hurl, not to mention the mountain curves at night. Besides, someone had to watch over the inn and lock up the Scotch.

****

With Poppy behind the wheel of her sports car, they made the trek to Brown's tree in record time. There was no other vehicle parked there, making a strong case for the theory that he'd found a way to venture from his post with no one any the wiser. Still, they'd need to look in the boat he was camped out in to be sure. The waning moon offered very little light in this small section of unscathed forest, so if they were going to check the boat out, they had to do it quickly but carefully.

Standing at the base of the tree, Mel blamed her quaking knees on the sharp hairpin turns they barely survived. Her trembling had nothing to do with gazing at the boat hanging what seemed like a lot higher than when she last visited. She'd climbed to the platform before, but that was in the daylight and night had thoroughly fallen, making it difficult to see her footholds. Poppy cupped her hands to give her a boost

288

again when she had an attack of vertigo. The tree, the boat, everything was spinning. She put a hand out to steady herself. "God dammit," she ground out, "I thought I was done being such a wuss."

"First off, just because you have a phobia doesn't make you weak." Still using her faux British accent, but in a softer tone, her friend put her hand on Mel's shoulder. "And secondly...or is it second off? Anyway, the spins are probably a result of the concussion you deny, but almost certainly do have. Let me do this for you?"

She gave a shaky nod of agreement. She'd wanted to do this, to prove to herself she was normal again, but the speed with which the slender woman made the climb proved she'd made the right choice. "What are you, part freaking squirrel?"

Moments later, the brunette popped her head over the side of the boat. "He's not here. You were right, he must have a video loop he sets to play on his Friends page, freeing him to pop wherever he pleases on his murder spree." She put the extra emphasis on "murder," in that distinctly British way. Mel chuckled.

"Take a picture of the scene so we can text it to Deputy Marks as proof that he's not here even when Friends says he is," she instructed.

From out of nowhere, a whisper quiet, two-toned electric SUV appeared on the scene. He turned off the headlights that would have warned her a car was coming in an obvious and successful attempt to come and go undetected. Oliver Brown jumped out and slammed the door.

"You just couldn't leave it alone, could you?" The fury in the man's voice combined with the familiar sound of the racking of a gun as he loaded a round in the chamber shot icy cold fear down her spine. He approached her, careful to stay more than an arm's length away. "I tried to warn you off with that little fireworks show, but you just can't take a hint. Put your hands where I can see them."

"Little fireworks?" she screeched as she complied with his demand. "You blew up *Innisfree*, you dick." She realized scolding a killer wasn't her smartest move, but the words escaped before she could stop them.

His rage turned into confusion, so maybe it wasn't such a terrible choice after all. "Who the fuck is Innisfree? I made sure the cabin was empty. I didn't want to hurt anyone."

"Really? Tell that to Kyle Lange and Leigh Pemberton." She hadn't meant to say that part out loud, but from his hard expression, she must have. "Sorry," she said in all sincerity, "I hit my head in your explosion and I think it rattled my brain more than I realized."

She schooled herself not to look at the tree. The smartest thing Poppy could do was hide there and call for help. Her best shot would be if she kept him talking. "Why did you do it? Why kill Lange after he turned over a new leaf and was working to save the environment, not destroy it?"

"Because he's a lying piece of shit," he spat at her. "The enzyme? All part of his con to trick people who care about this planet to donate to develop it. His magical cure never existed." His cool, professional grip on the gun tightened until his knuckles shown white.

"So, what was the necklace for?" She knew exactly what the necklace was now—a Macguffin, a prop to fool gullible, kind donors into padding his bank account. But the more enraged Oliver, got the more distracted he became.

"It was garbage! The reason he had that thief steal the thing was to keep me from getting it and revealing his pack of lies. And she'd better get down out of that tree in the next five minutes or I'll blow your head off."

*Shit.* She'd hoped he'd arrived too late to notice Poppy. The leaves on the tree rustled and her friend dropped to the ground in one of those super hero landings. She rose and stood shoulder to shoulder with Mel, then took a half step behind her. She glared at her, getting a shrug in return as she raised her hands.

"I warned him not to go through with his plan for one last funding push or I would destroy him. I gave him a chance, and he threw it in my face." Oliver circled around, his back to the tree as he faced both women.

"Oh, *you* left him that note," Poppy said with a sigh of relief. "It has been driving me barmy since we found it. But it wasn't much of a warning if he never got it, was it? It was still in the envelope taped to the bathroom mirror of his cabin."

"That's how big of an arrogant asshole he was. He *called* me to say he read my note weeks ago and kept it because my threat made him laugh every time he saw it. He brought it with him when he came to Pine Cove with his boyfriend and they both got a great big guffaw over the idea a dumb Army grunt like me could take him down. Well, who's laughing now?"

Yikes, Peter Mullins was smart to leave town when he did, or he really might have been next. She was sweating from fear and tension as he carelessly waved the gun, but her curiosity overruled caution. "But why kill Pemberton?

"I warned her she'd be next if she didn't return the money, but she refused. She left me no choice. Talk about gullible. I convinced her to meet me here, that I'd found the formula. Killed her right over there, in fact." He pointed to a nearby tree.

That answered the question of whether she was in on the con. She believed there was a formula and died trying to profit from it. "So the story about Lange's car being vandalized was a lie?"

His smirk made her want to slap him except for the gun in his hand. "You were so busy playing detective, I had you chasing your tail all over town." He didn't add the words "stupid idiot," but the curl of his upper lip did the talking for him.

The darkness was suddenly illuminated by two sheriffs' department vehicles. Mel squinted at the bright lights and saw a familiar tall, broad-shouldered figure in a cowboy hat behind the door of one of them, weapon at the ready.

"Turns out she isn't such a bad detective after all. Drop the gun and keep your hands where I can see them."

In the tense moments as Brown seemed to weigh his options, Mel interjected, "Jesus took you long enough, Marks." Her words were harsh, but her smile was meant to soften the blow. "Were you going to wait until he shot me before popping out of the woods?"

"The idea had occurred to me," a grin played on his lips before returning his focus to the man still holding a gun. "Drop the weapon now, sir. I won't ask again."

Both women's bodies sagged in relief at the heavy

thud of Brown's gun hitting the dirt. The deputies from the second car swarmed him, cuffed him, and read him his rights as they hustled him toward their SUV with practiced precision. Gregg Marks bagged the weapon before facing Mel.

"This was a nice bit of detective work, especially the part where you called for backup and gave us time to get into position. I still don't understand why you had to be here at all." His right eyebrow slashed upward as he glared at her.

"Stop trying to scare me with your mean scowl. You know perfectly well he was never going to confess to you and if the only proof we had was that he's a dipshit who lied to his fans and left his tree to get some food. He'd never go down for the murders."

He shook his head but let out a pent-up sigh/chuckle combination that meant things were okay between them. "We had the footage from the road cameras that proved he was in the area of both crimes."

"Oh, you mean the road cameras I suggested you check out?" She crossed her arms, knowing she was pushing it, poking the bear, and was relieved when he rolled his eyes but kept smiling. "Which only confirmed he was in the area. You needed this confession and you're welcome."

Gregg Marks put his hands on her shoulders and studied her with such sincerity, she squirmed in discomfort. "Mel, you're a good cop, but you take way too many chances. Promise me you won't pull a crazy stunt like this again."

"Don't worry, Deputy, I'm leaving all the detecting to big strong men like you," she said sarcastically, and hoped her rebuttal wasn't too subtle for him. "I'll stick with learning how to run my inn. Know anything about branding?"

"Not unless you're talking about a hot iron to a cow's behind." He grinned at her with, she had to admit, a charming twinkle in those blue eyes.

Chapter Twenty

The bed-and-breakfast was fully booked for their first Valentine's Day extravaganza. That meant Mel had to share her quarters with her cousin Gemma, who had come up early to help oversee the event she'd been so critical to making happen. The small space was a little crowded, but she was happy to get to spend some alone time with another member of her tribe. The days flew by, and before she knew it, the big night was here. They were both giddy with a mix of fear and excitement.

"You must be proud. Your debut solo social media campaign is a tremendous success," she complimented the younger woman. Gemma had the characteristic O'Rourke auburn hair, although hers was a shade or two darker than Mel's and shown more coppery in the afternoon sun as the two of them finished decorating the Great Room for tonight's pre-dinner wine and cheese tasting.

"A bit more to the right, love," Poppy called out, limiting her assistance to telling them what to do.

"Who made you the boss?" Mel scowled, but nobody bought the grumpy act, particularly not the ex-cat burglar. Shortly after they helped bring Oliver Brown to justice, she disappeared after lunch one day. The hole her absence left was painful, and she could have kicked herself for getting so attached to the thief. She'd been clear from the start she wanted to return to

L.A. as soon as she could, so why did she feel so abandoned?

Hours later, when she reappeared with a few bags containing the rest of her belongings, Mel was embarrassed at her relief and joy. Poppy informed her she had a new assistant manager whether she wanted one or not, but the truth was she desperately did. She needed the extra pair of hands while she took her first hospitality management course.

Not that Grandma O'Rourke wasn't a big help. She'd made the startling declaration that she refused to go back home, having found a purpose in life at the inn. Her untapped computer talents came in handy doing the bookkeeping her granddaughter despised. Oddly, the busier she was, the less cranky she became. But, as much as she loved having her family with her, she'd come to value Poppy as a friend. An annoying, pushy, and at times flakey friend, yet someone she could count on when it mattered. Not to mention she created mouth-watering breakfasts that earned them those all-important five-star reviews on travel sites.

Her brother Liam had gone back home to L.A. soon after the embers from *Innisfree* had cooled enough to be hauled away. A successful contractor with his own booming business, he couldn't stay forever, but she was grateful for the time he gave the inn. However, considering the budding romance he had going on with Poppy, she wasn't surprised he returned for the Valentine's promotion. When she told him they didn't have any rooms to spare for him, he'd given a throaty chuckle and informed her it wouldn't be a problem. She appreciated the extra hands pulling the wine tasting and dinner event together and tried not to dwell too much on the sleeping arrangement.

"Look, it really *is* Christ on a cracker," Grandma O exclaimed as she set out the snacks for the afternoon's festivities. They had teamed with On Cloud Wine to throw the wine and cheese tasting, exclusively for their guests. Mel checked the clock on the wall and sighed. Any minute now, Geoff, the wine bar's manager, would be here with the wine and glasses and none of them were dressed yet. However, the wonder in her grandmother's usually surly voice demanded their attention. Exchanging dubious glances, the other four dropped the decorations they were hanging to see what she was talking about.

On the long table that normally held their breakfast beverages, now covered with a tablecloth sporting hearts and cupids, was a platter of locally made water crackers their grandmother had arranged in an artful display. She gestured to one in the center. "See, it's Jesus!"

They bent over, peering at the cracker in question. There was nothing there but some vague tan splotches, reminding her she really did need to get her grandmother's eyesight checked out. She debated whether they should murmur agreement when the old woman cackled.

"Suckers," she snorted before returning to the kitchen for the rest of the food. The four chuckled at Grandma O's prank, but when Gemma and Poppy went back to finish decorating, Liam put his hand on Mel's arm.

"I missed this Mel, the one who smiles so easily. And I don't mean since your accident. The past few years, you were always so stressed, so serious."

"I was a little busy busting bad guys," she replied without anger or bitterness.

"Whatever you do, you're all in, one hundred percent, and I think that's great," her brother added hurriedly when she started to protest, "but you know the picture of us climbing together? Where you have a big shit-eating grin? We took it four years ago. You hadn't taken any time off to have fun after that until you were forced to. Murdering psychos aside, you seem carefree, more relaxed here. I'm happy for you."

Then he surprised her with a hug before returning to the rest of the decorating committee, brushing Poppy's lips with a light kiss as they strung the last of the hearts from the fake stuffed bear head hanging on the wall. She'd be nauseated at this side of him that she'd never seen before if it wasn't so sweet.

Finished dressing the tables, her younger cousin sidled next to Mel and the two of them took in the fruits of everyone's labors. "You ready?" Gemma asked.

"No time like the present, right?" She squeezed her cousin's hand, as exhilarated as the day they bought the place, excited about the start of a new adventure.

"Hey everyone, before you all go to change—and yes, Grandma, you have to put on something nice," she over-rode the protest she knew was coming the moment the old woman opened her mouth. "I have a small announcement to make. As you know, Gemma here browbeat me into this branding nonsense, and together, we think we've found the answer. Let me officially welcome you to The Brook."

Off to the side, her cousin hoisted a mockup of the new name and logo. Written in maroon letters against a forest green background, the look was simple and clean.

Two things she valued highly, according to the workbook she'd finally filled out.

"Thank the Good Lord Baby Jesus," her grandmother said, "that Babbling Brook thing was a mouthful to say when you answered the phone." Everyone laughed. More than once Mel had flubbed it herself.

"Aw, those are the same colors as your Ren Faire outfit," Poppy cooed. Her cheeks flamed hot in embarrassment as Liam hooted and even her cousin bit back a laugh.

"You didn't tell me you had a Ren Faire outfit." Gemma's words were filled with awe and a little envy.

She rubbed her hand over her right eye to keep it from twitching, as it was wont to do in times of stress or humiliation. "How the hell did you find out about that?"

"Poppet, if you don't want people to know, you shouldn't post photos on social media."

Before they could all check out the pictures on their phones, Mel regained control of this impromptu meeting. "Okay, okay, settle down, there's more. Since it was brought to my attention that cabin numbers aren't very whimsical and are definitely off-brand, in honor of Grandpa O'Rourke we're going to give each room and cabin a name taken from the poetry of William Butler Yeats, his favorite writer."

"Great, back to the tongue-twisters," her grandmother grumbled, but at the same time wiped a tear from her eye.

"We'll choose the easy ones, I promise. I wanted to to celebrate him even though he's no longer with us because at the end of the day, the brand for this place is family." At the mention of family, Poppy's smile faded, so she added, "All of our family, the ones we're born to and the ones we choose." Her friend's face brightened as she gave Liam's hand a little squeeze. "All right, let's clean up and get ready to welcome our guests."

\*\*\*\*

Nothing with the O'Rourkes ever went off without a hitch. One guest ate some bleu cheese without realizing what it was and broke out in hives. Liam did a spit take when he found out how much per bottle the wine he was sipping cost and Gemma, unused to drinking alcohol since she'd just turned twenty-one, got tipsy. Her grandmother, however, was on her best behavior, charming even, which frightened Mel all the more.

The event was more or less a success for the local winery and cheese maker as they gave out over a dozen cards to guests who vowed to come and buy their wares during their stay in Pine Cove.

The dinner at The Hungry Puppy was all that she had hoped for and then some. Jackson and his staff outdid themselves with decorations, three courses of delicious California cuisine, and an inviting atmosphere. They'd gone so far as to light a fire in the café's fireplace, the flickering flames adding to the romance of the night.

The only sad part was it would be the last meal he'd be making for a while. At least here in Pine Cove. His plane to New Orleans would leave in a couple of days. As the servers passed out the dessert choices, Mel glanced around, hoping to spot their host.

"Relax, Baker Boy will put in an appearance. He always does," Gregg cynically assured her. Since

Gemma opted to stay at The Brook to nurse her baby hangover, when the deputy appeared at the door, Poppy brazenly flagged him down to take the empty seat. She'd been surprised to see him at a Valentine's Day dinner without a date, let alone in a suit and tie. It seemed like a long way to go if he didn't have a woman to impress, but to each his own. Then she spotted Jackson heading toward them and forgot all about the deputy's civilian attire.

He must have made some very Gregg-ish remark she missed, because her grandmother said, "Don't worry son, you'll have two weeks while he's gone to get her to gawk at you like that. Unless they're right and absence makes the heart grow fonder. Then you're screwed."

"Grandma!" she hissed, embarrassed and sympathetic as Gregg's face turned pink. Eager to escape whatever that was all about, she stood and met Jackson halfway across the dining room.

"Well, get a load of you," he murmured seductively, "don't you clean up nice?"

She'd let Poppy talk her into a deep maroon colored dress for the occasion that complimented her red hair. The A-line shape and velvet material accentuated all the right curves. It was too bad the vintage styled garb would have to go back to the store after tonight, especially from his appreciative smile. The hunger in his eyes was almost enough to take her mind off the painful high heels that, although difficult to walk in, raised her to the correct height to reach those kissable lips.

"Thanks, you don't look too bad yourself." He'd ditched the plaid shirt, jeans, and chef's apron she saw him in earlier in favor of a tailored charcoal grey suit. His tie and pocket square were almost the same shade of red as her dress.

"What, this ol' thing?" He gave her a slow, sexy grin. "The food's all made, the kids can handle the service, and I thought being with a pretty lady dressed in such finery called for something more…grown up." They stood there for a moment, wrapped in awkward silence.

If there'd been music, they might have danced, but Mrs. Oberdingle held them to the strict letter of the law, which meant food and alcohol only. A dance floor apparently would have been a public safety hazard. And there she was, sitting with her husband near the windows, keeping an eye out to make sure the fun factor didn't get out of control. She childishly stuck her tongue out at the woman, who blinked back in shock, before dragging him to her table.

In her absence, Doc Hart had joined the family. "So, did the ballistics match?" she asked Gregg, "Was Oliver Brown's gun the weapon used to murder Lange?"

Ever since she'd returned to the table with Jackson, Gregg had this weird, lost demeanor. He snatched hold of the question about the case like a lifeline. "Yep. We used his recorded confession as leverage to get an official statement, and he admitted to everything. I won't go into the details about Ms. Pemberton's demise since we just got through eating, but needless to say Brown used skills as a hunter who was used to field dressing his kills."

Mel scrunched her face in disgust. "Thanks for *not* going into it, Marks."

He gave her a casual shrug, the corner of his mouth kicking upward. "What can I say, detective? So far you're batting two for two. What's your next case, finding D. B. Cooper? Recovering the Nazi gold train?"

"You are such an ass, but I've got enough on my plate learning to run an inn. You were right. From now on I'm leaving solving crimes to you professionals." And she meant every word. So why was everyone shaking their heads and smirking at her?

"Can I borrow you for a moment?" Jackson murmured in her ear, but then he needed to be close to be heard over the hoots of derision from her brother. She nodded and followed him out the door to the front porch, stepping outside of the circle of light.

"When you come back from New Orleans, are you going to be all '*chere*' this '*mon ami*'—" She never got to finish her sentence as he crushed her against his chest and covered her mouth with his own. His lips were as soft yet demanding as she remembered, and the intensity of his kiss took her breath away. When he finally broke it off, she teetered unsteadily in those damnable heels.

"We may not get to have much alone time together before I leave, and I've been wanting to do that ever since I saw you walk in the door." He rested his forehead against hers and she breathed in the smells of pine, fresh baked bread, and cinnamon that made up his own unique fragrance.

"I'm going to miss you, Jackson Thibodeaux. You'd better come back home."

He threw his head back and laughed before his aquamarine eyes met hers. She was serious. Not prone to believing in premonitions, she did believe in hunches and her gut warned her something would keep him in New Orleans. Knowing his mother, it would include a boatload of guilt and possibly even a length of chain. He tried to lighten her darkening mood.

"Sweetheart, I'm just helping my mother until she's back on her feet from her surgery. Two weeks, tops. I swear." Then he kissed her again and despite the chilly temperatures, she would have been happy to stay where they were except the first of the dinner guests clomped out the door. Their lips parted, but he kept his arms circled around her. She was sure he meant what he said, but she couldn't shake the feeling something was going to go wrong.

Epilogue

For a Friday night, the Pine Cove climbing gym was packed with families, a scout pack, a few teenage jocks, and the brood from The Brook. Their eyes bore into her back as she stood three handholds from the top of the fake vertical face wall. Sweat dripped down her spine even though the air conditioning was on full blast. Heart thundering, her hands were clammy and, oh goody, her left leg started to shake.

"C'mon love, you got this!" Poppy cheered from below. Doc Hart added an ear-piercing whistle for encouragement.

She willed her legs to push up from her crouched position to get her in range of the second to last handhold, but they just weren't listening.

"Are you climbing that wall or dry humping it?" her grandmother barked. Gasps from shocked parents echoed off the walls of the gym. Mel hung her head in embarrassment, although secretly laughing at the same time,

Gritting her teeth, she pulled herself to the final toehold, stretched out her right hand, then her left and she'd done it—she made it to the top! The applause from her fan club buoyed her spirits for a moment until she remembered whose voice wasn't there.

Three months ago, Jackson assured her he'd only be gone two weeks and yet he still had no set date for his return. Worse, he usually joined her weekly climbs by video chat, but today he left a voicemail saying he couldn't make it but would talk soon. *Crap.* She was mooning like a teenager. If she didn't snap out of this funk, the next thing you know, she'd start crying. She had to accept he was gone. That's okay, she didn't need him, anyway.

"Look at me, at the top of the climbing wall. I'm king of the world," she murmured under her breath to psych herself up.

And then two little girls chased each other to the top of the wall and then back down again like monkeys, giggling the whole way. She sighed, resisting the urge to bang her head against the wall. Careful not to glance down, she peered over her shoulder and shouted, "I'm coming down so mind the belay line."

"What? I'm not holding your rope, you pussy. Rappel down like a badass." There was friendly laughter in Gregg's voice, rather than his usual snark.

*Seriously?* However, he had a point. It would be faster, but the last time she tried she let go of the rope by accident and plummeted most of the remaining forty feet of wall before catching herself. As luck would have it, she'd packed a change of clothes that day but hadn't done so tonight.

"Please God, don't let me pee myself in front of these little kids," she whispered and pushed off. She soared out about ten feet from the wall and fed the rope through the belay device, allowing herself to drop at a quick but controlled pace before putting her feet back on the wall halfway down. Bending her knees, she pushed off even harder to make sure she had plenty of room to reach the floor without smacking into the wall.

With her feet on solid ground, she wriggled out of the climbing gear, gave Gregg the stink eye. "Asshole," she said, although her playful wink contradicted the insult.

She clocked Grandma's sly exchange with Poppy. "If a certain baker doesn't get his scrawny butt back home, he might find someone stole his gal," Grandma muttered, not nearly as quietly as she thought. Or she did it on purpose. Both Mel and Gregg turned pink and glanced away.

"Dinner's on me," he offered as she got out of her gear and stuffed it in her duffel. "Anywhere but the sushi and spaghetti place. That combination is just wrong on so many levels."

Everyone nodded their agreement. "That leaves pizza, Mexican, the other pizza place, or the really expensive fancy joint on Ash," Doc said with the enthusiasm of someone waiting in line at the DMV. Dining choices had gotten limited with The Hungry Puppy closed for dinner. Hugo and the staff could handle a scaled back breakfast and sandwiches for lunch, but their skills weren't up for anything more complicated.

Grabbing her duffel, Mel fished her phone out of her purse in case a guest called. She checked the screen and her breath caught. There was a text from Jackson sent twenty minutes ago. She opened it and gasped again at his message.

*—I need your help.—*

## A word about the author...

Marla White started her illustrious career as a storyteller at age four by drawing on the TV screen to help Winky Dink get out of mortal danger. It earned her a firm spanking. Deterred by the negative feedback, she studied to be a park ranger instead. Later, she realized it was really a TV show about park rangers she liked, not the actual outdoors.

Since then, she's been involved in several award-winning television movies for ABC, CBS, USA, and HBO. Later she became the head of television for an Emmy Award-winning writer/producer. She currently teaches story analysis and story workshops at UCLA. She's also a frequent mentor at retreats run by the CineStory Foundation.

Those retreats, held in beautiful Idyllwild, California, were the impetus for the Pine Cove mystery series. A stay in a rustic inn, not all that different from the one Mel owns with her family, inspired the book that started it all, "The Starlight Mint Surprise Murder". Marla goes to Idyllwild at least twice a year despite sharing Mel's absolute discomfort driving the twisty, winding two-lane road to get there.

\*\*\*\*

Do you want to keep up with the latest news from Marla, free stories, and favorite cocktail recipes? Sign up for my newsletter at:

https://landingpage.marlaawhite.com/h5m2o0.

Thank you for reading! If you've enjoyed this book, please help other readers discover this series by leaving a review on your favorite bookselling site.

Or visit my website at MarlaAWhite.com

Do you love mysteries, horses, and romance? Turn the page for a sneak peek of Marla White's award-winning *Cause for Elimination* available now.

Cause for Elimination

Chapter One

Alone in the spacious public barn, Emily Conners tried not to think about the body at the end of the aisle. Dust motes swirled around her in the dim, early morning light as she drummed the worn heels of her ankle-high paddock boots on the large wooden tack box she used as a bench. God, what an awful way to start the day. Of course, not as awful as it had been for Pamela Yates, whose bits of brain and gore clung to the toe of her weathered leather shoe.

She couldn't remember the last time she'd cleaned her boots, let alone polished them. There had been a time when things like that mattered to her. Now layers of mud and dust collected on the dried, cracked leather, along with whatever she'd stepped on in Feneatha's stall with a nauseating squish.

Good job, Em, step on your boss's brains.

The memory of Pamela, or what was left of her, laying in stall thirty-eight made Emily's vision slide again for a moment. She gripped the edge of the tack trunk, determined not to faint. Not now. Not when all that stood between the little gray mare and a syringe of whatever they used to kill horses these days was her.

She folded her arms and huddled against the bite of the January wind. The cold sliced right through her threadbare work shirt and sweater but failed to penetrate the wooly layer around her brain.

Who could have killed Pamela?

Did they really mean to frame the horse for the crime? Or was it serendipity that the cops who arrived in response to her 911 call assumed her boss had been kicked to death by the horse, then called Animal Control to have the 'vicious' animal destroyed?

No one who understood anything about horses would have jumped to that conclusion.

No, Emily was certain the only animal capable of the brutality done to Pamela was the two-legged kind.

She glanced up at the collection of uniformed cops who had arranged themselves across the barn aisle wide enough to drive a truck through. In the soft light, the tall, balding one reminded her of the actor who'd starred in the old TV show ER. This being LA, maybe it really was him. A giggle escaped, despite her efforts to bite it back. You are definitely losing it, Conners.

Possibly, taking the pill she found in Pam's desk hadn't been such a good idea. For Feneatha's sake, she willed herself to keep her shit together until the detective arrived.

\*\*\*\*

Justin Butler could have satisfied his need for a tall, strong drip coffee at any of the dozens of designer coffee shops he passed, but he was too irritated to enjoy a cup now. He normally stopped at the Brew House near the station where the tall, blonde barista with the slightly crooked eye tooth worked. But no, he had to go to the Los Angeles Equestrian Center and talk to a drama queen who had demanded an investigation into what was an unfortunate accident. The disturbance to his morning ritual, which also screwed up his plan to ask the blonde out, left him cranky and sullen.

Why him? As a member of L.A.'s elite Robbery-Homicide Division, he handled high-profile cases, not freakish mishaps. Why didn't his boss, Lieutenant

Placer, give the handholding-shoulder-to-cry-on gig to someone else? Someone who didn't already have the murder of a city commissioner's son on his desk?

He got why RHD caught this 'death by horse' case. Every movie producer, real estate mogul, and reality star who boarded their horses at the large equestrian facility had learned about the death minutes after the police, then woke up the mayor with frantic phone calls. Worried about the safety of their children/spouse/partner who rode at the Center, they demanded police action. Since RHD was the best, the mayor assigned the case to them personally. Justin suspected the lieutenant had passed the task on to him because Placer resented the way rich people got special treatment and considered Justin one of 'those people.' Sticking him with the case must have seemed like poetic justice.

With a couple of half-assed centering breaths, he tried finding his calm, peaceful place his dojo master lectured him about as he turned onto the Equestrian Center's tree-lined driveway. Instead of serenity, a growl of frustration rose as he realized he had no idea where in the seventy-five-acre park filled with dozens of barns and arenas he was supposed to go. Then he saw the black-and-whites parked in front of one of three huge wooden barns just off the driveway. Bingo. He pulled into a parking spot and stepped out of his car, only to squash a not quite dry pile of horseshit with his favorite pair of Italian loafers. Great, his morning was now complete.

Inside, one of the unis filled him in on the situation. "Sorry to call you in on this, sir, but the lady over there refused to let Animal Control take custody of the horse until she talked to a homicide detective."

The cop shrugged, embarrassed by the whole thing. Justin dialed back his scowl. None of this was their fault. He peered down the dimly lit aisle of the barn and found the current bane of his existence, sitting on a large wooden box. What startled him was that she studied him right back. There was a shaken air about her. Could be the shock of finding a dead body, but her glassy expression struck him as odd.

"Ma'am? I'm Detective Butler. I understand you asked to speak to a homicide detective?"

He walked across the dirt floor of the barn to stand in front of her. The woman gazed up from under a mop of auburn curls, revealing the most amazing gray-green eyes he'd ever seen. All of a sudden, missing out on his barista didn't seem like such a big deal. Her feet didn't quite meet the ground from her seat atop the wooden chest, so she had to jump down to stand. All five feet four inches of her slender build reached his chin.

She offered her hand. "Emily Conners," she stammered. "Sorry, this is my first…um, I'm not sure what the protocol is in this sort of circumstance." Trying to ease the tension, he shook her hand. She was trembling. Why wasn't she wearing a jacket?

"Ms. Conners, my condolences. This must have been quite a shock, finding your friend's body."

****

Emily pulled her hand out of his grasp with a weary sigh. She recognized the tall, arrogant type from the moment she saw him. He even draped himself in the same type of designer suit that her ex-husband favored. True, it looked a lot better on the detective than it ever did on Nick, but clearly the two of them were cut from the same literal and figurative cloth.

"You can save your smarmy charms for someone else. I'm not crazy. There's no way that horse kicked Pamela to death."

"No one is saying you're crazy, Ms. Conners," he explained in a tone which implied exactly the opposite. "I understand how difficult this must be for you, but as you must be aware, horses can be unpredictable. Isn't it possible your friend—"

"Her name was Pamela Yates. I'm—was, I guess— her assistant."

"Excuse me, ma'am, of course. Isn't it possible Miss Yates startled the horse, and the animal kicked out as a natural response, injuring her and causing her death?"

Injured? Pamela's brains were on the wall. On three of them, as a matter of fact. "Have you actually seen her body, detective?"

"I thought it would be best if we talked first."

The man's soothing voice made her want to scream. Instead, she fought to maintain a reasonable tone of her own. The last thing she needed was to antagonize him, erasing all hope of keeping Feneatha off the endangered species list.

"Why don't we do this," she said, keeping the you patronizing, pompous ass comment to herself. "Why don't we take a look at the...at her...at the stall." If it doesn't put too much of a dent in your morning, detective, sir.

Emily clenched her fist so hard that her fingernails bit into her palm. "If after seeing her you decide it was an accident, I'll move aside and let Animal Control do their job."

"Fair enough," the detective agreed and followed her down the barn aisle to an open stall.

"I swapped the mare to another stall so she wouldn't keep stepping in...on..." Her hands fluttered, dreading the scene that awaited them.

Pamela lay sprawled on her back a few feet inside the enclosed space. Afraid to speak for fear the bile rising in her throat would come spewing out, she gestured at the wall. Bits of brain, bone, hair, and blood speckled the polished wood planks. Poor Pamela must have been standing almost exactly where Emily stood now when something hit her face so hard it left nothing recognizable behind.

An icy chill that had nothing to do with the weather caused her to tremble. The detective took off his coat and wrapped it around her shoulders. She'd given up her own jacket to cover the pulpy remains of Pamela's head in a sentimental gesture she'd almost come to regret. Dammit, she really liked that jacket. This time, when the cop gave her shoulder a comforting squeeze, she didn't pull away.

"Sometimes I didn't even like her, you know?" she whispered as unwanted tears rolled down her cheeks. "But no one deserves..."

Unable to finish, she huddled tight against the detective's chest.

\*\*\*\*

Justin held her close, hoping to keep her from seeing what his practiced eye recognized immediately. The pattern of gore continued in a graceful, macabre arc onto the ceiling and the opposite wall. The blood splatter was a classic pattern created by a heavy object being swung at a head and bursting it like an over-ripe melon. Even if the horse had kicked her, the motion would have been straight back, splattering the blood in one direction. Unless the horse knew Tae Bo, it didn't kill the woman.

"I'm afraid the good and the bad news is I agree with you, Ms. Conners. Pamela Yates was murdered."

Thank you for purchasing
this publication of The Wild Rose Press, Inc.

For questions or more information
contact us at
info@thewildrosepress.com.

The Wild Rose Press, Inc.
www.thewildrosepress.com